UNHOLY SUNDERING

A DARK RISING NOVEL

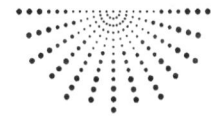

DEANNA BROWNE

CELTIC
MOON
PRESS

Copyright © 2018 by Celtic Moon Press
All rights reserved.
Unholy Sundering - Dark Rising - Book 2
Celtic Moon Press
ISBN: 978-1-948884-11-2

Cover Art: Copyright © 2018 Killion Design, Inc.

ALSO BY DEANNA BROWNE

DARK RISING TRILOGY

Evil Etched in Gold - novella

Demon Rising

Unholy Sundering

Dark Alliance - coming Spring 2019

HARD-WIRED TRILOGY

Hooked

Synched - coming Spring 2019

To Spencer,
for still believing.

ACKNOWLEDGMENTS

I'm so grateful for all the help I've had while writing this book. It started with writing partners and early readers who helped keep me check, especially Jami Gray, Dave Benneman, Betsy Love, and Lorelei Mote. I also couldn't have written this book without the other half of my tribe, who helps watch kiddos, makes dinner, and cheers me on when I want to quit. These include but are not limited to my parents, my sister Sharla, Tammy for her endless optimism, Penny for being a backup taxi driver, and Spencer for all the above. I couldn't have kept my sanity without you all. Thank you isn't nearly adequate, but I'll say it anyways.

CHAPTER ONE

Becca shoved her way through the throng of people, fighting towards the execution platform. It stood tall and withered in the center of the dilapidated town, an effigy to the gods above or, in this case, the devils below. The afternoon sky rumbled its dissent, a storm threatening in the distance.

"Damn rebel," a ragged man hollered. "String him up for the devil to devour."

City guards, in their green uniforms, hoisted the prisoner up on the stage. The young man strained against his captors as they tied him to a flat board. He couldn't be older than twenty.

In the corner perched a black dragon-like demon, long and lithe with an even longer wingspan. Its fangs poked out from beneath massive black lips.

"Watch it," a guy shouted at Becca as she passed.

Someone yanked her backwards by her hair. Pain shot through her scalp as she regained her footing. Her long black hair escaped her ponytail and fell into her face. The hum of magic vibrated in her hands. A thick, rugged man glared down at her, as ugly as he was probably stupid.

Should she end this fight the fast way, with magic, or the more satisfying way, with her fists? At least this would be one fight she could win. She cocked an arm back, ready to strike, when someone approached from behind.

"Don't start this now," Caleb spoke in her ear. "Not here."

"They're setting him out as dinner for that demon." Revulsion tasted sour in her mouth.

"We have other responsibilities." He took her hand and pulled her away from the stage, levelheaded as always.

He didn't have to explain Becca's other responsibilities. Her gnawing guilt was a constant companion. But he was right: Darion and Liz counted on her to return. She needed answers and couldn't afford to be sidetracked.

Caleb and Becca had been on their way to a pawnshop to follow a lead when the crowd for the execution had separated them.

Cheers erupted from the crowd, and she picked up her pace. Caleb's hand tightened on hers. The demon on the stage bellowed, piercing the air over the boisterous voices. It had begun.

They passed a mage on their way out. His pleasant grin and the Soultorn at his side told Becca he must be a member of the city coven. She lowered her eyes and buried her repulsion. Soultorns, demon-possessed humans with pitch-black eyes, were expensive and hard to make. Even harder to unmake. She should know—her sister, Liz, was one of them.

Once past the magician, they hurried, almost running. Caleb's clenched jaw and tight shoulders indicated this execution bothered him as much as it did her.

Several blocks later, the cheers and screams of the

execution finally died away. They slowed to a walk on the crumbling asphalt road as they drew closer to the pawnshop. Many of the stores in the strip mall were dark and vacant, like a beggar child with missing teeth. The cheap green lights on the sign that read Pawn $$$ flickered on and off. Heavy bars covered the crumbling stucco.

Caleb curled his lips in a concerned look.

"I've gone to worse stores," she told him as they approached.

Just then, the *n* in Pawn flashed out. Now it glowed Paw $$$.

He gave a short laugh. "That's a great selling point."

Becca paused and stared at him. It had been weeks since he'd laughed, since his tanned face lifted in a real smile...since his parents' death. He'd lost a lot. They all had.

"What?" He brushed back his dirty blond hair. It had grown, curling a bit at his temple now.

"Nothing. Let's go."

They pushed through the front door and bells chimed. The shop might have been small, but every inch was crammed full. Floor-to-ceiling shelves held electronics, weapons, and random household items. Hopefully among the clutter of junk were the answers they sought.

A short man with a thick beard sat behind a glass jewelry counter. He didn't greet them, but his dark eyes framed by heavy brows watched their every step. His only remarkable characteristic was the fifteen or more gold hoops that lined one ear.

Becca approached the counter. Incense burned nearby, trying to cover an old, dank smell. "We're looking for someone," Becca started.

They were met with silence.

"Are you Boone?" she asked, understanding his caution.

Boone was supposedly a mediocre magician who heard things. They had been searching for a month for a rogue around here, a rogue who kept his or her distance from coven influence. There were rumors now and again, but no one with real answers.

"We're looking for someone." Becca slipped him a small coin, hoping it would help.

"I am Boone." The man looked Caleb and Becca over with an experienced eye. His hands carefully tapped the glass counter. Littered below the counter, expensive stones lay in random settings.

She didn't even see him pocket the coin. "A friend said you could help us find an older rogue living nearby."

"There are many rogues. They're killing one this morning." He spread a hand along the counter. "How about some jewelry? This man here could buy you a pretty ring. Show his affection."

"No thanks." Becca stifled her impatience. They didn't need to get into that right now.

"Just answers." Standing a good foot taller than her with shoulders to match, Caleb's intimidating presence often helped encourage cooperation, despite his lack of magic. They'd been best friends for years, and she relied on him to watch her back. Which, as the only Mundane in their group, he did surprisingly well.

Despite their protests, Boone bent down to open the cabinet. Caleb looked over his shoulder at the front door, his gaze skittering around the room. He never did like magicians—he made an exception for Becca though.

Boone brought out a large ring, with an amber stone.

"Look, if you want money, we'll get you some." Becca

placed both of her hands down on the glass in frustration. "I don't want jewelry, just information."

Without hesitation, the man gripped Becca's hand, something cold pressed around her finger, and a searing pain shot up her arm.

Caleb had a knife at the man's throat. "Let go."

"If you kill me, your girl dies." Boone spoke to Caleb, but his eyes remained locked on Becca.

Becca fought back the pain while focusing on her magic. She was stupid not to be more prepared for an attack, but this man was supposed to be weak.

"Becca? You okay?"

Not trusting her voice, she shook her head. The pain in her hand traveled up her arm then down into her gut, twisting into a pit of agony.

Caleb pressed the knife a little farther, a thin red line beading at the blade's edge. "If she dies, you will too."

"I'm not going to kill her," Boone scoffed. "I just want to borrow something from her."

He slipped the metal ring farther up her finger, and the pain intensified all the way to her core, to where her magic lay deep inside her. The magical sensation paralyzed her body.

"No!" Her voice grated. "Not that."

A few months ago when she first learned about her magic, she might have gladly gotten rid of it, but now his parasitic touch invaded her very soul, seeking to take what wasn't his. She remembered her defenses, the magical barriers Darion had taught her. But every wall she put up, Boone easily knocked down.

His grip tightened, and he lowered his face to Becca's, ignoring Caleb's knife and the blood trickling down his neck. "I felt your power when you first stepped into the store. So strong and fragrant." He inhaled deeply as if smelling a bouquet.

"Kill him!" Becca screamed.

"Then you'll die too." The man's dark eyes bore deep as if seeing beyond physical layers. "Your choice, but then you'll never get to see your rogue. So close, too."

Caleb ran to one of the nearby shelves, knocking things aside. Boone yanked her closer again. He pushed the ring farther up her finger, and Becca's legs crumpled underneath her. Somehow, though, he kept her up and connected to that ring.

Her magic, which was usually a low humming sensation she found deep within, now screamed out, pain lighting every nerve ending on fire.

Caleb returned with something large in his hands. Then, with a loud crash, the cabinet shattered underneath them, and Becca tumbled to the floor. The pain vanished, replaced by aching exhaustion. Boone's howls of pain filled the store.

Caleb reached down to lift her up. "You okay?"

She ripped the ring off of her finger, her hand still shaking. She glanced back and quickly wished she hadn't. Boone sat on the floor cradling a bloody stump where his hand used to be.

Bile rose in her throat, and she hurried out the door. Caleb stayed at her side since her steps were unsteady. She focused her energy on a defensive spell for both of them and cursed herself for not being more prepared in the first place. As they walked by a large dumpster, Becca dumped the ring, grateful to be rid of such a foul object.

"Did you really chop off that guy's hand?" Becca never imagined Caleb was capable of doing such a thing, but the last month had changed them all.

"It was the only way to break contact. He seemed only

able to hurt you when he touched you with that ring." Caleb spoke in a rush, his gaze darting around the passing streets and the people littering the storefronts.

Becca tried to shake the nightmare of that man's touch, and walked faster now that she trusted her legs. "Thank you."

"There is one good thing about today."

"What?" It was hard to imagine anything good between the execution, and the fiasco in the pawnshop.

"We now know the rogue is nearby."

After Boone's attack, she'd almost forgotten about the rogue. After weeks of searching, could he be within reach? Hope flared in her chest.

She flexed her hand, knowledge of what almost had happened sending a cold chill up her arm. She reached for her knife, the heavy metal a comfort in her hand. "Next time, let's buy the damn jewelry like he wants. Okay?"

A glimmer of amusement crossed his face. "Sure thing."

CHAPTER TWO

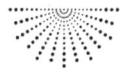

No matter how many times she climbed this mountain, Becca's legs complained. Caleb led the way up, his pack heavy with their purchased supplies. When the ground leveled out near the cave entrance, she paused to catch her breath. She slipped off her pack and stared out to the water.

With night fast approaching, the horizon and the water blended together in a dark blue infinity. Cool salt air brushed her face as the waves crashed into the rocky hillside. She would never tire of watching the ocean, an entity in its own accord. Another deep breath and the fear, wound tight in her belly from the incident at the pawnshop, floated out to sea. That had been too close.

"Beautiful, isn't it?" Becca glanced at Caleb, who stopped to wait for her.

"It's not home," he replied, a hollowness haunting his voice.

"Nothing ever will be." Nothing could ever compete with the comfort of being where you belonged. Unfortunately, the feeling of home was destroyed for Becca before her sixteenth birthday.

"You coming in?" Caleb adjusted the pack on his back.

"Yeah, in a sec."

Darion emerged from the cave, and headed straight for Becca. His pitch-black hair poked up in every direction, while stubble covered his jaw. Even with those weary eyes, Becca warmed at the sight of him despite her doubts.

"What happened?" His worried tone held a biting edge.

"Nothing." She didn't want to worry him.

Earlier, Darion complained about her going to town with Caleb, but left with no other options, he grudgingly agreed to stay behind. Darion had more control over magic and was the only one strong enough to watch over Becca's sister, Elizabeth.

For inside Elizabeth resided one of the most lethal demons in this dimension, Bael, the Duke of Hell himself. In an attempt to overthrow the coven leader, Ryma, their uncle bound Bael to Elizabeth. Becca and Darion killed her uncle, but now they struggled to deal with Bael and Ryma's wrath. Outgunned and outmanned, they'd been searching for answers ever since.

With magic being relatively new in the world, answers were sometimes hard to come by. Thirty years ago, a wizard named Lazario opened a portal that flooded the earth with magic, which gave him access to another dimension filled with demons. In the takeover, Lazario overthrew the major world governments and replaced them with his followers. He only shared with those loyal to him.

Becca glanced between the two boys, not sure what to say. A heavy weight settled onto her shoulders. Ever since they'd escaped the coven with her sister, Caleb had been distant. And Darion's affection didn't make it any easier.

Darion found when he was magically connected to her sister, Elizabeth, he could sense Becca's emotions through the sisters' shared blood bond. The bond came in handy when they fought their way free from Ryma's coven. The continued strength of it surprised them both as it drew them closer.

"I felt something when you were gone. Are you all right?"

"I'm fine," she lied.

Darion grabbed her shoulders, searching her face. His touch turned the conflicting emotions inside her. She was attracted to him, but with his lies and previous ties to the coven, she was hesitant to trust him. She didn't need any more complications in her life.

She struggled with her ties to both men. Caleb would always be her friend, her *best* friend. Hurting him because she couldn't determine Darion's place in her life was not an option.

Keeping Caleb in sight, she shuffled back a step. It was enough. Darion quickly dropped his hand.

Becca avoided his eyes as she spoke. "If Boone was your friend, then he isn't your friend anymore." Before he could ask more questions, she added, "We did hear that the rogue is nearby, though the source might be questionable."

"Really?" He cocked a brow and waited for more. Tired lines etched his face. Controlling the demon inside her sister drained him more than he admitted. "Don't think you're getting away with not telling me what happened with Boone."

"I'll talk while you eat."

Before she could pick up her pack, he took it from her. He brushed her hand as he slipped it onto his back. A warm sensation traveled up her arm. She told herself it was completely magical. Residual magic from the last fight, that was all.

Without a word, Caleb headed to the cave.

"I can carry my own pack. I'm fine. I was careless. There was an execution that set me off my game, so my guards weren't up when we met Boone."

"You should know better," he said without malice. The anger in his eyes was clearly not directed at her. "Did you kill him?"

"No."

"Then I will."

She held up a hand. "Boone got what he deserved. Caleb chopped off his hand."

Surprise flitted across his face, and he glanced to where Caleb had been, but he was already inside. "Really?"

Becca nodded.

"That Mundane constantly surprises me."

"Me too."

Darion stepped towards her, but before anything else happened, she started back to the cave. "Let's eat," she said.

"Sure." His casual response almost sounded like a question, but he followed her back inside.

At first glance, the cave appeared to be nothing more than a shallow rock overhang. As one explored farther, it opened to a cave, well hidden from below. The usual dank odor hung in the air.

Caleb was already unpacking, putting supplies in the back. The cave was barely large enough for the four of them, and gave no privacy. Her sister, Elizabeth, lay unconscious on a mat.

"How has she been doing?" Becca pushed out the

nagging guilt in her mind that whispered she'd put her sister here.

"Bael's restless," Darion said.

"What's new?" Becca set down her pack and went to her sister. Bael had been restless since day one.

Kneeling next to her, Becca grabbed the rag hanging in a cup of water and slowly dribbled some into Elizabeth's mouth. Darion said there was a chance they could remove the demon residing in her, but he wasn't sure what would be left of Elizabeth. They didn't know the spell to pull the demon out, and they needed help. Someone not bound to a coven, someone like a rogue. Unfortunately, most magicians weren't the helpful type.

"How much longer can it stay confined?" Worry knotted in Becca's stomach.

"Indefinitely. How long can I control him?" He ran his hands through his hair, leaving it mussed. "I don't know. Maybe if I call another demon to help boost my power, I can hold him in check. But that would mean we couldn't travel, not with another host to haul around."

"Don't look at me," Caleb said. "I'm allergic to demons."

"That's not funny. We're not making a Soultorn." Becca wasn't in the mood to joke about dark magic. "Elizabeth needs to eat."

"Okay. We can get ready to wake it."

Becca grimaced. She hated when he referred to Elizabeth as an "it," even though she knew he meant the demon inside. They were two separate beings. "Let's eat first. You'll need your strength."

"You're probably right." Darion grabbed a small can of peaches and slumped to the ground.

Caleb leaned back on top of his now empty pack and

bit into some jerky. Becca grabbed a can of food to eat and returned to Elizabeth's side.

"Caleb"—Darion paused with a peach halfway to his mouth—"thank you for what you did back at the pawnshop, for saving Becca."

"I didn't do it for you." Caleb stared out the cave opening then turned to face Darion. "But next time you send us to a friend, let us know if he'll kill us first, will ya'?"

"He didn't know he would do that," Becca protested.

Darion raised a hand, bringing her protest to a stop. "He's right. I'm sorry. He isn't a strong wizard, but his relics can be. I should have been there."

"We needed you to be here with Liz," Becca reminded him.

"All I asked was for a warning," Caleb interjected.

"Next time, we'll be more prepared," she promised.

"There won't be a next time." Darion's voice rose over the crash of waves outside. "We can't chance that."

Frustration burned under her skin. "We need answers, and soon, before Bael not only destroys Liz, but us as well."

"Stop." Caleb stood and then headed towards the cave opening. "What's happening to the waves?"

Becca had been too distracted to notice the sound of the waves growing louder. Turning to look outside, she noted the skies were dark with heavy clouds. Was a storm blowing in?

Becca and Darion joined Caleb at the cave's entrance. The waves crashed into the wall below with a fierce determination. Hit after hit, they clawed their way up the side of the cliff, rising over twenty feet in the air. She wrapped her arms around her stomach to protect against the striking cold.

"This is one hell of a storm." Becca had never lived by the ocean and wondered if this was normal.

"I don't think this is just a storm." Caleb searched the horizon.

The roar of the ocean echoed off the cave walls, and the mist sprayed her clothes. Lightning struck nearby. Becca flinched.

"Is it possible that Ryma could be behind this?" The idea brought a whole new level of fear in play for Becca.

"Grab the bags." Darion dropped his can on the ground. "We gotta run."

CHAPTER THREE

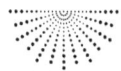

Becca slung on her pack and took out her knife. Caleb already had Elizabeth in his arms, while Darion stayed by the cave's entrance. After living together on the run for these past months, they automatically moved to their given roles.

As water flowed over her boots, she realized this was an enemy they didn't know how to fight. The frigid water easily penetrated her boots, and a chill crawled up her spine. They had been camping here for a week with no problems. Could someone have followed them? She thought they covered their tracks, both magically and physically.

"What is this?" she asked.

Darion didn't answer, his intent gaze focused on something beyond the cliff. In between one eye-searing strike and the next, a large man covered in camouflage rushed into the cave and slammed Darion into the wall.

Swallowing her anger and shock, Becca took aim and threw her knife through the air. The attacker spun at the last second, and the knife clattered against the cave wall.

There was no time to worry about Darion as three more men stormed the small cave. Caleb pushed Elizabeth into Becca's arms, and she staggered under the additional weight. He spun with a knife in each hand and met the group of attackers head-on.

As much as she hated to do it, she shrugged off her pack, letting it slide down the rock wall and propped her unconscious sister against it. Caleb had bought her mere seconds, and she wasn't going to waste them.

She reached down to grab a the extra knife out of her boot, ignoring the curl of cold water lapping at her feet. Before she rose, a large man grabbed her from the side. He easily lifted her off the ground and pinned her arms to her sides. Unable to use her knife, she mentally protected herself against his attacking magic then slammed her head into his nose.

He swore, but didn't loosen his hold. The water steadily rose in an unnatural column, wrapping around her legs and sending a frightening chill up Becca's spine. An inhuman scream tore through the night. It was Elizabeth, who now sat straight up, her pitch-black eyes open with water rising up to her chest.

Shit. Not now. Bael could destroy everyone in the room if given the chance. Becca focused her magic, and with a spell, forced Elizabeth's body unconscious again. They had to get out of here.

"Darion!" Becca shouted. Why wasn't he burning all of these men to a crisp? Granted, the water didn't help things.

Trapped in her attacker's thick arms, she didn't hear a reply, only the grunts of the fight ensuing behind her. He began lugging her towards the entrance of the cave. She caught sight of Caleb, partially submerged but still fighting another man. A large dark man used both hands to hold Darion's head under the water.

This couldn't be happening. Not now. When every muscle wanted to fight, Becca closed her eyes and focused on her magic, the humming deep within her. Frustration built and the spell tangled in her mind. Dammit.

Water ebbed and surged, pushing the man off balance, giving Becca a spare inch or two to move. And she could do a lot with an inch. She turned the knife in her hand and slammed it into his thigh. His pain-filled scream pierced her ears as he stumbled back, and released his hold.

Off-balance, Becca plunged into the cold water. She struggled to keep her footing on the wet cave floor. With the water near her waist and almost to Liz's neck, Becca started to wade toward her sister. *Hold on, Liz. I'm almost there.*

I'll survive if you free me. The voice crawled inside Becca's mind. It wasn't Elizabeth, but Bael, the demon dwelling inside her. Despite her revulsion to the voice, the offer was tempting, but she knew better. Once released, Bael would destroy with no regard for who or what. Rule number one: never trust a blood-sucking demon from another dimension.

Becca never got the chance to reply to Bael because a large wave crashed over her head. It pushed her forward as she reached out for her sister. Before she could grab onto Liz, the current's force dragged Becca back under.

A monster of its own accord, the cold water swallowed her whole. She screamed for her sister, for Darion, for Caleb. They were all that she had left. Water rushed in, taking her screams and burning her throat. Her head cracked against something hard, and her world turned black.

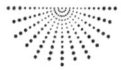

CHAPTER FOUR

G ritty sand rubbed against Caleb's cheek. His stomach rolled in tandem with the memory of the wave, its endless spinning and spinning before it spat him upon the shore. It brought to mind the stories his mother used to tell him, stories of Jonah being swallowed by a whale. Now, he could empathize. He felt like regurgitated fish food. He couldn't stop the spins long enough to stand or even open his eyes.

"We get them all?" The man's voice was deep and rich.

"Yes. All four," another man answered, annoyance tingeing his words. "I told you we could have handled it. We didn't need a tsunami. Man, I hate that ride."

"We didn't have a clue what we stumbled upon. I felt this demon over a mile away when it woke. You're lucky, brother. It could have been worse."

Caleb tried to rise, but instead rolled over to his stomach and threw up. The salt burned as it came out his mouth and nose. He tried to blink, to pry his stinging eyes open. What had just happened? What ride?

"Not time to wake yet." The growl came from

someone nearby, and then without a word, unconsciousness consumed Caleb.

~

The next time awareness hit, Caleb squeezed his eyes shut
against a bright light. His whole body ached as if it had
been through a washing machine. A soft hand brushed his
hair, tucking it behind his ears.

He moaned softly and leaned into the hand.
"Rebecca."

He cursed himself for giving in to her touch. He'd kept
his distance for weeks, giving her space to make a decision,
and her decision had been obvious. But now, he didn't
care.

"Are you in any pain?" a soft voiced asked, a soft voice
that *didn't* belong to Rebecca.

It took him a bit to sit up. He was on a tall, thin bed,
but he got there, taking in the gray room spinning around
him. "Who are you? Where's Becca?"

A woman sat next to him, young, pretty. There were no
restraints, no magical barriers. Where was he?

"I'm Nikki." She wore a wide smile with eyes that were
soft and reassuring. The white coat she wore stood out
against her dark skin.

This wasn't a prison. This looked more like a medical
unit of some kind, complete with blinding overhead lights.
A red-headed man in a similar white coat stood on the
other side of the room with a patient. Caleb recognized
the patient from the fight in the cave. He scanned the
room, looking for Becca and the others. Instead, he found
another man from the cave, standing at the foot of his bed,
a gun at the ready.

"Relax." Nikki placed a hand on Caleb's arm. "You're safe here."

"Tell that to your buddy over there." He motioned to the man with the gun.

He stood over six feet tall, with huge shoulders and dark skin. A cut above his eye was stitched, and by the look on the man's face, Caleb thought the cut was his doing.

"Where are my friends?" Caleb noticed the cotton shirt and pants he wore. Someone had changed his clothes. "How long have I been out?"

"Careful," the man with the gun said to Nikki. "He's stronger than he looks."

The girl stayed seated nearby despite the warning.

"Don't mind Leon," she said. "He doesn't like to lose a fight."

"I didn't lose."

She ignored the comment. "He won't hold a grudge for too long."

The scowl on Leon's face said otherwise.

"You've been out through the entire night. It's after ten in the morning now." Her calm voice did nothing to settle his nerves.

Why wouldn't she give him answers? Did they know about Elizabeth? Caleb gripped her arms, struggling to keep the panic at bay. "What about my friends?"

"Let her go," ordered Leon.

Her eyes held no fear. Caleb dropped his hold. He stumbled out of bed and caught himself on the bed's metal frame. There had to be an exit or weapon, something. He lunged for a pair of scissors. He didn't know or care what relationship these two people had. He wasn't going to stand in the same room as that soldier without a weapon.

"Drop it."

Caleb whipped around to find a rifle leveled at his chest. He didn't expect any less. "If you were going to shoot me, why didn't you do it in the cave?" As he stared at the barrel, though, he wondered why the man had a gun. Magicians didn't carry guns. Out of the corner of his eye, he watched the other two men enter in the room, blocking the door.

Nikki stepped in front of Caleb, blocking the gun. "Leon! I was doing fine without you."

"Were you?" Leon boomed.

"Jemi said he doesn't mean us harm," she said.

How would they know that? What did they do to him when he was unconscious? Adrenaline raced through his veins, and he wondered how this girl could be so naive. Even armed only with scissors, he could easily use her as a hostage.

"Jemi can't predict the future. Get away from him," Leon ordered.

"What are you talking about?" Thoughts of old sci-fi stories haunted Caleb.

Nikki turned towards him, biting her lower lip and not quite meeting his eyes. "We have someone that can read minds. She did it while you slept. It's completely harm-less." If Nikki didn't act so guilty, Caleb may have believed it were so simple. "We're not going to kill you. Ignore Uncle Leon. Muscles and guns are second nature to him."

That, he had no trouble believing. Caleb's body ached from his fight in the cave with these men. "Why did you attack us? Where are my friends?"

Nikki grabbed his hand and led him back to the bed. He still clung to the scissors, but his tired body followed her. "Your friends are in containment. They are too powerful to be let free, until we can trust them."

"Trust them?" He stopped pulling away and dug his

heels in, trying to stop her. "You guys are the ones that attacked us."

"You strayed too close to our compound. We have to protect ourselves. I've tried to get them to change their methods, but they prefer to contain magicians first for safety." She helped him into the bed.

Leon lowered the rifle, but kept it out, watching their every move.

"Relax. Doc wanted to stitch up one of your wounds, and then I will answer all of your questions," Nikki said.

The man with red hair gave a brief wave, and then returned to his patient.

Caleb looked down, only then noticing the blood seeping through the cotton of his pant leg. There was a cut on his thigh, but not too deep. He reclined against the wall behind him, trying to find a position to rest but also to get to his feet quickly if needed.

Then his thoughts returned to Elizabeth, and his stomach clenched. "What about Elizabeth? People aren't safe."

A puzzled look briefly crossed her face. "You mean the Soultorn?"

"She's a friend. We're trying to save her."

Leon gave a dry chuckle.

Nikki shot him a look before turning back to Caleb. "It's in containment."

It. She was only a demon to these people.

Before he could argue, Leon stepped closer. "Nikki, your father wanted to speak to you. It's rude to keep him waiting. I'll watch over him."

Caleb's gut tightened, despite the pain. He didn't trust Leon not to unload that gun into him.

"When can I see my friends?" He needed to see Becca for himself.

"I'll ask." Nikki laid a hand on his knee. "You'll be okay. Just rest."

She walked out of the room, her long black ponytail swishing as she walked. He turned to Leon who lugged the rifle over his shoulder.

"Rest." His lips pressed tight in a grimace.

Yeah right. Rest.

Becca bit her lip, focusing all of her magic on the man standing guard outside her cell. She'd been practicing with Darion for the last month to control and focus her newfound magic, but the guard outside the barred door remained stoic, unbothered. She was in way over her head.

She rubbed the scar on her back, a habit from when she had her tattoo. A tattoo she'd had since before she could remember. When it was burned off over a month ago, it opened magical abilities she never knew she had. Abilities she still was trying to figure out and control. With Darion's coaching, she'd been improving.

Despite all that she'd learned, she'd never seen anything like what happened with the ocean in the cave. She wouldn't have believed it possible if she hadn't seen it herself. Saltwater still clung to her clothes, and with a hand through her stiff hair, she shook more sand free. Were magicians powerful enough to move the ocean? She didn't like to think about what demons such a magician would have in his back pocket.

And if the water show wasn't scary enough, this cell had its own peculiarities. Pacing back and forth, she searched for any clue or possibility of escape. It was more of a hovel than a cell, really. Dirt and rock formed the walls with no seams anywhere. Some type of clear plastic or glass sheet took the place of a door, but the ward or invisible barrier wouldn't let her get close enough to figure out how to open it. On the side of the wall, a magicked light was encased in glass. No electricity, then. Were they underground or in some type of cave? The dark hole near the back of this room told her they hadn't even figured out plumbing in this place.

She'd already spent the first ten minutes or so screaming for Elizabeth, Darion, and Caleb to no avail. If anyone were stupid enough to touch or wake Elizabeth, they would get what they deserved. But any connection she usually felt with Elizabeth was dead, same with Darion. She refused to let herself think the worst. They had to be okay. Maybe this cave was a black hole for powers. It could explain the guard outside not even flinching at her spells.

She slumped down, settling her butt on the floor. Needing an outlet for her frustration, she began dragging her fingers through the dirt. Something sharp scraped across her palm. After several minutes of digging and a few broken nails, she unearthed a jagged stone. Nothing great, but the cold stone in her palm comforted her. The only physical weapon she possessed. Darion had repeatedly told her to rely on her magic, not muscle, but after living on the streets for years, some habits were hard to lose.

With a renewed sense of purpose, she stood and headed to the door, stopping just shy of the ward. "Hey, psychos," she hollered. "Are we waiting for the next wave to come get me? Did I get abducted by a coven of mermaids?" The bitter edge in her voice echoed off the walls. "Come on. I don't bite."

A tall man with short graying hair and deep mahogany skin approached. He wore a loose cotton shirt and light pants. "I'll take it from here."

The guard's shoulders sagged with relief. "Thanks, boss."

Boss? At first glance, he dressed more like a clergyman or a janitor than a "boss." As he drew near, though, she didn't miss the confidence in his wide, relaxed shoulders. He had a high brow and wide nose. It wasn't how he appeared, but more an instinct an animal might have that told Becca there was more to this man than he displayed.

With a wave of his hands, the door disappeared, and he ducked his head to enter her cell. She didn't waste time with magic—she wasn't that strong. Instead, she charged him, hoping to throw him off balance.

She made it two steps before a light flashed and something jerked her backwards, slamming her back to the wall. It was the rock, now warm in her hand. She dropped it quickly, but not before her head smacked against the wall. Ignoring her throbbing head, she scooted back and readied herself.

He lifted a hand. "I would like to speak. No weapons involved."

Cold seeped into her bones at this man's casual display of power. She was at his mercy. "Easy for you to say. You have more weapons in your arsenal."

"I do. But I was more concerned with the weapon you have. Your Soultorn is stronger than you know what to do with."

Becca flinched at the word Soultorn. "Don't kill her. She's my sister."

His brows lifted. "Your sister."

"Yes. Elizabeth. We keep her unconscious. She's not a threat."

He chuckled. "You are naive if you think it's not a threat." He spoke a command, then the wall of the cave moved.

The ground vibrated underneath her. "What are you doing?"

A lower portion of dirt protruded out of the wall, creating a bench of sorts. "Getting comfortable."

"Who are you?" Becca tried to hide her amazement.

"I forgot to introduce myself. I'm Andre." He took a seat on the bench, like he was visiting a friend, not a prisoner. "And you are?"

Not seeing a reason to lie at this point, she told him. "Becca. Where are my friends?"

"They're safe. Even your sister is alive, for the moment."

At his confirmation that Elizabeth still lived, Becca's breath left in a rush. At least everyone was alive...for the moment. "I want to see them."

He watched her in silence before answering. "I need to be able to trust you first."

"Just let us leave. We have no desire to hurt you."

He picked up a nearby rock, tossed it in the air, and caught it. He closed his eyes briefly and took a deep breath. "You've probably guessed my powers lie with the land and water. While things may look simple"—he nodded at the rock lying flat on his palm—"they are not. This is my home, filled with runaways, magicians, and Mundanes alike. The slightest pressure in the wrong spot can crumble all I've built." He closed his hand and opened it. Where the rock had once been, now fine sand poured through his fingers. He blew the grains off his hand. "That is something I can't allow."

"We're only trying to help my sister." She stood, unable to sit by while he performed magic tricks.

"Hopefully in time, you can join our community or go on your way." He rose and dusted off his pants. "But you're not leaving with that demon. That I cannot allow.

The best thing you can do for your sister is to provide the peace only death can bring." He raised a hand, halting her objection. "I'm not saying we won't help. In fact, here's Jemi now."

Becca turned to the woman entering the cell. Dressed in dark, fitted clothes with lace-up black boots, she looked like a soldier. Short-cropped hair and a lithe, muscular frame finished the look. Her face held sharp pointed features, almost pixie-like. She'd call Jemi almost beautiful if not for the disdain on her face.

"Can you restrain her?" She turned slightly to Andre.

"Restrain?" Becca tried to hide the panic in her voice.

"Becca, this is Jemi. She is gifted in reading people. With a slight touch, she can read your intentions for us. It'll be easier if you don't fight her."

Becca glanced at the door. No chance of making it past combat-girl here. "What's to say she'll only look at my intentions? Maybe she'll stay and play a bit."

Jemi stepped forward, a wicked smile creeping on her lips. "Let's do this the hard way, then."

Becca struck out at her, but a debilitating pain in her temple brought her to her knees. She heard Andre's deep voice from somewhere, but it was distant. Cold hands forced themselves against her mind. She remembered her defenses and built wall after wall to keep these people out. But their power pressed down on her, wiping out any protective spell she could remember. Soon, the past few months flew in front of her eyes. Glimpses of her sister, Darion, and Caleb scattered across her mind.

Then her uncle appeared, the one devil she'd killed months ago and never wanted to see again. He had stolen Becca's innocence as a teenager, and returned to their family to kill her parents and take Elizabeth for his Soul-torn. His haughty laugh told Becca that despite his death, she didn't have her sister back and never would. A scream ripped out of her throat, and she slumped to the ground. The cold ground seeped into her body as echoes of the past reverberated in her mind.

Andre spoke, but Becca was beyond listening. They finally left, leaving her to her own demons.

CHAPTER FIVE

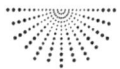

Peter's steps were slow and measured as he moved up the marble staircase, sharp needles of pain shooting up his legs with each step. The guards on either side of the door quickly averted their eyes. Too quick. Disgust stabbed him. He couldn't blame others for turning their heads. The first time he looked in a mirror after the fire, he's thrown up.

The guard kept his gaze lowered as he opened the door for Peter.

"Mr. Weston." The elderly servant greeted Peter without any hesitation or reaction. "May I take your jacket?"

Peter shrugged out of it, pain running across his shoulder as the scarred skin pinched.

"I will let my lord know you are here." With a nod, the servant left with Peter's jacket folded over one arm.

Peter turned, searching Ryma's opulent estate for any evidence of the attack. The hall held the elegance and beauty of the past with the promise of tomorrow. Large paintings covered tall walls, and a luxurious chandelier glittered above him. All evidence of the fight was wiped clean. Ryma, the coven leader and high priest, had quickly repaired the damage and downplayed the situation. If only Peter's wounds were so easily healed.

Peter had missed the fight here since he was almost killed days before, burned beyond recognition by a pyromancer. Despite magic and medications, months later his wounds remained puckered, red, and inflamed, making him some freak monster. Magical wounds were harder to heal. People said he was lucky to be alive. It didn't feel like luck.

The attendant returned. "Ryma is ready for you."

Peter followed him down the hall. The servant opened the door, and Peter strode in, his head high. Ryma had taught him at a young age to be proud and confident. He was a magician, and part of one of the greatest covens in the world. Peter had buried his past long ago and embraced the coven when Ryma discovered him at ten years old and had been bound to him since.

Ryma stood to greet him, his magic permeating the room. He wasn't a tall man, and he didn't need to be. He had an exotic Middle Eastern look about him with extremely short hair. Ryma kept it short on purpose, displaying the gaping scar across his scalp as a badge of honor. It gave Peter hope that he could someday wear his scars in much the same way.

Faced with Peter's grotesque scars, Ryma didn't flinch. It showed what kind of man he was.

"Peter, my dear boy. It's so great to see you up. How are you feeling?" Ryma shook his hand gently.

Peter paused to consider the dreaded question. What was he supposed to say? He felt like a demon with a tongue of thorns had dragged it across his whole body. Instead, he answered, "It is bearable, my lord."

"Good to hear. Please sit. We have much to discuss. What do you want to drink?" Ryma headed over to the liquor cabinet. He always loved his drinks. Some used to say he would poison whomever he disliked, but to refuse a drink would mean certain death as well.

Peter never cared to turn him down. "I'll take the strongest stuff you have."

Ryma chuckled. "Of course. Are you still in pain? The doctors said you were improving."

It was Peter's turn to laugh, but his sounded bitter and sharp. Improving? Perhaps, but he was barely better than the mass of bloody burns when he'd first arrived at the healing center. He was nowhere near completely healed though.

At the perplexed look on Ryma's face, Peter restrained himself. He already looked crazy. He didn't need to act the part. "The doctors are competent, but there is much for them to learn in healing."

"True. It was an art without much practice, but your doctors are the best." Ryma handed him his drink and sat down. His pristine suit and crystal glasses spoke of a wealth that Peter envied. Ryma paid him, but it was crumbs compared to this.

"Yes. Thank you for the care." Peter drank down half the glass in one gulp. Then he carefully lowered himself into the chair, his skin aching in protest.

"Of course. I've put a great deal into your well-being. I couldn't stop now. We have much to accomplish."

"Accomplish?"

Ryma led one of the governing thirteen covens in Northern America. What more was he aiming for?

"Yes. We need to purify our ranks. These wayward brothers of ours need to be taken care of."

"You mean Darion."

Ryma tightened his jaw, and with a twist of his wrist, stirred the ice in his drink. "Yes, Darion."

"He needs to pay for his crimes with a slow, painful death."

"I agree he needs to pay. I wouldn't be sad to string up his dead body in the middle of the market, but I'd rather use his power."

"He would make a powerful addition," Peter said. "Though I'd rather the birds pick the flesh off his skin." Darion had given him this hell he was forced to live with. Peter couldn't look at Darion's face again without wanting to rip it apart.

"I knew you'd be motivated to help."

"Motivated, yes. Whether I can is another question." This trip alone had drained Peter more than he cared to admit. He finished off his drink, relishing the warm liquor down his throat. "I am far from inconspicuous."

"I understand." Ryma took another sip. "I've been thinking on that. I've recently corralled a wayward illusionist back into our flock who should be able to help you. You may know him. A talented boy, Nevada."

CHAPTER SIX

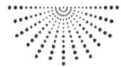

Darion walked down the narrow corridor lit with witch lights, the end of a rifle pointed at his back. They called the man behind him Leon, the same one that Darion couldn't touch with magic during the fight at the cave. Beneath all those muscles, Leon must have some type of defense or immunity to magic, something Darion had never encountered before.

Walking next to him was the mind reader, Jemi. She had a brisk manner about her, but was talented enough. When she pried into his mind, she focused on his intentions, motivations, and strong feelings. The sensation unsettled his defenses, but it wasn't the first time someone had scanned his mind. He knew he was overmatched, and playing nice for a few minutes might give him the upper hand later on. Darion would do what he had to do to get to Becca.

"Do you ever get tired of fighting magicians? Not being able to wield any true power?" Darion turned slightly back to Leon, trying to find out more about this anomaly.

Leon motioned with his gun. "Keep facing forward. Jemi may trust you, but I'm still waiting for an opinion that counts."

Darion warmed Leon's gun slightly. He didn't want to startle him, but was testing how far this man's immunity covered.

Leon jabbed the gun into his neck. "Cut it out if you ever want to see your friends again."

"Okay." Darion raised his hands in innocence.

At the thought of Becca, Darion's chest tightened. She was smart. Smart enough to not cause too much trouble. Maybe he was being too hopeful, since she seemed to fall into trouble on a regular basis. But it was his kind of trouble.

Darion tracked the turns and twists as they continued down the tunneled hall, trying to determine where they were at. "So where're we going? To your leader, the over-sized gopher?"

"You're a riot," Leon said with no humor. "Shut up. We're almost there."

They stopped in front of a heavy door, dark, made out of a similar material as the cave walls, but smoother. Leon put his hand on the door, and with a click, it opened.

"Come in," a deep voice said from inside.

A brush of power wafted over Darion as he entered the large room, similar almost to a den with several book-shelves and a couple of desks and chairs. In the center of the room sat an older magician behind a large desk. Darion didn't read magicians well—he never took to it in school—but he didn't need to. This man radiated power.

"Have a seat. I hope my brother wasn't too unwelcoming."

Brothers? At second glance, he could see the similarities past the tall frames and dark skin. Andre must've been older, his hair, closely shaved and speckled with gray, while Leon had the strength and power of someone younger, still in his thirties.

"If you call having a gun pressed into your neck welcoming, then he was perfect." Darion helped himself to the nearest chair.

"You need me anymore?" Leon asked. "I'm due back to scare some new recruits."

A flash of exasperation crossed Andre's face. "That will be all, thank you." Once Leon left, he turned his attention to Darion. "Welcome. I'm Andre and this is my home."

"Nice, if you don't like the sun."

Andre smiled. "We do have sunrooms and many amenities that would surprise you."

"Resort-style living for a coven. What will we think up next?" Darion lifted his feet up on the desk and relaxed back in his chair. If this man wanted him dead, he would be. It made him feel bold.

"We're not a coven. I don't call for blood oaths." Andre brushed his hand across his desk as if dusting off lint, but instead, a strong wave forced Darion's feet off the table.

Darion caught himself before he fell out of his chair.

"But I do demand respect, and usually get it."

Jemi chuckled lightly as she took a seat across from Darion.

"I see." Darion coughed slightly, covering his embarrassment. "What coven raised you?"

"My parents raised me. How about you?"

No obligations? No blood oath?

"Then you're the rogue I heard about." Darion never imagined the rogue would be this powerful. He imagined a rugged man with a dark cloak and a mangy beard down to his chest, nothing this organized or powerful.

"I'm no rogue. I run this community for humans with or without magical powers, as a safe haven of sorts."

"A safe haven?" He swallowed his surprise. One of the most powerful magicians Darion had ever met, and he ran an orphanage. "Why hide? With your power, you don't have to hide."

"You didn't answer my question." Andre leaned forward in his chair, elbows on the tables. He pressed his fingertips together. "Jemi said you were not bound to a coven. What coven raised you? Or should I ask Jemi?"

Darion nodded, trying to focus on the question instead of this rarity in front of him. "My parents were blood bound to Ryma. They died when I turned eighteen. Before he could tie me into servitude, I disappeared."

"And you've managed to stay hidden?"

"No. He's wanted me for years but was a busy man, and I wasn't worth his time. He has upped his search recently." Darion didn't think it smart to mention the price Ryma had on his head at the moment. "But I don't plan to be bound to anyone either." He stressed his point. Giving a blood oath to a high priest was signing a contract that couldn't be broken, tying two magicians together in more ways than one.

"I don't ask for blood bonds. My people take oaths sometimes, but they are not magically bound. We do have a very talented group of individuals. And while I don't force obedience, I have my ways of ensuring our safety." He leaned back in his chair.

"A mind reader is helpful." Darion glanced at Jemi.

"But you *are* bound in some way," Andre said.

Puzzled, Darion waited for him to continue.

"To Becca, who happens to be connected to the Soultorn."

"My connection to Becca is…" How could he explain

something he wasn't sure of himself? They'd joined powers when they escaped Ryma's estate, but their bond continued. It wasn't forced through blood, but tied through something else.

"It is something unique, from what Jemi tells me and what I sense. But I'm more concerned about her bond with the Soultorn."

"It's not a Soultorn to Becca. It's her sister. We've been trying to save her."

Andre cocked his head. "How do you think that's possible?"

"Ryma's been working on moving demons from one host to another. What is so different about shoving one out of someone who didn't ask for it?"

"That perhaps you want this host to stay alive when you've done so."

Darion let out a frustrated breath. "Yeah, if at all possible."

"Maybe." Andre pushed back from the desk and stood up. "Let's go see this demon for ourselves, and her witch."

Becca kept time by the meals sent through her door, always the same thing: some type of fishy soup and a roll. It was fresh, though, so she couldn't complain.

Sometime after lunch, the camo-wearing nightmare, Jemi, appeared to escort her out. In a fight, Becca may have taken her. But this witch now carried a gun. Guess even magicians liked back-up.

Becca tried to memorize the path they walked, but everything looked so similar. Witch lights hanging on the walls marked the tunnels, but with no apparent pattern. "Where are we going?"

"To see your Soultorn."

"My sister," Becca corrected.

"Whatever." Jemi brushed her off.

Becca bit her tongue, holding back what she really wanted to say. She was outmatched and outgunned right now. She needed to see Elizabeth.

They continued through the complex system of hallways, which were wide enough for two people to pass, but not comfortably. How could these people live like this, like rodents scurrying in the shadows?

The hallway widened into guarded doors. One man with a rifle stood watch. He lowered his head and stepped out of the way as Jemi approached.

She placed her palm on the door, and it opened under her touch to a bright room with neon lights and white walls. Andre stood waiting for her with Darion and Caleb.

"Becca." Darion came to her side. "You okay?"

Becca nodded and glanced between Darion and Caleb to make sure they were both all right. She started to answer them, but the words lodged in her throat. She noticed a glass barrier in the room, and on the other side lay Elizabeth, unconscious on a bed with a sheet covering her. Tubes ran out of her body to bags full of liquid hanging on metal stands. The disturbing picture looked like an experiment gone wrong. Elizabeth's pale skin had grayed, her eyes dark and sunken in.

"The tubes are to keep her fed and unconscious, even without magic." Andre stood next to Becca. "We can't chance waking her."

Becca wiped her cheeks, cursing herself for the tears. She couldn't help it. She could have sworn that these people had killed Elizabeth. Becca didn't believe their lies. It didn't make sense that they left her alive.

She stepped forward and placed a hand on the glass. A chill ran through her body.

"Why have you kept her alive?" She'd racked her brain for possibilities. The only one she could think of was collateral for bargaining. A level five Soultorn was worth more than a small town.

"I was under the impression that she was more than your Soultorn." Andre stepped beside Becca. "I thought you wanted her alive?"

"I do." Becca kept her gaze glued on her sister. "I just thought…"

"Who did this?"

As closed-mouthed as she normally was, she found herself telling him and hoped it would make a difference. "My uncle, a week or so after he killed my parents. Great wizarding etiquette.

"And yet here you are, one yourself."

"Lucky me." She knew her smile was nothing more than a bitter twist of lips. "So what happens now? You let us on our merry way, and no one is the wiser?" The moment she looked into his eyes, she knew that wasn't going to happen.

"I can't jeopardize my community. And I can't let her live. You'd be doing her a kindness."

"So after you kill my sister, we get an ultimatum. Join your little coven or die?" Becca's voice rose in tandem with her temper.

Darion stepped forward, addressing Andre. "Give us time to search for an answer, to remove the demon. Time won't hurt."

Darion gave this man too much credit. But hey, why not ask the man who'd just kidnapped them for a favor?

Andre watched Elizabeth, obviously considering the

proposition. Instead of answering, he turned to Darion. "She will probably die either way."

"I think it's worth the chance. Think of all the other Mundanes and magicians you could help," Darion said.

"Maybe, but is it worth the risk?"

"It is to me," Becca replied. They had come too far for her to stop now.

"Yes, I guess it would be to you." Andre stared between the two sisters.

Darion continued. "If you didn't already know, Bael is inside that girl. A demon guaranteed to give amazing power to those powerful enough to wield it. If you help us, you can have Bael."

Andre lowered his gaze at Darion.

"We don't negotiate." Jemi finally joined in the conversation. "If what you say is true, then we could take Bael for ourselves, and let the girl die."

"If that's how you work, then you're no better than Ryma," Caleb snapped back, a steady presence in the room.

"Quiet," Andre silenced them and watched Liz for a moment. "I will help you however I can. We'll research methods for separation, but you need to know it will probably mean death for your sister. Even in this state, she may not last the month."

"I know." Becca had been preparing herself for the inevitable.

"While I work on this, I expect full cooperation here in our community. Taking jobs and contributing where necessary. Then, if you choose to leave after the cold season, you can."

They were well into fall. After the cold season meant they would be here for months. If it meant a chance to save Liz, Becca would do what she had to.

"Do you actually believe this is even possible?" Jemi moved to Andre's side.

"Doesn't matter. I've never turned away a magician in need, and I won't do it today."

Jemi gave an exaggerated huff, but didn't argue further.

"We better get you situated in the dorms, then, and set you up on work rotations." Andre headed to the door.

Relief and hope flooded Becca's body. Were they finally catching a break? Somehow stumbling across a wizard to help them? Becca placed a hand on the glass barrier, and projected her thoughts to her sister. *I haven't forgotten about you. I'll save you.*

"Coming, Becca?" Darion asked as the others began filing out of the door.

"Yeah." The glass trembled under her hand, and a sharp crack gave way. A strong power stirred beyond the glass. "What the—"

Caleb pulled Becca away from the barrier.

Jemi spoke from behind them. "What the hell is happening?"

CHAPTER SEVEN

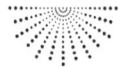

"Bael's awake," Becca said.

The crack continued to crawl across the glass, splintering like a glass spider web. Everyone stood quiet for a moment.

"We have her on some pretty heavy tranqs." Jemi pulled a handgun off her belt.

Andre approached the mirror with no trace of fear. "What's this tricky devil up to?"

The lights above them flickered.

Fear crept up Becca's spine. This was her sister. And the easiest way to get this demon under control would be to kill her. Becca wasn't sure how far Andre's power or hospitality would stretch if Bael pushed things.

"Darion." She grabbed his hand. Since their escape from the coven, they'd combined their power until they were strong enough to manage Bael. Maybe manage wasn't the right word, more like kept him sedated.

Darion tightened his hold and whispered the simple spell. His magical warmth flooded her system, and Becca closed her eyes at the familiar power flowing easily between them.

They had done this enough times so neither of them needed to speak. They pushed their magic forward, projecting it with a simple spell of unconsciousness. This time, though, it hit a brick wall.

Becca glanced at Darion.

"Again," he said.

They repeated the spell and struggled to gain power over Bael. Instead, the demon's power increased.

Becca's breath picked up as if she had been running a race. Her heart battered against her rib cage. Looking around, she noticed Andre staring at them. Jemi had the gun pointed at Elizabeth, and Caleb looked unsure whether to attack Jemi or Elizabeth first.

"You two share power so effortlessly," Andre said.

"It has been the only way to control the demon," Darion explained, wiping his brow. "He's been gaining strength."

"Probably feeding off of the girl," Andre suggested.

The idea sickened Becca, and she couldn't ignore the dark whisper that maybe her sister would be better off dead. No. She couldn't think like that, but the malignant thought lingered, a dark dread that constantly questioned if she was doing the right thing.

"Let me help." Andre's lips moved slightly, whispering a spell Becca couldn't hear.

After a long second or two, Elizabeth's clenched hands finally slackened as her body relaxed into the bed.

"So Bael is tired of playing dead, huh?" Andre offered.

"Guess so," Darion replied.

"How long have you been forcing it dormant?"

"A month or so. We only wake it slightly to feed, and that requires both of us."

"Those meds are strong enough to put one of us in a coma. Placing it in a pentagram will be our safest move."

"Then do it." Caleb's frustration was evident in his voice. Even though he may not have magic, Becca knew this demon drained Caleb too. It wore on all of them.

"Since the beast is tied to you, Becca, why don't you help me with the pentagram?" Andre turned from the viewing window. "We need to take care of this soon. The longer we wait, the less chance there'll be anything left of your sister to save."

He should get a medal in sugarcoating, Becca thought sarcastically, though she actually enjoyed his brutal honesty.

With a quick glance at his watch, he turned to Jemi. "Do you have the time?"

"As much as I'll have tomorrow."

Jemi and Andre retrieved the needed materials from the cabinets lining one wall, and they all moved into the room where Elizabeth lay behind the glass. Jemi carried five bowls, made from some sort of stone, and began placing them around Elizabeth. The two looked comfortable setting up the needed material: salt for the outline of the crisscrossing stars, and fire, water, earth, wind, and spirit represented in each of the bowls. Becca wondered how often these two did this sort of thing. Was that the true purpose of this room?

She hadn't created a pentagram since she was back at the cabin, learning magic for the first time from Darion—which felt like an eon ago. But it didn't stop her from picking up the second bag of salt and starting to work at the opposite end of where Andre worked. This pentagram had to include not only Becca and Liz, but the bed too.

Darion started the fire in one of the small bowls. Caleb stood watch, looking uncomfortable, like he often did when Becca's more magical side showed.

With all of them helping, they finished the oversized pentagram quickly. It sparked and snapped with magic. Power flowing through the room.

Andre stood next to Becca. "You ready?"

"Yeah." She bit the inside of her mouth, keeping her nerves at bay.

Andre looked to Becca. "One of your jobs will be to come in twice a day with the medical staff to keep her fed and hydrated. Jemi or I may also need to be here to help control Bael."

Jemi rolled her eyes, but Andre didn't notice.

"Okay." Becca was grateful to be given the chance to see her sister as often as she could. She hated the idea of locking her away in this cold little room.

Andre reviewed the spells for sealing the pentagram and breaking it with Becca, making sure every syllable was enunciated correctly. Then Becca drew on her power deep within, and sealed the pentagram with Andre. Fire snapped in the bowl, and a hot breeze blew across her face.

"Good job. Now let's get to work." Andre turned and started out the door. "I have assignments for all three of you."

Caleb, Darion, and Becca glanced at each other for a moment, each dazed by Andre's abrupt manner. Since their separation for the last day and a half, there were so many words left unsaid between them.

"Assignments?" Becca tentatively asked.

"No time like now. Everyone here earns their keep. Caleb, the guard outside the door will direct you to Leon for your assignment. Jemi, take Becca down with Lance and the others, and Darion, you're with me."

Before any of them could say more than goodbye, they all went their separate ways. Becca spared one last look at her sister, unconscious in the dim room. Liz should be safer here than before, right? Even though Becca felt grateful for Andre's help, leaving her sister behind, buried in this underground labyrinth, left an empty feeling in her gut.

CHAPTER EIGHT

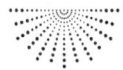

Peter headed down to the basement, dampness clinging to his skin. Sweat gathered on his brow with each step, a painful reminder of his limitations. Why were monsters always created in the basement? By all means, Peter felt and looked like the quintessential monster. Ryma must have watched too many scary movies. That, or he didn't trust the magic going on down here.

At the bottom of the stairs, a large room opened up, littered with old rugs and scattered seating. A minor winged demon sat in the corner, hiding in the shadows. Lamps dimly lit the room, adding to the eerie motif. There were a few doors branching off and a hallway leading into darkness. Peter had heard of the underground system under this estate, but had never seen it.

In the center of the room, Nevada, a boy Peter remembered from school, reclined in a chair, staring into a fire and cradling a drink. Gone was Nevada's jovial confidence from years ago. Peter felt no pity for him. Nevada had shirked his responsibility for long enough. The coven needed every magician they could get, especially illusionists.

As one of the most gifted illusionists around, Nevada's powerful creations were a valuable tool. Now, under Ryma's unrelenting influence, they discovered that Nevada could permanently change things, too, like faces. Granted, it required a great deal of magic. Of course, they wouldn't know how much until Nevada stopped sulking.

Peter cleared his throat.

"I heard ya'." Nevada sipped his drink again. He had on torn jeans and a bulky purple scarf. His black hair was growing out, thick and bushy, and needed to be washed.

"Then let's get to work. I'm not here for a social call."

"No one would call you the social type." Nevada turned to face him. A massive bruise covered the side of his face, one eye bloodshot and his lips split.

"Why don't you fix your face?" Peter remembered Nevada as a vain illusionist, his appearance always in perfect order.

Nevada shrugged and stood up. "Why?"

Peter shuddered. "Disgusting."

"Look who's calling who disgusting." Nevada smiled, the cut pulling at his lip.

Peter stilled at the insult. It was true. More than true. "Ryma wants you to fix my face. Permanently."

"So Ryma's huge scar is okay, but your kind of ugly is too much?" Nevada headed over to the cabinet to refill his glass.

Peter bristled. "I don't need the commentary. Just do your job."

"And you trust me? For this kind of work, it will take several weeks. Any little slip..." Nevada started to tilt his glass. "Could end in catastrophe."

"Which would end your life. Screw with me and I'll kill you." He meant it. His pulse raced with anger.

Nevada straightened his glass and chuckled softly.

Was this guy sober enough to do this? Peter would have to talk to Ryma about cutting off his alcohol.

"Don't worry," Nevada said. "I'm blood bound now. I can't go against Ryma's wishes even if I wanted. I'll make you back into whatever ugly bastard you want."

Rage poured over Peter, and before he could think twice, he punched Nevada in the face. He crumpled to the ground, his bulky bracelets clattering on the floor.

Guess they were starting tomorrow.

CHAPTER NINE

Caleb remained stone-faced while frustration boiled under his skin. After Becca worked her magic, Andre sent the three of them to work in separate directions. Caleb didn't even have a chance to talk to Becca, to see if everything was all right. But once they offered to stay in exchange for help with Elizabeth, they were expected to get to work. All Caleb heard was "earn your keep," and something about a "well-oiled machine."

They were doing fine earning their keep on their own, except for Liz. Maybe it would last and maybe not, but now they had a chance to save Liz, so he reminded himself they needed Andre, for the moment. He'd grown up with Elizabeth and Becca, and they were the closest thing to family he had left. He treated Elizabeth like a little sister, though he never thought of Becca like a sister. He was trying to now.

"Hey, Caleb, this way." Nikki stopped and pointed to a path branching off to the right.

Caught up in his own thoughts, Caleb walked ahead before noticing she wasn't following. He paused. "What?"

"Don't worry. If anyone can save your friend, it would be my dad. He's great."

He didn't reply. Did she really think he could do an about-face with the man who sent soldiers to attack them? She watched him, obviously waiting for a reply, which he didn't give. Her boldness was aggravating.

With one last frustrated glance, Nikki started back down the hall before explaining the history of the compound. A few years after the Magicians took over the government, her grandparents realized how powerful their son, Andre, was and took him into hiding. They didn't want him to be manipulated and used by the city covens. Her grandparents were long gone, but their memory remained strong in this underground haven for Mundanes and Magicians alike.

Nikki showed Caleb the cafeteria first. The great room spread wide and far, bigger than he thought possible underground. Huge pillars were stationed throughout the room, possibly providing support for the structure.

She offered him lunch. He declined, wanting this tour over as soon as possible.

They exited into the hall then took another path down to a set of rooms. "And here's your dorm room. They'll show you the showers and bathrooms."

"Everyone sleeps together?" He didn't mind the idea too much. Between Darion, Becca and himself, they could protect each other.

"No. There is one room for the men and another for the women. You can request your own room from Andre, but they take some time. They're mostly for couples or families." She glanced at him.

"Is that all?"

"Just one more, the training room." She headed off.

Caleb kept pace at her side. "What training? I don't have magic."

"It's not that kind of training." She didn't slow, her lips twitching as if hiding back a smile. Was she happy that she finally had his attention?

"Then what kind of training is it?"

"After you fought with Leon, he recommended you for combat training. You must have impressed him."

"Impressed him? He was trying to kill us."

"No. He was bringing you back alive."

Right, as if he'd believe that. "I'm not going to war for you people." He didn't run away from one ruler to get another.

"We don't go to war," she explained. "We defend ourselves."

"Like when you guys attacked me and my friends." Caleb's shoulder still ached from that fight.

Nikki stopped and turned. She closed the distance between them, and he could smell the cleaner from the medical room on her. For such a small person, she was intense. "We train to protect. We train to build, to help, to hunt for food."

Her face flushed slightly with frustration. It didn't look natural on her. He'd witnessed that when she tended to his wounds. But she wasn't weak either. And for some reason, now that she was standing up to him, he liked her for it. He still wasn't happy, but he couldn't blame her for his situation, at least not completely.

He tried to smooth out his features, and even offered a placating smile. "I'll go, but I can't make any promises."

"Sounds fair." She did an abrupt about-face and continued down the hall.

The noise of the water echoed down the tunnel to

greet them. Scones of witch light sent shadows dancing against the walls. Soon, a bright light grew in the distance.

"Are we going outside?" He thought he wouldn't see the sun until they left this crazy place.

"Yeah." Nikki grinned. "They train outside and in the surf."

"How can that be safe? Won't people see?"

"We're very secluded, and my father is alerted when any of our barriers are breached. That's how we found you and your friends." She glanced back, and an apologetic look crossed her face. "We have ways to protect ourselves."

"Looks like it."

They stepped out into the surf. The afternoon sun hiding behind the mountain cast shadows on the beach. Tall cliffs surrounded them, and the expanse of never-ending water shimmered in the sunlight. Actual sunlight on the ocean. The smell of saltwater brushed over him on a cool breeze.

"What guppy do we have here?" The deep, familiar voice of Leon rang out, breaking the beauty of the moment.

"Be nice, Uncle," Nikki warned.

"We're not playing patty-cake out here."

Dread bubbled in Caleb's empty stomach as Nikki laughed and patted her uncle on the arm. Nikki could get away with murder with that smile of hers. What was he getting into? He could be fish food by the end of the day.

CHAPTER TEN

"A re you coming or not?" Jemi snapped over her shoulder. For a small woman, she was fast. With her short blonde hair, she could almost pass for an evil pixie.

"Yeah, yeah," Becca mumbled and jogged a couple steps to close the distance.

Jemi had already showed her the supply room, where the woman behind the desk gave Becca a warmer jacket, thank God, then Jemi briefly pointed the way to the cafeteria and sleeping areas. She wasn't in a talkative mood.

"So what's the plan?" Becca sped up to stay at her side. "Am I meeting Andre later to research spells to help Elizabeth?"

Jemi scoffed. "Hardly. Unless you speak ancient Latin, Andre doesn't need your help. He needs you to learn what the hell you're doing with your powers before you get yourself killed."

"I've survived on my own for this long." Becca rubbed her face. Granted, she wasn't great with magic yet, but she knew enough to get by.

"Thanks to Darion." Jemi didn't give Becca time to

answer, but took a left down the next path. "The more you know your magic and its limits, the better chance you have."

"So, you're going to train me?"

"No," she said. "I'm dropping you off with Lance. He's in charge of all new recruits."

"What about Darion or Caleb's assignments?" She hated not saying goodbye or talking with them about her agreeing to stay with Andre. It felt…off.

Jemi shrugged. They turned another corner.

"So you say there are no blood oaths here, and you're in charge of this so-called mind security. Who checks *your* head?" After all Becca had been through, she couldn't help but wonder, and the mental ache from Jemi's probing in the cave was far from forgotten. Her hands curled into useless fists.

Jemi's gaze dropped to Becca's fists, then lifted as her lips curled in a sneer. "No one. One of the perks of being number two."

"If you say so." Becca took a deep breath and unclenched her hands. Despite her inclination otherwise, she had to work with these people. If Andre was who he appeared to be, he was the best hope for Liz. So she wouldn't push Jemi any more for now, but she wouldn't forget what Jemi had done to her either.

Jemi continued through the tunnels and soon dropped her off at a simple door. "Tell Lance that Andre sent you. He'll figure out what to do with you." She scowled at Becca and left.

Becca glared at Jemi's retreating form, and then turned to the door. No use in prolonging the inevitable. There was no security on the door, only a simple silver knob. When she walked through it, she struggled to keep her mouth closed.

The magic in the room was almost palpable, like a heavy fog causing the hairs on her arms to stand on end. The room was almost as large as the cafeteria. Its cavernous ceiling stretched high, and she couldn't see the back wall since it appeared to wind sideways. A small mob of people were strewn throughout the room. She didn't even attempt to follow the different threads of magic and fights carrying on inside. Blue mats littered the floor, and one wall was filled with metal lockers.

A white-haired woman sat on the floor with calico cats on her lap and shouted encouragement to a pair of young boys in front of her. "Curse the bastard. Get 'em good."

One of the boys flew to the floor. People were fighting, cursing, and one small girl almost appeared to be floating as everyone practiced magic. Controlled chaos at its best.

How does anyone think straight in this place?

A thin man in dark fatigues jogged towards her. His light hair was shaved short, and the start of a beard lined his face. "You must be the new girl I heard about. Come to join in the fun, huh?" He carried a heavy accent that she hadn't heard before.

"You call this fun?" she asked.

"Sure is." He nudged her slightly with his shoulder, like some schoolboy, not the thirty-something-year-old man he appeared to be. "I'm Lance. I run this zoo."

"Becca."

"So Andre tells me he caught you. Never know what that guy will turn up from the ocean."

"More like reeled in from the sea like a dead fish."

He laughed. "Come on. We're not a bad lot. At least not until you really get to know us."

"If you say so," Becca mumbled.

This man laughed more than anyone she knew. *Does Andre grow drugs down here or something?*

"I heard you specialize in the spirit element, right?" He arched a brow and kept his quirky grin.

"That's what they tell me."

For most people, magic was a general ability, like lighting a small fire or throwing a painful curse at an enemy. Others received specialties, or one specific magical area where they excelled. Like savants in music or math, magicians could specialize. For Darion, it was fire. Most of his curses revolved around fire because that was where his strength lay. For Becca, it was spirit. Whether she could read minds like Jemi, or some other manifestation, was still yet to be determined. The freaky powerful ones, like Andre or Ryma, had more than one specialty.

"Good, good." Lance waved a young girl over. "We'll go over basics and see what you got. We train a bit differently here."

He welcomed the young girl with long tawny-brown hair and big green eyes, and then turned to introduce her to Becca. "This here is Navina. She'll be your sparring partner for the rest of the afternoon. We don't use demons in here and no physical contact for the most part."

"Sparring without touching?" Even if there was contact, Becca couldn't hurt this young girl with freckles on her nose. She didn't even come up to Becca's chin.

"Navina, take it easy on her, okay?"

The girl batted her eyelashes and gave an innocent smile. "Of course."

"Off you go, then. I'll check on you in a minute." Lance jogged off to a boy screaming near the back. Soon, the noise was gone, but the teenage boy's face was twisted, contorted in pain.

Did anyone else find kids torturing each other...unsettling? Evidently not the old lady by the lockers. What was her deal?

"What's your name?" Navina started towards an empty mat by the wall.

Becca dragged her attention away from the injured boy and followed. "Becca."

"I'm twelve. How old are you?"

Becca smiled at her. "I'm twenty-four."

"So Andre found you?"

"That's one way to put it." Not used to children's forwardness, she wasn't sure how much she should tell this girl.

"That is not an answer." Navina was bright for her age.

Becca swallowed. "No. But maybe I don't want to talk about it."

The girl shrugged. "I heard you turned your sister into a Soultorn and needed Andre's help."

"I didn't turn my sister." Becca's face burned at the stupid rumor. Lowering her voice, she added, "My uncle did."

"Yeah. My dad tried to turn my mom into one. I stopped him. That's why we're here." Navina looked proud.

Becca scanned the room, and for the first time, realized how many people found refuge here. Most people here were outcasts, runaways from a world that didn't play fair. "Sorry to hear that."

"It happens," she said with a maturity way beyond her years. "Let's see what you've got."

Becca wasn't sure if she should be curious or nervous. "What are we going to do?"

"Fight. Lance says the best way to practice is to pretend we're outside of these caves. Pretend we're fighting for our lives."

"Okay."

"Ready?"

Becca mentally put up her walls, hoping this would only be defensive. "Yes, ready."

Navina spoke in Latin, the language curling off her tongue. Becca took a step backwards. It felt like a battering ram knocking at her defenses. How could this girl be so strong?

Becca retreated again and again until her back hit the wall. Then, in an instant, a gush of wind hit Becca, flipping her in the air. She landed with a thud.

The pigtailed Navina appeared above her. "Wanna go again?"

Becca nodded, pain tingling down her spine. Navina held out her hand with a wide grin.

After the fourth time of losing to little miss pigtails, Lance was the one to offer Becca a hand. "Having fun?"

"Getting my butt kicked by a kid? I've had better days." *And worse*, she reminded herself. At least Navina had been nice. Nice and relentless. Becca stood and dusted off her pants.

"Andre told me you often combine power with another more experienced wizard," Lance said.

"Yeah. My powers were sealed, and I didn't have time to train. That's how I stayed alive." She couldn't help the defensiveness straightening her spine.

"It's dangerous, you know. When you combine powers, you give a wizard free reign of your magic, your soul. Now that you have the time, you need to learn how to survive on your own."

She swallowed hard. She couldn't deny she relied on Darion more than she should, but Lance was right. Darion wasn't necessarily always going to be there.

"Then teach me." Warm determination grew in her muscles, which wanted to be used. She might have been forced there, and might not completely trust these rebels, but she was being handed tools to grow. She'd stay for as long as it took to learn all she could about her power and abilities from these people. She needed to be strong, not only for herself, but for those she loved.

Lance's face lit up with a smile. "See? It only took getting your butt kicked by a twelve-year-old *several times* for you to be eager to learn."

CHAPTER ELEVEN

With a bowl of clam chowder in one hand and a roll in the other, Becca stared into a sea of people, searching for Darion or Caleb. The huge cafeteria buzzed with people visiting over a warm dinner. She was impressed with their kitchens and how they fed this many people, especially existing underground. There had to be at least fifty or more gathered here at the moment, and there were still others scheduled for the later dinner shift.

"Becca, over here." Navina stood on her chair and hollered across the cafeteria, waving.

Navina was definitely not shy. Warmth spread over Becca's face as numerous sets of eyes focused on her. The new girl in town. After one more glance, Becca headed over to Navina's table. People slowly turned their eyes away and resumed their dinner.

Becca slid into the bench seat across from Navina.

"Mom, this is Becca. My partner I told you about."

"Pleased to meet you. I'm Bree," she said, while struggling with a wiggly toddler on her lap. Bree looked young for a mom, with a thin frame and brown hair braided down her back. "And this little monster is Thomas."

Thomas had brown curls covering his head and clam chowder plastered on his face.

"Hi, Thomas," Becca said.

He stuck out his little tongue.

"Nice to meet you too." She stuck her tongue out in a playful return.

"I heard you had a rough first day of training," Bree said.

"Only because Navina kicked my—" She stopped herself before swearing.

Bree laughed. "Don't worry. I heard all about it. I know it can be rough, but if it keeps us safe, it's worth it."

Becca wanted to ask if they were really safe. She guessed they were safer hiding here than struggling out in the wild or surviving in the city. Becca couldn't let herself completely relax though. Not when the true monsters were still out there.

"So what do you do here? I'm curious to know what comes after training." Becca wondered what all those kids would do with their skills.

"Everyone has a different job to contribute to the community. I'm what you call a Mundane. I work in the nursery with the young children." Bree quickly grabbed the roll her son tried to chuck across the table. "They keep me busy, for sure."

Navina spoke up. "I got my magic from my dad."

Becca remembered Navina's earlier comment that her dad had tried to turn her mom into a Soultorn. Bree looked down at her son and didn't speak.

Caleb then crashed down into the seat next to Becca's, with two bowls of soup and a handful of rolls. "I was looking all over for you."

"Got enough food?" Becca eyed his overflowing plate.

"Those training with Leon get doubles. His orders."

"Leon?"

Before Becca could get an answer, Navina chimed in. "Leon's the top military commander, and Andre's brother." She turned to Caleb. "I'm Navina."

"I'm Caleb. Nice to meet you."

"This is my mom, Bree."

As if on cue, Thomas chucked the bowl across the table. Caleb caught it before it clattered to the floor. The toddler erupted in laughter.

"I think that's Thomas's cue we need to leave," she told Navina. "Nice to meet you, Becca and Caleb. I'm sure we'll see you around."

"But, Mom..." Navina complained.

Bree lowered her eyes, and Navina quickly quieted.

"I'll see you tomorrow, Becca. Wear some pads." Navina chuckled and grabbed the plates. She and her mom walked away.

"Rough first day?" Caleb glanced at Becca before biting into a roll.

"Nothing bread and butter won't solve." Becca swiped one of his rolls, hers already finished. "Who makes this stuff? I'll marry them and live underground for the rest of my days."

Caleb stifled a laugh and ended up choking on his bread. It took him a couple moments to clear his mouth. "You must have had a good day."

"I got put in my place by a twelve-year-old." She swallowed a bite and continued. "One of my better days. What about you?"

"The person who trashed me was much older, Leon actually." Caleb pushed his hair out of his eyes as he dug into his soup. "Plus side is working on the beach."

"Security team? Isn't that dangerous?" She didn't like the idea of him being on the front lines of any conflict, especially if it didn't involve both of them.

"Not any more than usual." Caleb shoveled in a couple more bites.

The idea didn't settle well with Becca, but she couldn't blame him. Keeping up their strength and skills would only help them when they left. "Have you seen Darion yet?"

He shook his head.

"I'm sure he'll come around by nightfall." After the words left her mouth, she realized what they sounded like. She ducked her head. "I didn't mean that how it sounded."

"We're not on the run anymore, Becca."

"I know…" She couldn't remember when he started using Becca and stopped calling her Rebecca, the girl he first knew. The girl he had loved. She knew it was for the best, especially seeing she no longer was the girl he loved. Years in the city had changed her. They were friends, close friends, which was best for everyone, but these awkward moments still crept in now and again. "There are some rooms assigned to families and couples if you want, but that's Andre's call."

It was Caleb's turn to avoid her gaze.

"N-no, I'm not saying that," she stammered. "We were prisoners last night. I'm still getting used to all this."

"I get it." He lifted his eyes, and despite the dirt and grime on his face, there was a peace there she hadn't seen for ages. "It's hard to trust even those who feel trustworthy, but maybe, just maybe, we can make a difference here."

Becca was happy for Caleb and hoped these people were as good as they seemed. She just wanted Bael out of her sister. She couldn't imagine anything more beyond that, because if her sister died… Well, she couldn't think beyond that.

"I'm tired. I think I'm going to crash." She grabbed her dishes.

Caleb snagged her arm and studied her with comforting concern. "Are you okay?"

"Yeah, I'm fine." Some of her hair escaped its ponytail and fell into her face. She was grateful for the cover. "And Caleb, you always made a difference to me."

For Becca, the next couple of days sped by in a blur. She trained early in the morning, only taking breaks to meet up with Nikki and help feed Elizabeth. Despite her frail frame, her sister looked a little better. The vitamins in the feeding solution helped.

By evening, Becca's body was exhausted. When she wasn't dueling, she was memorizing spells. Lance gave her a small book listing the basic curses and defenses. She enjoyed the hard work, but something was missing. Some*one*, to be exact.

Darion had missed meals. Caleb had said Darion only made it to his dorm room after he fell asleep. Caleb reportedly woke him in the mornings before he headed off to train. Becca could understand Darion being busy—they all were—but too busy to come by and say hi to her?

Her fears from when they were first dating started creeping back in. When they first met, he lied about being a magician. He said it was to protect her. Now the feeling like she was missing something important reappeared. It could be Darion. After spending day after day with him for months, an empty space in her chest ached to see him.

She didn't say anything about it, but continued training, pouring all of her anger into it and then falling asleep as soon as her head hit the pillow.

That night, after training and before dinner, she headed down to meet Nikki at Elizabeth's room. Jemi usually met them there as well to help if Bael started to get restless.

"Hey, Becca." Nikki greeted her with two liquid feeding bags in each hand.

"Hi. Still waiting on Jemi?"

"Yeah."

Becca and Nikki had no reason to hate each other, and they didn't, but an awkwardness always hung between them. Neither girl spoke of it, but neither tried for small talk either. It could be neither trusted the other. Becca's previous difficult behavior in the cell had gotten around, and she'd caught more than one sideways glance. Or maybe it had something to do with how Nikki looked at Caleb.

Jemi appeared around the corner. She bypassed any pleasantries or greetings and headed to the door. Becca hadn't figured out how these doors worked. They must have been forged from some type of clay, but the smooth finish made it look like wood. The doors to the dorm and cafeteria swung open, available to all. But these doors, with a clear pane in the middle, only opened to those with access.

Jemi placed her palm on the glass. Her magic must have a signature that unlocked the door. The magic amazed Becca, and annoyed her too. Since she didn't have unlimited access to her sister, it meant they didn't trust her. She'd often found armed security guarding the door.

Before they entered the room, Andre appeared behind them. "Jemi, Lance needs you."

"Again?"

Andre smiled, like he usually did when Jemi got grumpy.

"Okay." She stepped around him to leave. "If I don't help now, I'll have to clean it up later."

"Probably."

Nikki held the door ajar, and Andre and Becca followed her in. Becca took her place at the head of the pentagram, where the point of the star representing spirit lay, and she released the pentagram with a spell. With Andre present, Becca had no trouble holding Bael inside. Nikki quickly went to work, unusually quiet.

"How are things going in the hospital?" Andre asked his daughter.

"Good." Nikki had already removed the old bag connected to the tubing and was in the process of replacing it.

"Doc isn't keeping you too busy?"

Nikki didn't answer. She faced away from her father and worked on Liz's legs, exercising and moving them. Her annoyance etched in her tight brows. Obviously Andre's little community down here wasn't as perfect as he portrayed.

Becca interrupted the silence with her own question for Andre. "What is Darion doing for you?"

Andre stole his gaze from his daughter. "What?"

"I haven't seen Darion for days. Not even at meals. What is he doing for you that requires monk-like seclusion?"

"Research."

"Research?" Surprise and anger battled for dominance in her mind. "Like reading old books or dissecting demon rats? Be more specific."

"Why don't you close the pentagram first please, Becca. Your temper can affect the demon."

She did feel a pulse of power, but with her frustration

riding her, she didn't mind it. She closed the pentagram, stepped back, and then looked at Andre expectantly.

"He's been researching old books for me. His knowledge of dead languages is impressive."

Dead languages? Becca kept her face stoic, not wanting to show her surprise or how much she didn't know about Darion. When they dated the first time, he hid what magic he had. And since they'd been back together, well…they'd been busy.

"He still has to eat," she said.

"I don't restrict his hours. If he's skipping meals, it's of his own choosing." He turned to the door and opened it with his palm. "Now if we may, I do have a camp to run, as you put it."

Becca's face burned with embarrassment. She mumbled "thanks" to Nikki and hurried into the dim corridors. Unaware of her destination, she walked and walked, not ready to face training or anyone.

Why was Darion keeping his distance? Hopefully he had a good answer.

The lines of Latin blurred together as the dusty smell of books filled the room. Sitting in Andre's library, Darion shut the heavy old book and closed his eyes, pinching the bridge of his nose to relieve an oncoming headache. He should have stopped hours ago. He promised himself he'd make it to dinner tonight to see Becca, but he wanted to have good news.

The morning was promising as he found his first reference to removing a demon, a spell called *disrupit.* Continuing his search throughout the day, the only other reference he found was a grimoire written by a man named

Imar. Darion scoured the library for the book and then searched his notes and remaining books for any other reference to the man. No luck.

The candles burned low, and Darion wondered how late it was. His watch had broken the day the rebels first brought them in.

A slight buzz of magic, and the door opened behind him. Andre strode in with a young woman following. Darion's mouth watered at the sight of the food on her tray. He gathered up the books and papers to make room for the food. His grumbling stomach wouldn't even let him complain about it being fish again.

"Thank you," he told the girl, accepting the food.

"You're welcome." The girl nodded and quickly left.

"I figured you needed to be fed soon or you'd turn on my books." Andre sat in his usual place behind his desk. "Going stir crazy in here yet?"

"More frustrated than anything." Darion rubbed his tired neck. "I finally found one that references the spell and the grimoire, but nothing else. We need to find that grimoire, but I haven't read anything about Imar or the book in the past three days. Unless you have more books somewhere, I don't have a clue where to find it."

"I do."

Darion paused, fork in hand. "What? Where?"

"Not here, unfortunately. I saw it once, years ago."

"Why didn't you say anything if you knew about this?"

"I didn't know it held the information we sought, but I wondered. I needed your expertise in languages to make sure," Andre explained.

"Who has it?"

"You may know him from Ryma's coven, an old mage named Abel."

"Abel." Darion repeated the name, remembering the

last time he saw Abel. It had been when he and Becca rescued Caleb from the slavers' auction. "At least he is not closely tied to Ryma."

"Do not forget, he is bonded to the coven. The only reason Ryma leaves him alone is because he is an ornery old cuss. Ryma could change that if he really wanted to."

"Well, if Abel let you see it before, it shouldn't be too hard to see it again."

"No. Rumor is Ryma's been on edge since you escaped his estate. I can't risk entering his city."

Darion didn't have to ask who he wanted to send. Andre's direct stare told it all. While Darion wasn't eager to head back to Ryma's area, he couldn't think of who else would be better suited to the job. Darion knew Abel as a child, and maybe he'd let him in. Now inspecting the ancient texts Abel owned…that was a different matter.

"I should leave tomorrow," he said.

Andre looked mildly surprised for a moment. "It's the girl, isn't it?"

"What?"

"I'm surprised you're willing to go back there so quickly."

Darion wasn't. Ever since he found Becca again, a guilty ache for all he'd done gnawed at him. He'd stripped Elizabeth's protective tattoo so Jeremiah could force her to be a Soultorn. Granted, he hadn't known that Liz was Becca's little sister or what Jeremiah had intended, but that didn't matter. Darion had bloodied his hands enough working for the coven. It would take years before it would wash that away.

He cleared his throat, realizing Andre was waiting for a response. "Speaking of Becca, I should go tell her what we know."

"She's probably asleep. It's past twelve, and she's been training all day."

"That late?" Darion's aching back was the only true way to keep time, he guessed.

"They reheated up your food a couple times, but I was busy."

"How's she doing?"

"Doing well, but I'm worried we may be getting her hopes up." Andre exhaled and a heavy weight appeared to pull on his shoulders.

Darion leaned forward. "How so?"

"Bael is growing stronger every day, and Elizabeth weakens. We can't wait much longer if there is any chance to revive the girl."

"I'll leave at first light, then."

"No, you need your sleep. Tomorrow night, a team is leaving on a supply run. You can go then. You'll have to be blindfolded as you leave."

"Really?" After spending days in Andre's personal library, Darion thought he had earned some level of trust. Granted, there were so many wards in the place, he didn't dare explore.

Andre gave one of his notorious smiles, meant to placate others. "Leon wanted to knock you out."

"Thanks, I guess." Darion dug into his food, images of the city returning to him. He grew up in that city in the shadow of the coven, and yet somehow the dark memories overshadowed any of the happier ones.

CHAPTER TWELVE

After tossing and turning most of the night, Becca was the last one out of bed. Her normally crowded bunk room was nearly empty. Well, except for Jace who woke her a minute ago. The tall, lanky girl with small mousey features now sat on one of the low bunks, tying her boots.

"Training starts in ten minutes," she said. "Better hurry or you'll get latrine duty."

Becca rubbed her face, trying to wake up. "Think I have time for coffee?"

"Not sure I'd chance it." Jace stood and adjusted her pants. She was an earth witch, who drew her powers from the soil. Nowhere near as strong as Andre, but a lot friendlier. She'd shown Becca around a bit when she'd first moved into the dorm. Jace came to this hideout six months ago, when Leon found her hiding out in the wild, avoiding the gangs.

"See ya' there." Jace headed off.

Becca hurried to get ready and then raced out the door. She contemplated skipping coffee, but without the elixir of life, everything felt like latrine duty. She grabbed a cup, and as she was leaving, bumped into Caleb. He caught her by an elbow to help steady her, the brown liquid threatening to spill.

"Careful," she warned him. "This cup is worth its weight in gold today."

"Didn't sleep well, I take it?" He grinned even as Nikki in her white uniform, her hair combed back in a high ponytail, stood silently at his side. She glanced at Caleb's hand, still latched on to Becca's elbow, and then her eyes flashed up to Becca.

Since Becca couldn't shake Caleb off without spilling her coffee, and nothing was worth that, she offered an awkward smile, before turning back to answer Caleb. She didn't miss his concern underlying the forced humor.

"It's nothing, just still getting used to sleeping in the dorms."

Always great at smelling out Becca's lies, Caleb watched her for another second. Now wasn't the time to get into what really bothered her.

"I better go, or I get latrines." She turned to Nikki. "I'll see you at ten, right?"

"I'll see you then," Nikki replied formally, her face unreadable.

Becca left the cafeteria as quick as she could without spilling a drop. She'd have to return the mug later.

When she finished the drink, she ran the rest of the way to training. By the time she got to the big room, people were already partnering off. Lance didn't seem to notice her late arrival. Navina waved her over. She stood next to a type of wooden maze with a couple of mice.

"What happened to real-world scenarios?" Becca inspected the labyrinth.

"You never know when vermin can come in handy." Lance appeared behind her, almost making her jump.

"This is as much as a struggle with your partner as it is with the mice. Each of you tries to force your mouse to the center, while keeping the other out. We'll work up to other complex beings."

"Complex?"

"Yeah. How else do you think we get such great fish?" Lance quickly went to the next group and explained their assignments.

"You're welcome," Navina said.

"Thank you?" Becca racked her brain for why she should be thanking the young girl.

"I saved you from latrine duty."

Becca gave a big exhale. "I do owe you."

"I won't forget." Navina turned to the maze where the mice were contained.

Becca followed. "Doesn't mean I'm taking it easy on you today though."

Navina shot her a sideways glance. "Better not. My mouse will do an amazing victory dance. Watch." She squished up her freckled cheeks in a mocking smile.

"I'm ready for you." Becca mustered as much bravado as she could despite battling a twelve-year-old kid.

The intricate wooden maze held each of the mice in a container on the opposite end of the board. The goal sat in the center, a small compartment hidden with a small, painted white star. Both girls held a hand on the wooden slat that closed off the mice from the maze.

Navina's fighting face was set as she eyed Becca. "Ready, set, go."

They pulled the slats up. Becca closed her eyes and took a deep breath, clearing her mind. The more her emotions ruled her—which felt pretty constant for the last month or so—the less power she could gather. She focused on the humming magic inside and opened her eyes.

The mouse turned down a wrong path and found a dead end. With a simple spell, Becca projected her will at the mouse. It froze for a moment and then turned and scurried towards her without hesitation. It took a few seconds for Becca to get the hang of his erratic movements, but soon he was navigating the maze with her help and sat upon the white star.

"Rematch," Navina shouted instantly. She hated to lose. The age difference didn't matter to her. She fought with a fierce determination Becca understood came from a rough history. She would need a tough streak to survive outside these walls.

"Okay."

This time, Becca worked to control not only her mouse, but Navina's too. Navina's face turned red from exhaustion as she fought against Becca's hold. She directed the girl's mouse back into the starting room and easily won again.

"Maybe rats like you," Navina said sourly.

Becca tried not to laugh. "I wouldn't be surprised."

Her control over the animals, though, *was* a surprise. She and Navina had been battling with magic for a few days, and when it came to attacks against each other, they were about even. Obviously, this mental type of control came easier to Becca, something she found highly unsettling. Controlling others was some of the darkest magic, in her opinion.

Navina headed over to Lance. A few minutes later, Lance appeared with a cat. "I heard the furry rodents love you, Becca. Want to try your luck with something more finicky?"

"Sure."

"Okay, ladies." Lance's accent was growing on Becca. "Wait until my hands are off the feline."

Becca closed her eyes. She pushed her magic forward,

and for the first time could almost see with her magic. Lance's power pulsed, like gray clouds swirling around him. Without opening her eyes, she could feel him step away from the cat, whose energy was weak.

Navina's power pushed towards the cat, like a dense fog vying for territory. Magic thrummed through Becca's body as she countered the attack. This magic was more instinctual and less about precise words and spells.

The cat meowed loudly as he found his way to Becca and twirled around her legs. Eyes open, she reached down and picked him up. She wasn't sure how, but she knew the cat was male.

She glanced over at a sullen and angry Navina. "Don't feel bad. Everyone has different strengths."

"Tomorrow, it's back to fighting," Navina huffed. Her gaze traveled over Becca's shoulder, and her countenance changed to surprise. "Andre."

Becca's spine stiffened. He must have watched the whole encounter. She turned to find Darion standing beside him, his black hair perfectly messy and his eyes piercing. She couldn't help her heart fluttering, though part of her fought to remain aloof, still angry for his absence and his quick alliance with Andre. With her conflicting emotions, she lowered her eyes and buried her hand in the cat's soft fur.

Andre approached their small group with Darion following behind. "Good to see you, Navina. Have you been helping Becca with her magic?"

A bit of red crept in Navina's face as if embarrassed of her recent behavior. "I've tried."

"She's been great," Becca chimed in.

"Quick learner, this one is." Lance appeared beside her and placed an arm around her. His familiarity with her was uncomfortable, but he acted this way with everyone.

Someone shouted for him on the other side of the room.

Lance glanced toward the group in back before addressing Andre. "Did you need me, sir?"

"No, go take care of your students. Navina, why don't you show me what you were working on?" Andre motioned to the mouse maze.

Navina beamed. "Sure."

Andre obviously wanted to give Becca and Darion time to be alone.

"Hey, Bec." Darion approached her with a hesitant smile. "Wanna go grab a bite to eat?"

"Not really." It came out snippy, but since it matched how she felt, she didn't care. "I want answers. Like why you're here all of a sudden with Andre as an escort?" She fumed. "What's going on?"

"You always get to the point of things, huh?" His smile wavered, the hesitation in his eyes putting her on edge. He grimaced as he ran a hand through his hair. "I've been searching for answers in Andre's library, and I found some."

Excitement sparked, snapping her out of her self-pitying stupor. "What are you talking about?"

"It's a lead to a grimoire located in the city, which should give us the spell we need."

"Really? That's great." She couldn't help the smile creeping over her face. "When do we leave?"

Darion's smile didn't reappear and his gaze was wary. "I leave tonight. You need to stay here. Keep training."

"Keep training?" Disbelief vied with hurt, and her voice hitched. "No. I'm more help to you out there, covering your back."

He rubbed his neck, not looking her in the eyes. "I'm

going with Leon's team. They have supplies to get as well. I'll be back in a few days."

Her emotions flipped chaotically around her, not sure which way to land. "So after avoiding me for days, you came for a send-off, keeping the women and children at home while you fight the battle?" She hated the anger building up in her. Part of her anger was due to his avoidance, the rest for becoming buddy-buddy with the man who had kidnapped them days ago. How could he trust Andre or forgive him so easily? Darion was putting himself in danger, for her, and there was nothing she could do about it. "I'm more than capable, and you know it."

"Due to your bond with Liz and your magic, we're going to need you for this ceremony." He squeezed her hand. "You have to train. Listen to these people."

Becca nodded, not trusting herself to speak. She'd probably end up yelling at him. Easier to be angry than admit she'd missed him.

Lance and Andre approached, heads bent in deep discussion.

"I wish we could have spoken in a more private place." Darion kept her hand, but she wouldn't meet his eyes.

"Becca," Andre said. "I've been talking to Lance. He says you show promise."

"I've told you the same," Darion said.

"True." Andre nodded. "I think you would benefit working with another spirit magician. Focusing on those skills, especially since the ceremony with your sister needs to take place soon." His forehead creased with worry.

There was something he wasn't telling her. "What's wrong?"

"Bael is gaining strength."

Dread built in her stomach. She knew there was a limit

to how long Bael would remain passive, but being here with Andre, she thought it would be longer.

Even Lance was quiet. No jokes when a greater demon who currently resided in your sister was getting cranky.

"What can I do?"

"I spoke to Jemi about beginning training with you as soon as possible. Then hopefully when Darion gets back, we'll be ready."

"Jemi?" Becca cringed. Anybody but Jemi.

Caleb spit sand and then quickly rolled to avoid the wood staff aimed at his head.

"You have to be faster if you want to keep that pretty head of yours," Leon hollered a few feet away from the fight.

Caleb blinked against the sun reflecting off the water and rolled two more times for a better position. The staff followed his path. He bounced up into a low crouch and charged forward, head down. What he lacked in speed, he made up for in brute strength. The staff struck his side. He ignored the pain and tackled his opponent. They grappled in the sand, and Caleb ended up on top. It didn't take long before Caleb had his partner pinned.

"Give," Jake huffed. "Damn, you're heavy."

"You should have never let him get so close." Leon approached the pair.

A couple of onlookers mumbled their congratulations to Caleb before heading off to their own matches.

Jake stood, brushing the sand off his pants. "What do you do when a bull charges?"

"Move," Caleb advised. "You're faster than me." He reached for his drink, his muscles tingling from exertion.

He wiped at the sweat and sand covering his face. It felt good to work out. Between the cold breeze of the ocean and the bright sun above, he felt a sense of contentment for the first time since his parents had died. Of course having that thought meant it was quickly replaced by guilt. They would have wanted him to be happy, he reminded himself.

"Hey, newbie, over here," Leon hollered.

Caleb jogged towards where Leon stood in the shade talking to Andre and Darion. This couldn't be a social call. "What's up?"

"Leon says you're very competent in training," Andre said. "So that means you really must be spectacular. Competent is one of the highest compliments my brother can give."

Caleb laughed, caught Leon's scowl, and quickly quieted. Guess only Andre could joke about his brother and get away with it.

"We have a supply run tonight," Leon said. "And they want you to go on it, even if you aren't ready."

"I'm ready." He'd been training for days, and a supply run didn't sound so bad. But if it was simple supplies, then why was Darion there? "What's the catch?"

"No catch," Andre answered. "Some of the items are of a magical nature, so I'm sending Darion along. He requested you be on the team."

"Okay," Caleb replied and turned to Darion. Physically, he looked better. The dark circles from their time on the run had faded some. So while Caleb hadn't been thrilled watching Darion and Becca grow closer these last couple months, Caleb trusted him with more than his life. Becca's too. Thinking of Becca, he had to ask, "Any other magicians going?"

"No. We can't spare anyone else."

"So you're sending me with this pyro and his friend. Oh, that'll be good." Leon rolled his eyes.

"They both have been vetted through Jemi," Andre replied.

"You put too much trust in Jemi."

"Maybe, but I trust you as well. You can pick the rest of the team. Be ready to leave at dark."

"Yes, sir." Leon turned to leave.

"I need to leave as well." Andre turned to Darion. "Let me know if you'll need anything else."

"Will do." Darion watched as Andre left, leaving the two boys standing in the sand. He squinted against the afternoon sun. "Is this your training room? I'll admit I'm jealous."

"Yeah, it's great." The wind brushed over Caleb, cooling the sweat from the fight. He'd grown accustomed to it these past days, the steady rhythm pushing him on. He needed to focus on the task ahead though. "What are we going to steal?"

"You always assume the worst."

Caleb glanced over, his brow furrowing in disbelief.

"You're usually right, but we can't steal this," Darion said. "We have to talk to a colleague. Another wizard in Ryma's city."

"What? You're crazy!" Caleb had no wish to end up hanging on a rope or trapped as a Soultorn. Even if Ryma forgot about Caleb, the price on Darion's head had to be big enough to make any man rich.

"There's an old magician, from the days of the takeover. Andre says he has the book we need. Who knows, maybe he can even help Elizabeth." Darion talked as if he was still convincing himself.

"That's a lot to risk for a maybe." Caleb hadn't forgotten about Elizabeth. He would do anything to save her, but every risk needed to be calculated. He wanted to know what he was walking into.

"It's our last hope. She won't last much longer." Darion stared at the ocean, not meeting his eyes. "You don't have to come."

"I know, but I will." While Caleb watched the expanse of the ocean, never-ending, churning and flowing to lands he couldn't imagine, he wondered if they were closer to the beginning or at the end of it all.

Leon gave Caleb the rest of the afternoon off to shower, eat, and get packed. It felt good to rid himself of the sand that crept into every crevice. Dinner was another couple hours away, and he had to figure out how to find a pack. All the other people in his bunk were still out, and his team was busy. He didn't know many other people here, or where Darion or Becca were, which left him with Nikki.

With her friendly personality and bright smile, she was usually more than willing to help him. Why did that scare him to death? Maybe because his heart had been trampled on, chewed up, and spit out? He wasn't ready for a relationship or to get close to anyone. He didn't want to care about someone who could be taken away from him again. And just because a pretty girl was nice to him didn't mean she had any feelings for him.

With limited options, he headed down to the medical unit. He followed the tunnels with ease now, thanks to the trick Nikki had taught him when he arrived in their underground community. It was a wheel, a circular maze. Many spokes ran from the center of the wheel, where the cafeteria and dorm rooms were, but most of the training rooms were set away from the center. The main circle was wider than the rest and easy to find. He curved around the main corridor until he found the door to the hospital. He entered to find Doc reading in his chair while Nikki sorted bandages. Always a good sign when the hospital was empty.

Doc's eyes lifted from his book. "What can we do you for?"

Nikki turned in his direction with a welcoming smile. "Caleb."

"Leon wanted me to get a pack ready. I thought maybe you would point me in the direction of the supply room." He shifted his weight to the other foot. He should have asked a stranger in the hall. Why had he not thought of that until now?

"Already? I didn't hear about a run." She looked away, her brow lowered in confusion.

"I just learned about it. We have to set off tonight. Do you know where the supplies are?"

She waved away his concern. "Yeah. I'll take you there myself. I need to talk to Leon too. There are needed medical supplies. I usually go along to help with the drugs."

"I have the list here." Doc started digging through a pile of papers in his desk.

"I'm not sure this is the usual supply run. It's for Elizabeth," Caleb explained.

Nikki gave a slow blink. "All the more reason for me to talk to Leon before you go. We'll need supplies to take care of her. IV fluids are difficult to find these days." She set down the bandages. "Let's go. We're both going to need supplies."

"Both?"

"Come on. I have gone on several supply runs. They probably forgot to tell me about it."

Caleb wasn't sure Leon would be excited about this, but better to let him deal with it. He followed her out the door.

Doc mumbled, "Good luck."

They both went to the supply room. The older woman in charge checked them out packs with water and a three-day supply of dried food. They found Leon outside of his room.

"Leon." Nikki caught his arm. "I have a list of medical supplies that I need to get on the run tonight."

"Who said anything about a run?" He caught sight of Caleb and glowered.

Caleb flashed a quick look at Nikki who was standing there clearly unconcerned with Leon's dark mood. "We need IV fluids and antibiotics, especially with winter coming up."

"And you'll get them next week." Leon folded his arms over his chest. "This isn't the usual supply run. There is no way your father would let you come, and I won't either."

Nikki's eyes narrowed and her spine straightened. "If it's that dangerous, then why is the new guy coming?"

"Bring that up with your father. It wasn't my call. I don't have time for this, Nikki. Caleb, are you ready?"

"Yes, sir. Nikki helped me find a pack." He wanted to explain himself.

"Next time, ask me. Go eat, and we'll leave in twenty." Leon nodded, signaling the end of any more discussion.

Caleb headed down the hall while Nikki stomped along behind him.

She seethed in silence to the cafeteria. It wasn't until they were seated with packs at their feet that she spoke. "You know why I'm stuck in the medical unit?" A sharp edge of anger cut at every word.

It wasn't aimed at Caleb, but he trod carefully. "I

assumed your magic helps you in healing." He took a bite of dinner, some sort of creamy sauce with shrimp.

"Most do. But my magic isn't in healing. My father stuck me in there to train as a nurse." She gripped her fork as if she were strangling the life out of it. "I finally convinced Leon that I'd be useful on supply runs, finding medicine others aren't trained on. It's my only way to see what is beyond these walls."

"Trust me. You're not missing much. The world is not what it once was." Caleb's parents would often talk about life before the takeover. The movies, amusement parks, and fireworks. Back when Mundanes had a chance to thrive on their own measure.

"But we're not going to change anything hiding behind these walls." Nikki's knuckles whitened as she gripped the fork.

Caleb's seat began to tremble underneath him. He held tight to the bench. She must be more like her father than Caleb knew. "What's going on?"

She snapped back to the present. "Sorry."

A couple of people grumbled nearby.

"I do have better control of my powers. It's my father. He drives me crazy sometimes."

"It's what parents do. At least you have one." He didn't mean for the last part to slip out like that. He would complain about his dad, too, when he was alive. Guilt pinched at his heart for not appreciating what he had while he had it.

"Sorry. I forgot." She reached out and placed her hand over his. She did it so casually that he wondered if it meant anything to her.

He withdrew his hand, picked up his fork, and went back to work on his food. "Don't worry about it. Just remember you're lucky to actually have a dad that loves you."

"I know." She lowered her eyes and started on dinner.

He didn't mean to hurt her, only remind her of what she still had. He ate fast, hoping to head out soon. It would be nice to stretch his legs for a bit and see the stars at night.

The ground below him started to shake again, stronger than before. Caleb could hear the waves crashing loudly outside. He'd never heard it this far inside the cave.

"Is this you again?" he asked Nikki.

She shook her head. "The alarm's up. Only my dad can do that."

People grabbed their plates and rushed to the exit.

"To your rooms," someone shouted above the crowd. "You know the drill."

"Is this a drill?" Already on his feet, Caleb pulled on his pack.

"I don't think so. Or I would've been warned."

"So we head to our rooms?" Caleb dreaded the idea of hiding underground while being attacked.

"Not us. Let's go." Nikki slung on her pack. Her lips pressed into a firm line.

CHAPTER THIRTEEN

"Back to your rooms," Lance shouted to Becca and the rest of the practicing group.

Waves crashed near the back of the caves, their force jolting the walls and echoing throughout the room. The temperature dropped, the chill causing Becca to zip up her jacket and pull on her gloves.

"Has this happened before?" she asked Navina.

The unsettling rattle of the walls reminded her that they were underground. Enough shaking and they would be buried.

"Probably another drill," Navina mumbled. She was getting grumpier as Becca's magic increased. "Andre pulls up the ocean and seals the exits, hence the rattling. It'll pass soon. I usually head to the nursery and hang out with my mom and the kids that haven't been picked up yet." She grabbed her bottle of water.

If there were kids still in the nursery, then the alarm couldn't be that bad.

"Hurry up, you two," Lance barked at them, his usual jovial expression gone.

"See ya' tomorrow," Becca told the girl and then took off to her dorm. She made it halfway there before running into Darion.

"There you are." He gripped her shoulder, and his familiar warmth and magic flooded her senses.

With reluctance, she distanced herself slightly, and he dropped his hands. She thought he would have already left, and she had spent the last couple of hours kicking herself on how she'd left things. Maybe she'd have a minute to explain herself and really talk. "I was heading to my room for the drill. Want to grab a drink before you go?"

"This isn't a drill." He ignored the space she'd put between them and pulled her down the hall. "Someone triggered Andre's wards, and they shouldn't even have been able to make it that far."

They pressed together to maneuver around a thick group headed in the opposite direction.

After the crowd passed, she sped up to walk beside him. "Thanks, Darion."

"For what?"

"For coming to get me. I was starting to feel like the redheaded stepchild."

His step faltered slightly. Stopping, he turned to her. "I'm sorry for not coming earlier."

"The alarm only now sounded. I don't know how you'd come sooner." She wasn't sure exactly what he meant.

"No, not today, but last night and the night before." He brought her close, his familiar musky sent comforting her. "I've missed you, but wanted to find answers. I know I've been caught up with everything, but…"

The short distance between them held a palpable energy. Driven by desire, her thoughts and emotions flew around her mind. Things between them were still raw and unsettled. They needed to figure things out between them.

Looking up into his eyes, she knew she should step back. She was drawn like a moth to the flame, but she couldn't afford to be burned. The words she'd planned fled with all sense of reason.

"Rooms, now!" someone shouted down the hall.

Released from her hormone-induced stupor, she stepped back. "We'll talk later. We better go."

Grabbing her hand, he kept moving.

"Are we going to be safe here?" Being buried by land or sea didn't appeal to Becca.

"Not sure. Either way, we need to stick together in case we have to run for it."

"What about Elizabeth and Caleb?" If they had to run, they all needed to be together.

"We'll find them if it comes to that. For now, let's find Andre." Darion steered them to Andre's door.

Leon opened it and scowled at the sight of Becca. "I don't remember her being invited."

Darion ignored the comment and continued inside with Becca. Andre's office was full. Caleb stood next to Nikki. Jemi took her place beside Andre, who sat at his desk, while Leon and two other men stood against the wall.

"Did you find out who it is?" Darion asked.

Andre leaned forward on his desk. "We haven't had a chance. I strengthened our defenses, but these aren't lost Mundanes."

"We need to take them out now. The longer we wait, the more time they have to tell others," Leon said.

"He's right," Jemi agreed.

"I know." Andre settled his chin on folded hands, and for the first time, he looked his age, stress tightening his shoulders and face. "And we need to get the team out."

"I'm coming," Becca blurted out. She shot Darion a quick glance, hoping he would back her up. "Ask Darion or Caleb, I know my way around the city better than either of them. I was a runner for years with the black market."

Leon started to protest but Darion interrupted. "If you expect me to convince Richard to help us, having Leon there with an automatic rifle isn't going to help me. He's met Becca before and found her quite interesting."

"He did?" She racked her brain to remember who he was talking about.

"He was the old man at the market."

"Oh, yeah." She didn't bother to tell Andre that when they went to rescue Caleb, she bore an illusion of an Asian seductress at the time so she doubted Richard would remember her at all.

"I'm not taking all three of them," Leon argued. "They'll run for it."

"Not without my sister," Becca replied.

"I've seen people do worse to family," Jemi cut in. "She has no training."

"Oh, I've had training and not the kind where we use mats." She survived in the city by herself for years.

"You're a liability," Leon protested.

Andre raised a hand, and everyone fell silent. He took a deep breath, and a chill permeated the room.

"Leon, take your men, Darion, Becca, and Jemi. I will bind Darion and Becca with a promise to not reveal or show others our location."

Several people spoke at once.

"Silence." Andre spoke quietly, but the power behind it was felt by everyone. "You'll need Jemi and Becca in case those magicians up there are powerful, which is what I'm expecting. Caleb can stay back. We'll need the extra manpower here."

"Okay," Caleb said, stone-faced.

"Please return to your station," Andre said, dismissing him. "You too, Nikki."

She began to argue, but her father stared at her with a cold, unwavering command.

"Leave your packs for the others," Andre told them.

Caleb and Nikki took off their packs. On their way out, Caleb briefly grasped Becca's arm. "Be careful. You too, Pyro."

"We will," she promised. "Watch Elizabeth for me, and take care of yourself."

"I will." Caleb and Nikki left, the door closing behind them with a loud click.

Andre addressed Becca. "I will watch over Elizabeth, and Doc said he had some sedatives he could try."

Becca nodded, and for the first time wondered if she'd made the right decision demanding to go. This was for Elizabeth, she reminded herself. No one was as determined as she was to get that book.

Andre stood. "Leon, you take point on this mission. Go now. I'll watch and assist from the lookout. Any survivors I'll bring back onto the beach."

Leon approached Becca and Darion. "Remember, I'm point. You obey my command. Otherwise, when you die, I won't feel guilty. And if your actions injure any of my men, there will be no help for you." He brushed past them.

She picked up the extra pack and lugged it over her shoulder. "I can see who got the personality in the family."

Darion carried a ball of fire above his palm as their group twisted and turned through the dark, unfamiliar path. Leon and his men, Marcus and Alex, led the group, carrying a torch fueled by witch light. Burly and strong, Marcus was nearly as big as Leon. Alex might have been smaller, closer to Darion's height, but his arms and shoulders bulged under his uniform. Both men sported shaved heads. Their strength impressed Darion, at least for Mundanes, of course.

Water dripped down the walls, and the smell of algae and ocean greeted them. A bright light slowly appeared ahead, and everyone extinguished their flames.

There was a sharp turn that opened to a rocky platform extending to the ocean floor. Small wet shells littered the floor, and barnacles grew on the walls. This must've been how Andre protected this exit. He could pull back the tide when needed, or flood the doorway. Amazing. In the shadows of the falling sun, the switchbacks lined the steep path up the cliff face.

"Gather round," Leon said. "Jemi says the men are about twenty yards from the top of the trail. Since I've never worked with either of you two before, stay behind us and try not to die. If you can shield any of my men from magical attacks, do it.

"I'll take point. Jemi behind me. We're not here to kill, but if it's us or them, better make it them. At this distance, Jemi can read vague intentions and give us a signal. Don't be afraid to have them come to the edge. It'll be easier to push them into Andre's waves and let him deal with them." Leon tightened the straps on his back. "Ready?"

"I can help." Darion's frustration grew. Did they not know what he was capable of? "Your magic and Jemi's are more defensive. Let me fight."

Leon's jaw tightened as he stared at Darion. "We can't burn down the whole forest. And remember, they may be friendly."

Why did extra muscles mean less brain cells? Darion seethed.

"Stay close," he told Becca. They took the rear as the party headed up the side of the mountain.

By the time they made it halfway up, his legs burned and he fought to calm his labored breaths. He reached out, pushing to see if he could feel any magic ahead, but there was nothing. Either these guys were Mundanes looking for help, or practiced magicians who knew how to hide. Worried about the latter, Dorian created a simple spell to quiet the party's passage up the cliff.

Jemi must have felt the ripple in the air. She turned back. He put a finger to his lips. She nodded and resumed her climb.

Near the top, Leon waited for the rest of the party to join him. Climbing out to the unknown and exposing themselves would be the hardest part. Andre's home forged a great, defensible community; a straight attack would prove difficult.

Realizing he didn't have the power to protect the whole group, Darion's stomach knotted. Trained to attack, not protect, he'd only focused on individual defenses in school.

Leon signaled to his men, then rushed forward, and the others quickly followed. Everyone except Darion and Becca, who were already on top when the shots rang out. Leon might have been immune to magic, but that didn't apply to gunpowder.

"Stay here," Darion told Becca, praying she'd listen, and then hoisted himself up and crawled forward.

Several men were scattered in the trees and brush ahead of them. To the right, Leon lay on his stomach, firing his weapon. On the left, Jemi and Alex crouched behind a large bush. The sound of guns firing exploded all around him. Marcus, the big guy, leaned against the base of a tree, his shoulder bleeding.

Within the chaos surrounding him, it took Darion a

minute to gather himself. Ignoring the shouts and blasts of gunfire, he continued forward on his stomach. The constant magical attacks against his shield meant they were facing at least one magician he could sense. Alex and Marcus appeared frozen in place. Darion needed to find the source of the spell.

A couple feet away, dust shot up. A bullet must have missed its mark. Ignoring his body's desire for survival, he searched for the shooter. There, up ahead, someone on the ground in fatigues. The black tip of the barrel lay on a branch, blending in. Darion focused on the gun, and before it could get off another shot, the rifle exploded in the man's face. Screams rang out through the trees.

"They can't escape," Jemi yelled from behind the tree. Her eyes widened in fear as she repeated herself. "Don't let them escape."

Darion wished he knew how many men they actually faced. He glanced over to find Becca next to Marcus, and his heart stalled. Was it too much to ask her to stay behind? Knowing her, probably. There was a bandage on Marcus's shoulder, and Becca took aim with Marcus's weapon.

Leon signaled to the others to cover him and then sprinted forward. Bullets whizzed past while he continued to charge forward. Reinforcing his physical wards, Darion ran after him.

Fifty feet ahead, a man sprinted out of his hiding spot. Darion pushed forward, and the gun exploded in the soldier's hand. The flames, a power in itself, reached for the man to consume as much as it could. Darion squelched the flames and left the man screaming on the ground. Another attacker was perched up in the tree, and Darion quickly disabled him. These were only Mundanes, though, easy to overpower. Where was the magician?

Darion stayed tight on Leon's tail. A man, not ten feet

from them, stood up. Before Darion or Leon attacked, the man dropped his weapon and raised his hands. A glazed expression crossed the attacker's face. Was this Jemi or...could this be Becca's power?

As Leon approached, the man didn't falter, still bound by a spell. Leon slammed the butt of his gun into the base of his skull, and the man crumpled to the ground. "We may need him later. The others will collect him."

Before they continued, Leon lifted a hand. Silence fell upon the forest. Their breaths came out in quiet gasps, turning into fog in the cold air.

Someone else was out there, someone strong whose magical presence emanated through the forest. Darion pointed in the direction of the pulsating magic, though he couldn't see a thing.

Leon charged forward, dodging around fallen trees and bushes in his path.

Before Darion could follow, a surge of power yanked him down to the earth, pressing on his throat. He fought back, but his defenses failed. Without a demon tied to him, Darion wasn't a match. He'd only survive if Leon found the magician first.

Darion turned his head and watched Leon's boots take off. Darkness ate at the edges of his mind as he tried to fight back. A figure sprinted out from behind a tree, Leon only feet away. The wizard had waited too long to run. Most magicians were not familiar with someone like Leon, someone immune to magic.

The invisible bands on his throat tightened, and Darion struggled to speak. He wanted to warn Leon that the gun wouldn't work. This level of magic would have protection spells stronger than most arsenals.

As Leon raised his gun, a large rock smashed into the

side of his head. It continued to pummel Leon as he stumbled, falling to the ground.

The man behind the spell straightened, mere feet from Leon, and stared at Darion. His face was scarred, deep red welts covering his face. His blond hair, short and bright, and focused eyes told Darion at once who it was: an old schoolmate he'd thought dead. Peter.

Becca was yelling for him, running through the woods. As black spots danced in his vision, he wanted to call her off. With the revenge and loathing in Peter's eyes, Darion knew he wouldn't be content with one death.

Jemi and Becca rushed to his side. Darion lost track of Peter as Becca and Jemi blocked his line of sight. Becca sank down and grabbed his hands. With a quick spell, she linked their magic. Like food for a starving man, the driving magic gave him enough power to release Peter's bonds. Darion gasped, sucking in deep breaths.

"Leon and another wizard." He pointed through the woods. When he searched for Peter, Darion couldn't find him anywhere. He didn't think Peter would give up so easily.

"I'll take care of it." Jemi took off running.

"Are you okay?" Becca bent over him, a worried expression creasing her brow.

"Yeah." His voice came out rough due to his abused throat. "Just took me off guard."

"What did I tell you about your guard?" Becca scowled, giving him the same lecture he'd given her after her fight in the pawn shop.

"He's stronger than before." He remembered Peter's strength, and it hadn't been anywhere near this strong. Granted, Darion no longer had a demon to draw from. Maybe something about sacrificing most of your body in a fire fueled Peter's powers? A cold chill ran over Darion. He never would have thought Peter would have survived the blast or inferno that almost took Becca and Darion. He would have felt sorry for Peter, if it wasn't the second time Peter had tried to kill him.

"Who was he?" Becca asked.

"Yeah, who was that devil?" Leon approached with Jemi at his side. He held a cloth to his head, blood dripping down the side of his face. The fact Leon could stand after that attack surprised Darion.

"An old acquaintance, you could say." Darion stood up, still scanning the surrounding area. He didn't sense Peter nearby but didn't let go of Becca's hand. He strengthened a shield around them both.

"What happened to the others?" Leon dabbed at his head.

"The shot went straight through Marcus's shoulder," Jemi answered. "And Alex is watching our prisoner. Marcus will be fine, but needs to go back. So do you," she said to Leon.

He brushed her off. "I'm fine."

"Then we need to find that wizard. He knows too much."

"Who does he belong to?" Becca kept a firm grip on the knife at her side. She must have left the gun with Marcus.

"Ryma." A familiar dread settled in Darion's stomach.

"Great. Ryma." Jemi ran a hand through her short hair. "We can't be found on Ryma's radar. Andre needs to know about this now."

"Go tell him," Leon ordered. "Take Marcus and the prisoner back with you. We're going to complete the mission and hopefully track this Peter down in the process."

Jemi hesitated for a moment. "You sure about this?"

"No," Leon said, "but we can't lose any time."

Darion couldn't agree more.

Becca went with Alex to retrieve the packs from the cliff face. As the adrenaline from the fight fled her system, her hands trembled. Determined, she gripped Darion's bag in her hands. As they headed back, Becca couldn't miss the guy's cussing and complaining. When they returned, Marcus was bandaged and standing up, pointing a gun into the prisoner's back. With some magic on Jemi's part, Becca eventually got the prisoner to shut up.

"Will you be okay heading back?" Leon asked Jemi.

"Sure. Andre's still watching for us. If he gets bad"— she motioned to the prisoner—"I'll push him over the edge."

The man, forced mute by magic, flashed Jemi a concerned look.

She sneered and then nudged him forward. "Move it."

The three of them headed back to the compound

With her pack against her back, Becca itched to take off as well. Now that Peter and Ryma knew where Becca and Darion were, there was a new timeline for her sister.

"Better get moving. If we plan on tracking Peter, we've got a lot of ground to cover." Leon started off through the woods, stepping over a fallen tree.

"We won't find him," Darion said. "If he covered his power this well from Andre when searching out this place, there is no way I can find him. Not unless someone grabbed something of his. Did you get anything, Leon?"

Leon dabbed at the cut on his head. It was thankfully only a surface wound. Leon's arms took most of the beating as he'd covered his head. "No. We'll head to the city and keep our eyes open. Maybe we'll get lucky."

"How did you get injured?" Becca asked Leon as they hiked. "I thought you were immune to magic?"

"I am. No one can change my mind, make me see other things, or hurt me physically. They can't get in my head, but they can use other objects or people to hurt me," Leon grumbled.

Remembering the scene when she'd found Darion, fear coiled in Becca's stomach. She motioned Darion to the side, hoping for a bit of privacy.

Darion appeared to get the idea and slowed slightly.

She kept her voice low but sharp. "Don't ever do that again." Now that they were safe, the volatile emotions from the fight came flooding back.

"What?" He actually looked confused.

"Ask me to stay behind. We've been in tough spots before, and probably will be again." She gripped her bag and struggled to keep her voice steady. "But don't ever order me to stay behind again. First, I won't do it."

"Yeah, I noticed."

"Second, we're in this together. I'm not weak. We fight together. We..." She almost said die together, but couldn't let the words out for fear of jinxing things. "We stick together. Got it?"

Darion leaned over and bumped her with his shoulder. "Got it."

She nodded, glad to have a clear understanding. This was how the problems with their previous relationship had started. He'd said he was trying to protect her when he lied about having magic and his involvement with the coven. He needed to understand she wasn't looking to be his protector but his partner.

"You two done back there?" Leon turned. "And here I thought we were in a hurry."

They picked up their pace and caught up to the others. Becca already missed Darion's touch.

Coming up alongside Leon, she asked, "Are we really going to follow Peter all the way to Ryma's? That's more than a three-day hike. He couldn't have walked the whole way either."

"No. Peter's gone. We need to decide our next course. I only say 'we' because it depends on you, Becca."

"Me?" Becca never thought he cared a bit for her opinions.

"If we press forward to Ryma's city, we should get there by tomorrow, and our contact will have information. But if Peter gets there first, there may be a surprise waiting for us. Or we can go get the needed medical supplies that may keep your sister unconscious but demon-possessed for another week. If she lasts another week."

"How can we get there in a day?" There was no way they could travel that fast on foot.

"We can get there by morning," Leon assured her without really answering. "Do we chance the city? If we don't make it back, she'll probably die."

"Or do we return to the caves and keep her alive, but sacrifice our chance in finding how to get rid of the demon?" Darion asked.

Becca realized there really wasn't a choice because there might not be another chance to get this book. "Let's go. Show us what chariot is taking us to the city." She wasn't sure what lay ahead, but they wouldn't find anything helpful behind them.

CHAPTER FOURTEEN

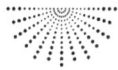

Caleb followed Nikki's tight shoulders and brisk pace down the tunnels. She hadn't said a word since they'd left Andre. Not that Caleb was too happy at being left behind either. Once it had been Becca and Caleb, and they worked well together. Now? Well, the only reason he agreed to stay behind was because he trusted Darion to watch Becca's back. Otherwise, no way would he have let her go.

He slowed as the turn for his dorms and the cafeteria approached.

Several feet ahead, Nikki stopped and turned to him. "What?"

"This is my stop."

Confusion crossed her brow as if her mind was elsewhere. "Yeah, okay."

"Hey, do you need any help in the hospital? I have nothing to do for the rest of the night. I can fold towels, clean bedpans, that kind of fun stuff." He hated to ask, but he didn't want to face a night of sitting on his bunk worrying.

She gave him a surprised look. "Man, you must be desperate. Come on. Doc probably has something for us to do." Her steps lightened slightly. Maybe she needed a distraction as well. "If nothing else, I could always use someone to practice stitches on."

"Never took you for a sadist."

"You never know." Her lips twitched slightly. "You'd be much more fun than oranges."

"Oranges?" His voice rose in excitement. He could almost smell the clean citrus flavor. "You guys get oranges?"

"When they're around. They're not as good as a human patient, but they're the closest thing we can find around here."

He loved oranges, had even dreamed about them now and then. His father would sometimes bring one back from trading in the city. Caleb usually found one in his stocking every Christmas morning growing up. "Do you have any now?"

"Yeah. We should get our first batch in time for the party."

"Party?"

"Christmas or whatever you want to call it." She started back down to the hospital. "We'll have a party next week for Christmas. It's nothing big. Dancing, a small tree. There isn't much in the way of gifts."

"The idea of Christmas is just..." His mind traveled to home, and his throat tightened as he thought about the holidays without his parents.

"You okay?" Nikki paused with a hand on the door to the hospital.

"Yeah. Fine." He chased away the memories that would only bring heartache. "Let's get to work."

They entered the medical unit.

"Hey, Doc," Caleb said.

"Didn't think I'd see you two back so soon." He was filing papers in a cabinet. "Nikki can be quite convincing when getting her way."

"Not convincing enough. I even got Caleb kicked off the trip," Nikki said.

"I wanted to see if you needed any help in here." Caleb was grateful to find the beds empty. He was joking earlier about the bedpans.

Doc set down his papers and ran a hand through the red wavy mess on top of his head. "Their loss is our gain. If you want to finish filing these reports from last year, that would be perfect. I need to check up on the Thompson boy with croup."

"You still haven't finished filing those? You told me you had them done." Nikki placed her hands on her hips like she was scolding a child, not her boss.

"I finished the reports, but never filed them. You weren't specific." He grabbed his leather medical bag and headed towards the door. "I know, I know, I'm a mess. What would you do without me?" He left with a smile on his face.

"Ugghh, that man. I think he relies on me because he knows if he puts something off long enough, I'll do it."

Caleb grinned. "I think he knows you well." Then he picked up the papers with large black names printed on the top.

She glared at him.

He smiled. "You're a doer, Nikki. There's nothing wrong with that. You can't always fix the rest of the lazy bums out there."

She extended his arm and took half of the papers. "Great. I'll be picking up after people forever."

"Nah, you'll be in charge one day. Like your dad."

"If he has his way, I'll never leave the med unit." A frown tightened her forehead. "You really think so?"

"I do. But until then, get to work."

They worked together in comfortable silence filing papers, then organizing the supply closet in the back. When they finished, Caleb stood to stretch, his back sore from bending Nikki took out her ponytail and then gathered it back up to retie it. The witch light softened her features. Her beauty shone through, even while cleaning.

She noticed him staring. "You ready for a break yet? Maybe scrounge up some tea or something?"

"Yeah," he said and then reprimanded himself. He needed to keep his thoughts in check before they got him in trouble.

He followed her towards the back of the med unit for drinks when someone came in. At first, Caleb thought it was Doc coming back from his checkup. Nikki turned around and started to say something. Words were lost, and the cleaning rag she held in her hand dropped to the ground. Doc wasn't alone.

Jemi and Doc rushed in with Marcus hanging on their shoulders. Blood covered his clothes. Nikki rushed to grab a tray of medical supplies while they lifted the man onto the nearest bed.

"What happened? Are the others okay?" Caleb's voice rose, demanding an answer.

Doc continued talking over him, barking orders at Nikki for supplies and waving people out of his way.

Jemi backed up, her face tense. "He was conscious until we made it inside."

"I'm going to find Becca and the others." Caleb headed to the exit. Forget Andre's orders. They were now short two people, and they needed him.

Jemi locked onto his arm and took a deep breath.

Some of the lines in her face relaxed. She finally opened her eyes and let go of him. "Sorry about that. I've been so connected to Marcus who is in a lot of pain. It helps to get a different perspective."

Caleb didn't care about her magic; he cared about his friends. "They are down a man and a witch. They'll need me."

"No. They're fine and probably long gone by now."

"So what do we do? Just wait?" Caleb flexed his hands. He didn't know if he could do that.

A fierce determination burned in Jemi's eyes. "No. You train. You learn. You fight. So next time we're out there, this isn't you."

After hours of racing down the freeway in the dark of night, piled in a camo jeep, Becca assumed they had to be near the city. They kept all the lights off, and Becca prayed they didn't hit an animal. Leon and Alex took turns driving through the night while Becca slept in broken intervals.

Finally, Leon turned off the highway. Becca's body strained against her seat belt as they bounced along the forest floor. Her heart leapt as they headed towards a grove of trees and bushes. She closed her eyes in reflex and gripped the hand rails, but Leon turned the jeep quickly and they dropped into a small cave-like opening.

The engine cut out, and silence settled into the dark. They didn't waste time getting out of the jeep and readying to go.

"Come on, we still have a few miles to hike before we reach town. Leave the packs. Only take necessities." Leon jumped out of the jeep, took the large gun from his hip, and placed it in his bag. He removed a couple knives and hid them on his body.

Ryma didn't allow guns into his city, and the consequence was steep: death. Magicians could fight against guns, if a wizard's defenses were up. If not, they usually didn't have enough time to react.

Becca noticed Leon hiding a smaller gun inside his boot. She had a knife on her belt, but her back-up blade went swimming when they first came to the rebels' hideout. "Do you have an extra blade?"

"You know how to use one?" Leon asked.

"You can find out right now, if you want." She was tired and cranky, ready to strike out. A knife fight with Leon might help. He'd probably win, but she'd hold her own for a little while.

"We don't have time. Caleb said you could handle yourself." He handed her a long, dark blade.

"Glad you approve."

Before Leon could retort, Darion interrupted. "Do you know where Richard lives?"

"Andre gave me directions. We'll enter from the east."

"Really?" Becca wondered when Andre had last gone to the city since he seemed like the type to be content to hide out by the seashore for the rest of his life.

"We really do try to keep up with intelligence, to protect ourselves."

"When did Andre come to the city?" Darion asked. "I have a hard time seeing Ryma being okay with that."

"Over ten years ago. Andre can conceal what he is." Leon zipped up his jacket. "Come on, grab some nearby shrubs."

The four of them placed shrubs and plants near the back of the jeep to camouflage it. Becca stepped back to examine their handiwork and was impressed. This small cavern concealed most of the jeep, and unless someone walked into it, they wouldn't see it.

"Let's do this." Alex turned and started through the forest.

The rest of them followed. Leon constantly scanned the horizon. Becca tied her hair back into a braid and focused on where she was stepping. She wished she had dressed warmer. She wore the same pair of boots that had brought her this far, but her jacket wasn't much help. However, her jacket would blend in once they hit the city.

It felt good to hike, to wake up her tired muscles. By the time they made it to the gate, the sun was peeking through the trees.

The city had several points of entry, but the rest of the city limits were given an invisible border built with magic. It helped Ryma control who came and went.

Darion caught Becca's attention and mouthed, "You okay?"

Becca nodded and turned to the gate. A nervous energy pulsed through her body. She had been to a couple of other cities since they had been on the run, but not this city with a host of memories and people who wanted to kill them. Those memories haunted her. Eight years ago, she came to the city by herself for the first time. Young and alone, she'd been a target. But she survived then, and she'd do it again.

She glanced at Darion. His hair had grown from their time on the run, now brushing his ears. He met her eyes, and for the first time, she wished she had Jemi's powers to read others' thoughts.

"Maybe we should have disguised ourselves," she said. He was too recognizable, beautifully recognizable to her.

"We'll blend. Always have."

Alex yanked off his cap and tossed it at Darion. "She has a point."

Darion shoved it on his head. It helped, but probably not enough. Darion and Becca had spent years living in the city, under the radar, but now, with the price on their heads as a motivator, betraying eyes would be everywhere.

Several guards stood ready at the gate. Ryma must have increased security after the attack. The only plus was more guards possibly meant they were inexperienced.

A tall guard with freshly slicked back hair stepped in front of Leon. "State your business."

"Trade." Leon's voice kept its usual annoyed edge. "I have a business partner waiting for me."

"Who?"

"John." He didn't bat an eyelash.

The guard looked their group over, his gaze resting on Leon and the bandage on his temple. Several other people approached behind them.

"Go on." The guard waved them on.

After passing through the gate, Becca had to ask, "How long have you known this John?"

"There's a John in every city." Leon kept walking.

There were several more security guards positioned within the walls. Becca slid her hand in her pocket to grip her knife. The cold steel gave her comfort. She focused on her defenses, too, building up a magical wall in her mind to protect herself.

"Stop, you four," someone shouted behind them.

"Let me talk this time." Becca kept her voice quiet. "I have more contacts in the city besides John."

"We could run," Alex suggested. "Get lost in the crowd."

"I'll set a distraction." Darion eyed a tower in the distance.

Becca turned around to greet the two oncoming guards. "Give me a chance, but be prepared." If they had to run, they may not have time to find Richard before they'd have to leave.

"You have two minutes," Leon mumbled.

A witch approached, her face weathered and worn from years of city living. "We didn't get your names."

Traces of magic pushed at Becca's defenses, but she smiled back.

"Blake," Darion said. "I went to school here, and I'm coming back with friends for business."

"And you?" The witch watched Becca closely, ignoring Darion and Leon.

"Terry." Becca gave the name of an old friend.

Alex and Leon gave their real names, which surprised Becca until she remembered Alex had no defenses, so the closer he stuck to the truth the better. The witch didn't speak for a moment, but studied Becca with a cold detachment.

"We came up for some trading," Becca offered.

The witch hollered to the men behind her. "Something isn't right. Come with me, and we'll check your papers."

"I don't think so." Darion stepped in between them.

Becca put a hand on his shoulder. She wanted to push him out of the way, but instead, she combined their power, readying to fight their way out.

"Darling," someone shouted nearby. "What took you so long?"

At the sight of her old crime boss, Becca faltered for a moment, unable to complete the spell. His tattooed face had thinned, and his eyes were dark with more than makeup. Becca couldn't imagine what brought him here. His place was miles from here.

"Did you get my supplies?" Nikko demanded, ignoring

the witch seething behind him. When she remained mute, he snapped, "Well, did you?"

"Yeah. I thought we were meeting at John's." It was the first thing that popped into her head. Stupid Leon with his Johns.

"We can talk on the way. There's still a lot to gather for market next week." He turned back to the witch. "Don't you have a dog to neuter or something?"

"Watch yourself." She spit out the last word.

"Or what?" He straightened, the boss Becca knew emerging. "Ryma will take my business, my money, and force me to work with worthless scum. Too late."

He grabbed Becca's arm and strode away from the gate. "We don't have long, Becca."

"Okay," she mumbled, still in shock from seeing Nikko out in daylight. The last time she saw him, he turned her over to her uncle, the crazy magician. Conflicted emotions battled for space.

Darion stayed close to her side, while Leon and Alex muttered behind them.

Nikko shot Darion a look. "You need to get out of here fast. There is a hefty price on your pretty recognizable head."

Darion bristled. "We know."

"Simmer down, pyro. You're at the top of the list. It's only because these guards are inbred idiots that you got this far."

"What are you doing here?" Becca shook off Nikko's grip. "Are you a regular on the coven payroll now?"

"Long story. Ryma's tightening his reins on the city, and I got recruited."

"Why don't you leave?"

"Not so easy, but I'm still running things now and then. The black market is still alive, barely, but alive. You need to disguise yourself. I never thought you were so dense, girl. I taught you better."

He had. Nikko had taught her how to question everything and everyone, how to fight, survive, and blend in. Which is why it made no sense when he gave her up before. Now, when she had already written him off like so many others, here he was helping them.

Nikko stopped walking, but waved them on. "I gotta go back, before they put two and two together."

"Why are you doing this?" He didn't owe her. He did what he had to do. Not many people who said no to her uncle lived.

He gave her an unreadable look. "Because I couldn't before."

"I did lose your bike," Becca reminded him. He loved that motorcycle.

"You did indeed." He gave a short laugh. "Now, get out of here, and go raise whatever hell you're working on."

"Me?" Becca asked innocently.

"Always." With one last look, Nikko strode away. His black spiky hair and dark suit was something Becca thought she'd never see again.

"Wake up, princess. Time to move," Leon said.

She glared at him sideways and started into the city. "You did not just call me princess."

CHAPTER FIFTEEN

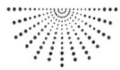

Every nerve ending on Peter's face burned, his scars more sensitive than ever since Nevada first worked on his face over a week ago. Peter gently touched the puckered wounds. His stomach churned, and he quickly dropped his hand. Night had fallen some time ago, and now he was waiting in the entry room of a local witch's home.

"Welcome." She appeared in the doorway and invited him into her study. Her haggard face had seen many years, and the scars on her arms, echoes of sacrificial offerings, were often done by weaker magicians.

Peter stood and pulled his hood down to cover his face.

"I have seen worse," she said. "Wear it as a badge of honor for service to your coven."

"Only one so ugly would say that," he snapped. "I need to use your phone. My cell gets no service in this Godforsaken place."

"No need to get nasty," she retorted. "I've let you in my home."

"If you didn't, I would have returned with reinforcements and destroyed it. You are a coven member. It is your duty."

"Of course." She lowered her head, submitting to Peter, the stronger magician, as etiquette dictated. "The phone is there by my desk. Anything else you require?"

"Your absence."

The door clicked behind him. He lowered his cloak, and a sigh of relief escaped him. The rough material scratched at his skin, a constant irritation.

At the desk, he picked up the phone and dialed Ryma's number. A servant picked it up and went to deliver it to Ryma. It took several long minutes. Peter's pulse quickened. He had actually found Darion.

"Peter." Ryma's cold calculated voice sounded on the phone. "What is your report?"

"We found him. Next to the ocean with other rebels like you heard."

He was rewarded with silence. Peter knew better than to push though. He slowed his breathing and waited.

"I'm wondering why your report didn't include his death. Here you are speaking to me in sound health, I assume, but yet he lives and is free."

Peter froze. The next words he spoke were important for his future. "Everyone on my team is dead or taken. I was in the clutches of a man immune to magic. I fled only to get this information to you."

Peter could hear Ryma's breath on the phone. He tightened his hold on the handle, waiting for a verdict.

"They are stronger than we expected. These rebels think they can live outside the law with such magic. Let me speak to Arturo. We need to see how far those underground rats go."

CHAPTER SIXTEEN

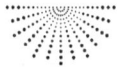

B ecca experienced an odd sense of déjà vu as they grabbed a cab and drove through the city in the early morning. Only months ago, she was grabbing coffee at Bonnie's and heading into work at Nikko's. She'd not only survived, but even prospered on these streets in an odd way. They never were quite home, but comfortably familiar.

Thankfully they had no other problems being recognized. Most people kept to themselves. It helped that the guards stuck to their regular routes Becca had memorized when she ran illegal goods for Nikko.

Leon stopped the cab a mile or so before Richard's estate and paid the driver—a kid with long, shaggy hair who couldn't be older than seventeen. He even gave him a tip to keep his mouth shut. Becca didn't approve, because the driver now knew they had something to hide, but it was too late to do anything about it, so she let it go.

In the northern-most part of the city, there were only old, large estates. The forest had begun to claim the streets as weeds grew between the broken asphalt. They walked to the side of the road, hoping to hide their presence in the foliage of the trees.

"So have you met Richard before?" Darion asked Leon, keeping his voice low.

"No. Only Andre met with him."

"I'd imagine magicians don't like you much," Becca mused.

"That's how I like it." Leon pulled out his small gun and kept it by his side.

"There isn't any use for our weapons here." Darion motioned at Leon's gun. "Richard is well guarded against any physical or magical threat."

"I'm not worried about Richard. It's others who may be here." Leon's pace picked up as his eyes roamed the woods. "What else can you tell me about him?"

"He's old." It was the first thing to pop into Becca's mind. "And confident." She remembered the oddly friendly magician with more wrinkles than she thought possible.

"He has a right to be," Darion said. "He fought on the front lines of the original takeover. My parents told me that's why Ryma had to put up with his eccentric behavior. He has old allies in covens all over the world. Too tired to be a high priest over a coven, he leaves Ryma alone and asks for nothing but solitude."

"So he'll be excited to see us, then. Great." Heavy sarcasm laced Alex's words.

Becca didn't care what it took. They weren't leaving here until they had that grimoire.

They turned down a dirt lane. The trees grew tall, creating a canopy over their head. Several birds hid amongst the branches. Becca made eye contact with two large black crows, perched on a limb. They tilted their heads back and forth a few times, and then with a short squawk, they both flew away towards the house.

They approached the gates that swung wide in silent invitation. Green vines covered the tall iron gates, entwined around the rusted bars.

Darion stuck a hand out. "Wait!"

It took a moment before Becca sensed the magical shield. "How strong is it?"

"Strong enough to kill anyone that crosses it."

Leon shifted his stance. "I can make it through. Then come back for you."

"You don't have to." Becca pointed ahead. "He knows we're here."

A large dog with curly, sandy hair trotted towards them. It almost came up to Becca's chest. The eyes were pitch black, a sign of possession. She grabbed her knife, but the dog didn't appear poised to attack. It barked twice, and the magic shield that had previously buzzed with power dissipated.

"I think this is our escort." Becca started forward.

Darion and Leon each put out an arm, as if to hold her back, but there was no harm. The dog quickly turned and headed toward the house. It looked back occasionally to make sure they were following.

"Not bad as far as help goes," Alex commented.

"Is everyone else seeing what I'm seeing?" Leon asked. "This rundown house may have been grand at one time, but the mice probably live better than any humans in there."

Leon was right; the mansion at one time must have been majestic. Now the wood shutters hung warped and crooked on the windows. An oversized porch wrapped around the house, and a large wood swing lay on its side. A gray cat currently sat on the broken swing, eyes open and alert. The two crows from before perched on the porch.

"You sure that's the place?" Alex asked.

Leon shrugged.

"Sounds like the Richard that I met," Becca said. "He liked everyone to know exactly how old he is. He'll probably tell us he built this by hand a hundred years ago, and that the dog is sixth generation."

Darion stayed close at her side. "You don't become a crazy hermit for fun."

"Is this a damn zoo or what?" Leon carefully followed the dog up the steps and tucked the gun into the back of his pants. Even though Becca knew their weapons would be useless here, she touched the familiar handle of her blade.

Unlike the rest of the home, the huge mahogany door stood proud, lacquered to a shine.

The dog barked at the door twice. A moment later, it opened.

Leon spoke first. "Richard?"

"And you are?" Richard lifted one of his graying eyebrows.

He hadn't changed since the market. His aging skin hung heavy, and his white hair remained short. An oversized nose took up major real estate on his face while his eyes peered from their deep openings. He wore simple, clean khaki pants and a flannel button-up shirt.

"I'm Andre's brother. You told him he could call on you again. He sent me in his stead," Leon said.

"I wasn't expecting visitors today, but a little variety at my age doesn't hurt. Please, come in." Richard held the door open for them.

They entered an aged hall perfect for any horror story. A gold dusty mirror hung next to an empty coat rack.

With a loud click, Richard closed the door behind him. "I wondered when I would get to meet you again." The statement was directed to Becca.

"Again?" Uneasiness turned Becca's stomach. The only time Richard had met her was when she'd donned the illusion of an Asian woman.

He stepped forward, crowding a bit too close. "Oh, I'd taste your flavor of magic anywhere." He turned towards Darion who hovered nearby. "And who else would be on the arm of the city's runaway pyro? You two are quite the scandalous couple. Let's get comfortable, shall we?"

He escorted them into a living room with matching faded floral sofas and chairs that surrounded a fireplace. She hesitated briefly, wondering at the age of the furniture and what other creatures took up residence there.

"I'm sorry. I don't have tea or something set out for you, but I don't have much in the way of human servants."

"No need. We can't stay long." Leon didn't look pleased with the situation.

"Well then, to what do I owe this visit?" Richard reclined in an armchair, and a plume of dust floated above him. The dog followed and sat at attention at his side. Richard dug his hand into its fur coat.

Becca finally perched at the edge of the sofa. Darion stood behind her, a hand on her shoulder. She felt a shield rise around her.

"We are in need of information on how to remove a demon from a human host," she said.

Richard's hand stilled. "Is this for your sister?"

"How do you—"

"Your fight with Ryma didn't spread too far through

the city since he didn't want to lose face. He came to me. He wanted to know how two magicians, one with no training, could overpower him and escape."

The dog lifted its head, and Richard began petting the dog again. "Ryma was quite put out." A small smile creased his face, and he nodded to the fireplace. "If you would, please," he said to Darion.

Without a word, fire soon roared in the brick fireplace, and Darion asked, "What did you tell him?"

"What I could. I didn't know much. Since the girls were sisters, they could have some old bond that her Uncle Jeremiah overlooked. Or maybe he planned it that way, and then his nieces turned on him."

She folded her arms, chasing off the memories of that night. "Jeremiah stole us. We fought back."

"No need to explain yourself. Jeremiah's despicable character will not be missed in this home."

"Can you help us?" Becca tried not to sound eager.

"Save your sister, the one containing Bael? Is she still alive?"

"Yes. She's becoming unstable though. We keep her unconscious most of the time. "

"We need to separate them soon," Darion added.

"What makes you think she can do it?" Richard asked Darion but motioned to Becca. "She is powerful, but doesn't know what to do with it."

Darion squeezed her shoulder. "So it has to be her?"

"I'm right here, you guys. You know that, right?" Becca bristled under their conversation.

Richard turned his gaze to her. "Even if you can pull this off, your sister won't be the same. She never will."

Becca glanced at Darion to see if Richard was telling the truth, but Darion gave nothing away. This had always been a fear of hers, but it didn't mean she'd stop trying to save Liz.

"I have to try." Becca's voice broke slightly as she fought to keep her emotions from slipping.

"I'm not sure you can manage Bael, but the replacement host would have to be strong, nothing lying around on the streets." Richard looked at Leon, as if he was pressing him.

Leon stood firm, his arms taut and ready for an attack.

"Interesting," Richard mumbled.

"We're not giving Bael another host," Becca said. "We're going to banish him."

"Shame." He stood, pressed a hand to his lips, and then headed out of the room, the large dog at his side.

All of them stood, uncertain on whether to follow Richard or not.

Richard returned with pen and paper in hand. He leaned on a nearby end table and wrote on the paper. When finished, he handed it to Darion. "Here's what I know. It requires a great deal of blood and sacrifice to entice Bael out of the body. And he will require a push."

Becca glanced at the dark ink hastily written across the paper in Darion's hand.

"We were hoping to get the grimoire." Darion folded the paper neatly.

"I burned my books." Richard said matter-of-factly. "I expect a promise that you'll do the same to that once you have it memorized."

A flash of surprise crossed Darion's face, but he looked the man in the eye. "I promise."

A small spark appeared in front of Darion and traveled over to Richard. It was more than a promise, more like some type of magical vow. Richard reached out and grabbed the spark, which vanished in his hand.

"Wait." Becca remembered that young mage at the marketplace, waiting for auction. "Why burn it? This could save people. Mundanes and wizards alike."

Richard creased his brow. For the first time, annoyance crossed his face. "Naive girl, Mundanes can't use this. Only magicians can. Their demons won't die. They will use and reuse every living thing on the planet to contain their pets until there is nothing left. If you ever want to limit a magician, this is the way to do it. When they kill a demon, they can't call it again. Why do you think the price of demon names is weighed in gold? Why Soultorns are younger and younger? They've played with demons for over thirty years now, and they are starting to realize they are a limited resource." He spat the last words.

Becca couldn't tell where the anger was coming from. Darion had said Richard had helped with The Rising. He stole the Mundanes' power and helped the magicians build secure cities. Becca stepped back, Richard's magic hanging heavy in the air, emanating from him.

Darion flashed her a warning in those dark eyes.

She ignored it. "Why do you care?"

Richard glared at her, and a small pecking noise sounded from the window. Like a light switch flipping, Richard's countenance shifted. He lifted his head back and laughed, actually laughed. "Oh, girl, you have the spirit of old Cleo here when she was a wee bitch." He placed a hand on the dog's head. "I wish we had more time to discuss the downfall of mankind, but alas I have more visitors."

Richard lifted his hand, and the hound headed towards the door. It swung open, and the dog trotted through. As its tail disappeared, it closed behind her.

"I have a feeling this will be Ryma's men checking up

on me. And if it is Ryma, I will have to tell him the truth, or as close of a version to it as I can manage."

The urge to flee readied her legs to run. Leon tightened his grip on the knife, and Alex's gun appeared at his side. Becca knew not many could lie to Ryma and was grateful for what little warning Richard had given them.

"No need for weapons. Not yet." Richard turned and left the room, then called after them. "Come on."

They followed him through a maze of rooms and hallways and out the back door. He whistled a particular tune, and another dog came running up to greet him, this one with darker fur. Again he placed a hand on its head. There must have been an exchange. Becca could only guess as she had never seen anything like it.

"He will lead you through the forest to an exit where you can bypass city guards out of the city." Richard nodded and the dog started off.

Leon and Alex followed the dog. Becca started down the porch but realized Darion wasn't coming and turned back.

At the top of the porch stairs, Darion turned to Richard. "Why are you helping us? You helped with The Rising, establishing the city covens, so why the change of heart?"

"You're still young. You imagine a better world, like I did, where people rise up to do it better than our fathers." He sighed, a tired, aged look on his face. "Let's hope you do a better job than we did."

"Then come with us. We may have a chance with you on our side," Becca said. With someone as powerful as Richard on their side the odds improved greatly.

"I don't have the stomach for dark magic like I once did, and I cannot oppose Ryma without it." Richard glanced at the forest, and then his gaze rested on Becca. "You better hurry. Ryma is out for more than blood."

"Thank you." Darion headed down the steps.

They took off at a fast pace to catch up to the others. Becca raced, not only from the oncoming threat, but from the memories of what Ryma could do.

CHAPTER SEVENTEEN

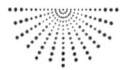

Becca's legs still ached from the five-mile run they took following that old pooch. The only solace she found was that Darion appeared to be just as winded. Leon and Alex trudged along like the soldiers they were without breathing hard.

Just like Richard had said, the dog led them to a section of city wall lying in ruin. Ryma didn't need a physical wall to keep his ward in place though. But for some reason, this section was void of magic.

"Walk carefully," Darion instructed. He pointed to bowls of salt and herbs. "Richard must have somehow provided a break in the circle. Not sure how."

Becca didn't care about the "how" as long as they could get out of there. Once past the city limits, they continued at a fast pace and straight back to the jeep.

Once they arrived, Leon slung his pack into the jeep and removed the camouflage, while Becca and Darion struggled for oxygen.

"You guys should really get in shape," Alex told them.

"We're not all allowed to play outside at the beach," Darion replied.

"It's not playing," Alex said.

"If you guys want to wake early, you're welcome to come on our morning run," Leon offered before buckling up.

Darion rolled his eyes and didn't bother with an answer. With the high sun, this jog was hard for him too.

Here was a time when Becca's life depended on her physical condition, not her magical one. She shouldn't have let herself relax lately. She never knew when she may need her fists. "I may take you up on that, Leon."

He looked back at her, as if checking to see if she was serious.

"We don't slow down for girls," Alex said.

Becca met his gaze. "I hope not."

"Good." The engine roared to life, and Leon drove out of the hiding spot. "We have one more stop on the way back." He tore through the forest before anyone could answer.

Darion pulled out the paper he'd received from Richard. Worry creased his face.

Becca held out her hand.

He glanced at her, then back at the paper.

"Come on. We knew it wouldn't be that easy." Becca spoke loudly, the wind tearing at the fabric roof. "We should both memorize it."

He nodded and handed over the spell.

It was hard to decipher the handwriting, but she recognized some English and Latin. One word stood off the page: blood. It required a lot of human blood and a human sacrifice. Anger built up in her throat, tightening as she tried to swallow. She must not be reading this right. They didn't get this far to find it impossible. Turning the spell over and over in her mind, she memorized the words.

She handed it back and kept her gaze straight ahead. Becca always thought she'd do anything to save her sister, but now she wondered just how far she was really willing to go.

Darion lowered his head and studied the spell.

She didn't want to think about what was on that piece of paper. Or what else lay between her and her sister.

They traveled in silence for almost an hour before pulling off the highway again. They followed a dirt path for several miles to an old warehouse. Leon parked behind it.

"What's this place?" Becca asked.

"Supplies for us from city dwellers," Alex answered.

Leon climbed out. "Come on. Also, don't use magic in here."

Darion climbed out of the jeep. "Even defensive? How can they tell?"

"Not sure. But they don't want anything influencing the bartering process. If they think you're using it, they'll shoot. We will be fine if we stick together."

"Easy for you to say with a gun in your hand." Becca shut the door behind her.

Leon gave an exasperated sigh. "Just keep your questions and hands to yourself."

Living by herself in the city for years didn't make her a complete idiot. She couldn't take too much offense though. Leon treated everyone like an idiot.

Inside the warehouse, long tables were laid out, holding a variety of goods from tools to cooking utensils. The only source of light were windows, or what used to be windows, lining the top of the walls, twenty feet or so above them. Light shined through the broken openings, throwing shadows across the room. With the tall ceilings and concrete floor, the chill bit through Becca's jacket.

Only a handful of people were scattered around the room. Most of them kept to themselves. Leon and Alex picked up several items, like cooking and medical supplies.

A couple of guys brushed past them, knocking into Becca's shoulder.

"Hey," Becca hollered.

The guys kept walking, ignoring her.

"You okay?" Darion asked.

"It was nothing," Becca mumbled.

Leon turned and glared.

"I kept my hands to myself." She raised her hands innocently.

Leon turned and said something too low to hear. At the checkout, Leon bargained on a couple of items while the others stood nearby quietly. Becca turned partly to scan the room. Alex set down the jug of gas he had been carrying.

Those same guys who knocked into her approached. There were only two of them, both tall and thin with greasy hair. She avoided their gazes, not wanting to put up with Leon's crap the whole way back if she got in a fight.

"So you think we can do it? Maybe with animals?" She aimed her question at Darion, referring to the spell.

"We need to talk to Andre. He'll know more—"

Alex shoved Darion aside, knocking him into Becca. A shots echoed in the air, accompanied by shouting. By the time Becca had her feet under her, Alex had his gun pointed at the two men from earlier. They lay on the concrete floor, blood seeping underneath them.

Darion pushed her forward. "Move!"

Crouching low, she rushed out of the building, Darion's hand on her back. Alex followed them to the jeep, gas container in hand.

"Is Leon okay?" Becca asked. *Why wasn't he coming out?* "When people start shooting, it's usually a good time to go."

"They were shooting at you, not him. Get in the jeep. He'll be here soon."

Alex opened the gas container, and Becca crawled into the back. Darion sucked in a sharp breath as he followed her into the back seat.

"What's wrong?" she asked as she scanned his body for injury.

There on his side, blood seeped through his shirt.

"Darion!"

"Easy, Bec." He carefully lowered himself on the seat.

"Alex, he's been shot."

Alex didn't seem surprised as he dumped the gas in the jeep. "First aid kit under the seat."

"It only skimmed my side." Darion tried to be reassuring, but his pale complexion and short breaths told a different story.

She ripped open the first aid kit. "How do you know?"

"I can sense metal, usually to heat it up or destroy it. There's nothing in me."

"Now you're a doctor? Who's to say it didn't go clean through?" It was easier for her to be mad than let the panic set in.

Darion grabbed her hand, and a warmth of magic flowed into her. "I'm okay, Becca. I promise."

She pressed a heavy bandage onto his stomach to stop the bleeding.

He winced. "Would I still have my magic if I was dying?"

"Maybe. I don't know." Her nerves were too on edge to think straight.

"Guess someone's been passing out wanted posters or something. We should feel flattered we're famous."

"Yeah, flattered." She placed another layer of gauze on the wound and taped it in place.

Leon and Alex climbed into the front seats without a word. They were out of sight of the warehouse in mere seconds.

"You alive back there?" Alex asked.

"Yeah. I'll survive." Darion's face whitened as the side of the jeep jerked and bounced.

"Can you take it easy on the roads?" Becca asked.

Leon didn't take his eyes off the road in front of him and kept his foot firmly pressed to the floor. "No."

Alex searched the road behind them. "If we slow up, we're more of a target. And the sooner we're back, the better your boy will do."

A feeling of total uselessness attacked Becca, then she thought of the one thing she could give him. Leaning back against the seat, she covered Darion's free hand on the seat with her palm. She briefly closed her eyes and spoke the spell to combine their magic. She wanted to give him whatever he needed. He couldn't heal with her magic, but maybe she could ease his pain.

It reminded her of the first time they'd tried it back at the cabin when he was training her. At the time, she didn't know then how rare and special it was. She hadn't seen any other magicians do it since. Probably because it opened a person up and lowered all their defensive magic. But now, Becca couldn't imagine not doing it. She felt the part of him that was free of the complications of the past.

"Thanks." His shoulders relaxed slightly, and he eased back into the seat.

The moon shone bright through the trees as they maneuvered their way back. She watched Darion drift in and out of sleep, his head now on her lap. The bleeding looked like it had slowed, but it was hard to tell without light. Keeping her hand on his shoulder, she prayed. Her parents were religious, but that didn't work out too great for them or her. She wasn't sure what she believed. But if there was a chance in heaven or hell that something could help Darion, she would try.

Somehow, Leon managed to maneuver through the dense trees in the dark as he parked the car. "Alex, finish storing the car. I'll take Darion in."

"Sure thing, boss."

They carefully maneuvered Darion out of the car. His quiet compliance worried her.

"Think you can walk?" Leon kept an arm around Darion and didn't give him a chance to answer. Leon carried most of his weight while Becca helped carefully with his injured side.

Darion winced slightly.

"Sorry." Becca tried to adjust her hold.

"No sorrys," Darion told her as they started forward.

Leon tried to keep a fast pace, but they had to maneuver around shrubs, trees, and fallen debris. They found the trail quickly. Thankfully, the ocean was already at low tide, the ground damp underfoot. Only two fit on the trail, so Leon helped him down, while Becca brought up the rear.

She peered into the darkness, listening for anything out of the ordinary. They hiked down carefully. She cringed with every sound that escaped Darion's lips. There weren't many, but there were enough. Soon, Alex caught up and continued ahead so Doc would be ready for them.

Darion's breath came in short gasps. She touched his neck to feel his magic. He was weaker than she'd ever felt him.

"Just tired," Darion said as if reading her thoughts.

She wanted to believe him, but the tightness in her chest wouldn't relax until she spoke to Doc. Ignoring her panicked thoughts, she kept moving. They squeezed through the dark caves and headed straight for the medical unit.

"Doc knows what he's doing," Leon told them as they approached the medical unit. "He's stitched me up plenty of times."

They pushed through the door, and a warm light greeted them. Doc waited for them, already dressed in scrubs, and Nikki waited beside him similarly dressed.

"Over there," Doc ordered. His usual relaxed jovial expression changed into stern concentration. "What do we have?"

"Bullet. Think it went straight through. Lost a lot of blood." Leon, with Alex's help, lifted Darion on the bed.

Doc quickly cut off his shirt and stripped off the bandages. "Did this happen in the city?"

"No, someone recognized us at the trading post."

Doc nodded and focused back on the wound in front of him.

Becca felt Caleb beside her, his tall frame a comfort. "You okay, Becca?"

"I will be, when he is." She motioned to Darion.

Caleb remained silent and placed an arm around her. She leaned into him. He'd been there for her for as long as she could remember. Caleb knew better than to push her or tell her lies that everything would be okay. He was her best friend for a reason.

Time passed slowly as Doc worked tirelessly. Leon left to report back, and Alex headed to the other side of the room to talk to Marcus who had a large bandage over one shoulder.

"How's Marcus?" Becca asked Caleb softly.

"Well. He'll regain full mobility in his shoulder."

"Good." She folded her arms to keep her hands from shaking.

Nikki approached Becca and Caleb. "It didn't hit any organs. We'll clean it out, then stitch him up. He'll make a full recovery. He's lucky."

Becca bit her tongue. Lucky was not a word she would use. Caleb's arm tightened around her.

"You can go rest," Nikki said. "I will come get you when he wakes."

"I'll wait." Becca stared at Darion's hands. They could be so gentle and so fierce.

"Come on, Becca." Caleb steered her into a chair.

She continued to watch Darion as others flitted in and out of her vision. Staring numbly, she began to realize a few things. First, despite her fears and Darion's past lies, she didn't want to live without him. He had woven himself into the fabric of her life, of her existence, and she didn't feel complete without him. And unfortunately, with this revelation, she knew her heart would never be the same.

Regardless of what came next with Elizabeth, she could no longer endanger Darion or Caleb. Saving Liz was Becca's job and her job alone. Today brought that into horrifying clarity.

CHAPTER EIGHTEEN

"You awake over there?" Nikki asked Caleb.

"Yeah. I'm worried about Darion." Caleb took another bite of breakfast, but his mind was in the medical unit. Becca had spent the night there, and he wanted to see how Darion was recovering.

"He'll be fine. I promise. Becca doesn't need to worry. He'll be back to his normal routine in a couple weeks."

"It's not only Becca worrying. We've survived weeks together, and he's saved my butt more than once." He couldn't help the heat rising to his face. Nikki had lived her entire life here in the safety of her father. Yes, he was jealous of it, but he also didn't think she could relate to many of these refugees.

Surprise crossed her features. "I didn't mean anything by it."

"I know, I—"

"Nikki." The young girl, Navina, appeared next to him, a small cat in her arms. "Is Becca okay? I heard someone was shot."

"Yeah, she's fine. Her friend Darion was shot."

"Her boyfriend? The one with messy black hair?" Navina struggled to keep the kitten in her arms.

Nikki nodded. "Yes, but he will make a full recovery."

He shoveled oatmeal into his mouth and tried to ignore the girl's comments.

"Maybe I'll go visit later." Navina turned to go.

"Wait until tomorrow," Nikki called to Navina's retreating figure. "And not with the cat."

Once Navina was out of earshot, Nikki put down her spoon and stared at him. "Are you in love with Becca?" she blurted out.

Caleb paused, his spoon in the air. The question took him by surprise, even when he was asking himself the same thing seconds ago. He took the bite of oatmeal to give him time to figure out how to clarify the mess of emotions going on inside of him. "I was at one time, years ago when we were still teenagers. But now we're friends, as close as family."

At first Nikki didn't reply, as if she were trying her next words to see how it tasted. "Okay… I guess I thought with all the time we've been spending together, there might be something between us…"

Caleb dropped his spoon. It bounced off his metal bowl and clattered to the ground. He bent over to pick it up and took a deep breath. He enjoyed Nikki but didn't think he was ready for something serious. How could he be, when he didn't know where he'd be in a month? He had nothing to offer.

He swallowed hard, his throat surprisingly dry. "I've enjoyed spending time with you, but…"

Her lips tightened as she waited for an answer.

"I don't know where I'll be in a month, or a week, and I don't want to get involved with anyone right now." The awkward words were painful to get out.

Before he could say anything else, she stood up and gathered her bowl. "Uh-huh. I understand."

"Becca!" Navina's voice rang out through the cafeteria.

Becca stood in the entrance, exhaustion darkening her eyes, her hair on top of her head in a bird's nest. Navina rushed to her side.

Unable to help himself, Caleb stood as well. He loved her, just not in the way Nikki might've thought.

As Nikki brushed past him on her way out, he couldn't find the words to make things right. Not that it really mattered. In the end, there was really nothing to say.

"You're back!" Navina rushed over with such excitement that Becca's mouth lifted into a grin.

"Yep." She reached out to pet the small kitten trying to claw its way out of Navina's arms. "What does your mom say about bringing this into the cafeteria?"

"I'm not eating, just looking for you. Wanted to make sure you were okay. Are you going to practice this afternoon?"

Becca hadn't slept much, and with every step she took, her sore legs protested. She'd also visited her sister this morning with Andre. Bael was gaining power, while Elizabeth deteriorated every second a little bit more. Becca came in for some coffee to help power her through the day.

At the sight of Navina, though, a distraction was tempting. "I have to go back to check on my friend, but I'll come a bit later."

"Good." Navina's mom entered the common room. The young girl's eyes widened. "Gotta go." She hurried out, the kitten in her arms.

Becca turned to find Caleb with a large, steaming cup of coffee. "Here you go."

"You're a lifesaver." She grabbed the mug, warming her hands.

"It's purely selfish. I know what you're like when you're tired." He shoved his hands in his jeans. "How's Darion?"

"Good. I'm heading back if you want to come visit," she offered.

"Sure, I have a few minutes 'til I'm due at training." He held the door out of the common room open for her. "Nikki says he's doing well."

"He harassed us all morning, so I'd say so." The hot liquid warmed a path straight to her stomach. Truly the nectar of the gods. "So what's going on with Nikki?" Becca glanced at him sideways.

He shrugged.

"She'd been great with Doc in taking care of Darion."

"Glad to hear it." His blank features and blunt tone told her there was more to the story, but she didn't want to push. They walked the rest of the way in silence.

In the small medical room, Andre and Doc were talking to Darion. Andre sat perched on the bed next to Darion while Doc held a chart in his hands. Nikki attended to Marcus a few beds down.

"Hey." Caleb approached Darion. "How's it going? They feeding you good?"

Darion looked as if he'd been run over by a truck. "Oh yeah, with this broth, I'm sure I'll be your size any day now."

Caleb had a good six inches and probably fifty pounds on Darion. He gave a light laugh. "I'll be ready for you."

"Glad you both came. We need to talk." Andre turned to Doc. "You said Marcus needed a walk today. Do you think you and my daughter could arrange that now?"

"Sure." Doc turned to Marcus. "Come on. No more lying around on the job."

Nikki helped him with Marcus, and the three of them left the room.

Caleb pulled up a chair, and Becca sat at the foot of Darion's bed. She placed a hand on his leg. His magic pulsed strong. If she could only keep a hand on him all the time, she wouldn't worry. Talk about smothering.

As soon as the others left, Andre spoke. "First, I wanted to ask you about the group that attacked us. Jemi got the impression they were searching for us specifically, and I'm trying to figure out how they found us. Could they have anything from you to track you specifically? Hair or blood? I protect against those kinds of spells, but I'm not sure what else it could be."

"I don't think so," Darion said. "I'm usually pretty careful."

"Maybe…" Becca's thoughts traveled to the last time she saw her uncle alive. She had woken up trapped in a cell. "I was unconscious around Jeremiah. He could have…"

"He's dead though. Ryma would have had to find it and know it was yours." Darion's voice tightened, proving he was just as unhappy about this topic of conversation as she was.

"And you haven't contacted anyone else?" Andre looked to each of them.

"No," she and Darion replied.

"I have no one to contact." Caleb shrugged, the emptiness in his voice making Becca's heart ache.

"Okay, then. I'll figure out that one later." Andre took a deep breath, a somberness falling on his features as he focused on Becca. "Darion showed me the spell you guys retrieved from Richard, and I'm sorry to say we won't be able to complete it, Becca. We need to discuss what we do next."

Becca bolted up. "What? We're giving up?"

His dark eyes bored into hers. "Did you really read this?"

"Yes." She'd actually memorized it. "I know it requires a blood sacrifice, but I saw a similar thing at Ryma's where they cut their arm to fulfill the sacrifice. I can do that." She wasn't afraid of a little blood, and Andre was far from a pacifist.

"No." He shook his head, pity seeping into his face. "It requires a complete blood sacrifice. And for a demon of this power, it will need to be quite a sacrifice. Someone relatively young, like your sister, and strong enough to attract the demon to the pentagram to trap him. Do you really want to kill a wizard on the slim chance your sister is still awake in there?"

A heavy weight pressed on Becca's chest, making it difficult to breathe. Caleb stood at her side, and Darion struggled to sit up. She searched their faces and found worry. For her. Not her sister, who lay dying in the nearby room. If they knew Elizabeth, or really knew Becca, they would realize they were worried about the wrong sister.

"We did all we could," Darion said. "We tried everything."

"Is that it, then?" Her voice broke under the pain threatening to explode.

Caleb took her hand, but it felt far away as if she were disconnected from her body.

"I'm sorry for your loss," Andre told her, so formal as if Elizabeth were already dead. In his eyes, she was.

Becca struggled to speak. "Can we do it tomorrow? I'd like to say goodbye."

Andre nodded. Becca backed up, wanting to run away from everyone's pitying gaze.

Caleb started to follow.

She raised her hand, palm up, stopping him. "I just need some time alone." She couldn't explain the pain in her chest about to explode, and she couldn't break down here.

Once she was out of the room, she took off, sprinting down the corridors. Welcoming the pain in her sore legs, she ran away from the eating and training areas through unknown paths with no sense of direction. She didn't care. She wanted to get lost, to be alone in the darkness like her sister had been for over a month. All of it had been for nothing.

Becca should have been the one trapped by the demon. The haunting accusations of her dead uncle came back to her—since Becca was ruined, he was forced to use Elizabeth. He was a monster. But maybe he was right. What if her choices caused her sister's death? Then who was the real monster?

CHAPTER NINETEEN

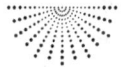

Before dinner, Caleb wandered the halls searching for Becca. She had wanted space, and he understood that. After his parents died, he needed time to scream at the world and curse God. But now as dinner was in full swing, he needed to make sure she was okay. He'd promised Darion.

Caleb caught sight of Navina's braids in the halls and caught up to her. "Have you seen Becca?"

"Yeah. She was in training."

"How was she?"

Navina shrugged. "Not too good. She even let me beat her a couple times."

"Thanks." He headed towards Becca's dormitory. He'd never been down here before, since it was for women only. He knocked on the metal door.

An older lady with graying hair opened it. "Yes?"

"I'm looking for Becca."

"Don't think she's up for company right now." She opened the door wider and motioned to Becca on a top bunk, back turned to him. "Said she wanted rest after training."

"I wanted to make sure she was okay."

"She's not, but she will be with time." The woman stepped farther into the hall and lowered her voice. "I spoke with Andre. We'll keep an eye on her tonight."

Caleb was grateful for their care, but it did nothing for the uneasiness in his stomach.

The woman placed a hand on his shoulder in a grand-motherly fashion. "She isn't the first one of us to lose a loved one. We'll take good care of her."

He nodded. "Of course. Thank you."

He slowly walked away, trying to reassure himself that Becca would get past this. She was the strongest person he knew. What was he going to do, watch her sleep all night? To be honest, he wanted to. It would be easier for him than trusting Becca to strangers.

Becca kept to her bed for the rest of the night. Someone brought her food, but she couldn't stomach it. There was too much on the line.

The other women assumed she was mourning, and in a way, she was. But not for Elizabeth. Not yet. She avoided Darion and Caleb. They knew her better than anyone, so lying wouldn't work. If things went wrong, she loathed the idea of not saying goodbye.

She drifted off once or twice as night fell. Not for long, just briefly. Images of her sister flooded her dreams, waking Becca to her real purpose. When the sounds of sleep filled the darkened room, she climbed out of bed. She'd have one chance at saving her sister, and it would have to be now.

Susan, the older widow, stirred slightly. "Is that you, Becca?"

"Yeah. I'm going to see Doc about getting something to help me sleep," Becca whispered so as to not wake the others.

"Okay. Ask him for something to eat too."

"I will," she lied and crept out the door.

The halls were bare and nearly dark to save energy. But after living down here for a week, she didn't need light.

She stopped by the kitchen, but not for food, and then continued on to Jemi's room. This was the hardest part of her plan—lying to Jemi. Becca could only hope that Jemi would chalk it up to crazy emotions at her sister's impending death.

Jemi lived alone, near Andre. Becca wondered at first why she didn't live in the dorms with the rest of the single women, but after dealing with Jemi's sharp demeanor, she stopped wondering and was grateful.

She knocked quietly, and didn't have to wait long before Jemi answered.

"What is it?" she asked.

Becca wasn't an actress, but she brought everything out for this performance. She had to. "I couldn't sleep and wondered if you could talk. Maybe explain why Andre won't save my sister. It's like he doesn't even want to try."

A mixture of emotions crossed Jemi's face as she struggled to wake up, annoyance the most prominent. "Sure, come on in." She rubbed her face with one hand. "Guess I'll make coffee."

Becca took two steps inside, and then without hesitation, raised the pan she'd stolen from the kitchen and slammed it into Jemi's head. Jemi collapsed in a boneless heap. Becca couldn't have countered Jemi's magic, but magicians often forgot about good old muscle.

"I'm so sorry, Jemi," Becca whispered as she dragged Jemi's body out into the hall. "I wouldn't have done it if there was any other way."

Jemi was the only person light enough for Becca to carry. She heaved the unconscious woman over her shoulder and staggered slightly under her weight. Bracing one hand on the wall, Becca continued down the path.

There it was. Elizabeth's room. One guard stood outside. He carried a rifle over his shoulder, which was a good sign that he was one of Leon's men. She didn't recognize him from Lance's training either.

Becca closed her eyes and focused her magic. She had been practicing with controlling animals. She was improving, more than she wanted to admit, because it scared her.

Today, regrettably, she even controlled Navina. The girl would go pick up the animal and then return to her spot, believing the animal had come to her. Normally Navina wouldn't be so susceptible, but the girl was focusing all her power at beating Becca, not protecting herself from Becca.

It sickened Becca to do it, but desperate times, desperate measures. Desperate to right the wrong she started all those years ago by running away, resulting in her parents' deaths and her sister becoming Soultorn. She needed to know if what she planned for tonight was even possible. If there was any chance of saving Liz, she had to take it.

Watching the guard, Becca projected her magic, pushing ideas of hunger, an uncontrollable hunger, into the mind of the guard. Flashes of food from the kitchen did the trick. Confusion clouded his vision. He shook his head a few times. Becca pushed harder, and then the guard snapped his head up and headed off right past Becca, towards the kitchen. She'd done it.

It left her breathing hard. Hopefully it didn't drain her too much. She needed her magic for what came next.

She lugged Jemi towards the door, struggling with Jemi's unconscious body. Finally, she propped Jemi against the wall and used her hand to open the door. It unlocked with a small click. She lay Jemi on the ground close to the wall so hopefully no one would step on her. Becca hated to leave Jemi where people could find her, but it wasn't safe inside, especially for an unconscious witch. What Becca had planned shouldn't take long.

Inside the room, Becca watched her sister. Elizabeth lay pale and still as if dead, except for the movement behind her eyelids. Her golden hair was braided to the side, soft pieces framing her face. Clear plastic tubing ran from her arm to a metal stand.

"Just hold on," Becca told her sister.

The next several minutes felt like hours as Becca opened the glass barrier with her magic. Then she carefully drew a pentagram next to the one she'd previously drawn. She took her time, making it perfect, with every grain of salt and every word. She had only one chance at this, and Elizabeth's life depended on it.

Bael's power thrummed inside the room, pulsating on her skin. Becca took off her jacket for the first time in weeks.

"I don't know if this will work," she told her unconscious sister. "But whatever happens, know I love you."

She stepped inside the pentagram and pulled out a knife she'd kept from Leon. Sitting with legs crossed, she locked the pentagram with a single word. Then she began the spell. She had ingrained the words into her mind the second she saw them. No one probably thought a person would use them on themselves.

She offered herself as the sacrifice to pull Bael out. She

opened her magic. It felt almost perverse. It was similar to the same spell she used with Darion. Except this time, she was pairing with a demon. A demon who could and probably would kill her. She drew the knife down her arm, blood quickly welling to drip onto the floor. The wound wasn't deep enough to kill her, but deep enough to entice this devil to leave her sister alone.

Gritting her teeth, she swallowed the pain blossoming in her arm. Blood pooled around her as she let it flow freely. The sight left her light-headed, but she wasn't done yet. This was the only way, she reminded herself. Her sister deserved to live.

The knife clattered to the floor as Becca finished the spell. "Come and get me, Bael, you devil."

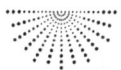

CHAPTER TWENTY

Darion thrummed his fingers on the edge of the bed. Trying to ignore the wound throbbing on his side, his frustration grew with every passing second.

"You need anything?" Doc grabbed his bag as if heading out.

Darion wanted to tell him to track down Becca, tie her up if he had to, and drag her back here. He hadn't seen her all day since she'd taken off. Instead, he replied, "No."

"Nikki will be here in a little bit. I have to go see a patient before I turn in. Will you be okay for a few minutes?" Doc covered a big yawn.

Marcus had moved out today, so Darion would be alone.

"Sure thing."

"Thanks. Nikki can give you more pain meds in an hour, and that should help you sleep. Night."

Despite Andre lending his magic to help Darion heal—something he'd never seen before—Darion was still sore as hell. But he didn't want pain meds. He'd feel better when he knew Becca was okay.

Caleb had checked on her and told Darion she was in her room. Andre had even assigned a woman in the dorm to watch over her. Though nice, it did nothing to ease the dread growing inside. She'd lost her sister. The only reason she was grieving now, instead of a couple months ago, was because of him. He gave her this crazy hope that Elizabeth had a chance.

Once that shattered, the last couple of months were meaningless torture for all of them. He had to talk to her, make it right, and if he was going to have a chance, it would be now.

He slowly rolled to his uninjured side. The wound throbbed every time he tried to use his stomach. He continued off the bed and collapsed on the ground, breathing through his teeth. A cold chill traveled up his back. He wore loose cotton pants, but no shirt. At least the large white bandage on his side held secure.

He used the bed to pull himself up and moaned in agony. Once up, moving was easier. He shuffled forward along the bed and searched for a cane or something, but no luck. With clumsy steps, he made it to the wall. Holding on to the jagged surface, he waited for the pain to pass before continuing out the door.

The corridors were nearly dark and empty, thankfully. He continued down the hall, trying to orient in the dark maze before him. It was his first time on his feet since the attack, and the walls lurched around him. He gripped the rocky surface, determined to stay upright.

Which way to the girls' dorms? They were on the other side of the cafeteria.

Low light barely illuminated the halls, but he could see his feet. Pushing out the pain, he focused on placing one foot in front of the other. Sweat dripped down his back despite the chill in the air.

With each step, the dread steadily grew to panic. He had to find Becca.

Someone approached. A guard. Darion held his hands open, magic ready. He wasn't going back to his room until he saw Becca. The guard approached, his gun slung on his back, and a look of confusion etched on his face. His eyes skittered across Darion, but he didn't speak. It was strange behavior.

Something in the air didn't sit right. Leon's men knew their jobs and performed them well.

"Where you going, soldier?" Darion steadied himself on the wall, hoping the young man wouldn't notice.

The soldier had a blank look in his eyes. "I'm hungry. So hungry. But the kitchen's closed. I don't know why I'm so hungry…"

Magic. There were only a few people who could have done this, and Becca was one of them. But why?

"Where are you supposed to be?"

The guard shook his head for a moment, as if trying to clear his mind. "Guarding the Soultorn. I need to get back there. It's my post."

"You may need help. Take me with you."

The guard looked Darion over. "I'm not sure about that."

Darion's temper heated. He may not have magic to influence people's decisions, but he damn well wasn't going to be left behind. "Unless you're a wizard, that pretty gun won't stop what's hiding behind that door. We need to move. Now." He gathered his strength and strode towards the man.

The soldier nodded and turned down the tunnel.

Darion quickly leaned on the soldier with an "umph."

"Are you sure you should be out of the medical wing?"

"Just keep moving." Darion tried to tell himself this wasn't Becca's doing. He gritted his jaw, and tried to hurry.

They arrived at the door, and everything was quiet.

The guard relaxed his stance. "Good. Everything's fine."

Darion noticed the small, unconscious lump hiding in the shadows. "Then why is Jemi unconscious on the ground? Open the door. Now."

A power radiated through the door that twisted Darion's insides. Something was terribly wrong.

"I can't open the door." The guard looked dumbfounded.

"What? Look, idiot, open the door, or I'll burn it down." He opened his free hand, and sparks jumped out of them. There was no time to waste.

Fear flared in the guards eyes. "I can't. I don't have access."

"Then go get Andre," he ordered. "Run!"

The guard took off, sprinting down the hall. Darion tried to focus beyond the fear building inside of him. He had to keep his head. A voice boomed inside, and a surge of magic pushed its way through the door. Bael.

Forget control. He raised his hands high overhead, sparks turning into flames. He screamed a spell and shot his magic straight through the door.

Power pulsed through his body, and the door blasted open. Fire clung to the frame. He extinguished the flames as he passed through. Taking in the scene before him, Darion sank to his knees.

It was Bael. The demon hovered in the air over the two sisters, its shape slowly emerging. Part man, part beast, this demon stretched his inhuman limbs, and a few heads even. The dark shape twisted and turned, changing shape as it grew in size.

A scream clawed its way up Darion's body. "No!"

Below him lay Becca in a pool of blood. It wasn't supposed to end this way. He wouldn't let it end this way.

Darion tried turning his pain into a sacrifice, giving anything and everything he had to stop this demon. But he was an empty vessel, hindered by his wounds and fatigue. He couldn't stop it. Bael spoke powerfully in a language Darion didn't recognize, the words reverberating through his mind, and the creature continued to grow in size. It absorbed Darion's attacks, almost feeding off his pain. He caught himself on his hands and knees, black dots filling his vision.

Shouts erupted behind him, and a cool wave of energy pooled over him. Andre approached, keeping his eyes focused on Bael, with Jemi at his side. One look at Becca, and Darion feared their help was too late.

"Save her," Darion pleaded, but wasn't sure if he spoke aloud. His side ached, and his body and magic were exhausted.

Andre shouted curses, his palms opened towards Bael. The cabinets lining the walls shook around them. Debris fell from the ceiling. Darion crawled towards Becca's body. The pentagram was broken from Bael's strength. The demon now focused on Andre and left Becca to bleed out below.

Darion moved slowly, the magic in the air thick. He moved another foot closer. He ached to touch her one more time. He realized she must have opened herself magically to Bael. Becca had presented a willing sacrifice to entice the demon out and save her sister.

A blast of power pressed down on Darion, flattening him on his back. Darion turned his head to see Bael explode into a black vapor. Andre had vanquished the demon. Its black miasma settled throughout the room on the wreckage. Both girls remained unmoving.

Bael might have been gone, but it didn't ease the pain as he watched Becca's still frame.

"Help her," he tried to shout, but it came out weak.

Doc ran past him with his black med bag. He yelled for Andre. The scene unfolded in slow motion. Doc pounded on Becca's chest, then breathed in her mouth. Muffled voices bounced off the wall. Nikki appeared at Doc's side, handing him a large needle. He uncapped the needle and slammed it into Becca's chest.

Darion's vision blurred, but somehow he crawled to Becca's side, across from Doc. Doc and Nikki continued working on her. She moved Becca's chest while he breathed air into her mouth. Darion reached out for her hand, and wished he had more power to give her.

"Fight, dammit," he whispered to her. As soon as he touched her skin, relief rushed through him. She was alive. Though her skin was cold to the touch, a small spark of magic thrummed inside her, tiny but there. Was it enough?

"She's alive," he told them.

Nikki looked at him with disbelief. Andre kept speaking over her body.

"She's still in there." He squeezed her hand.

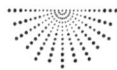

CHAPTER TWENTY-ONE

A dark mist surrounded Becca as she dreamed. She struggled for footing amid tall trees in an unfamiliar forest. Her throat tightened as a panicked scream struggled to escape. Before she could say anything, Elizabeth appeared beside her. Her sister didn't appear startled, or even frightened. Her large blue eyes held an empty look. Blue eyes. Demon-free eyes. Becca grabbed Liz's hand.

"At least we are together," Becca told her sister.

Liz didn't turn or even acknowledge that Becca spoke. Pushing down her fear, Becca moved forward. It didn't matter that they were alone or lost. She held her sister, not Bael or some other demented demon. Her sister.

Becca slowly began hearing things, voices calling for her. Darion. She leaned into his warm touch, though part of her felt guilty for leaving her sister. But that was just a dream, she told herself. This Darion, flesh-and-blood Darion, was real. He continued talking to her. A bright light burned behind her closed eyes.

Darion brushed back her hair, speaking to her. "Come on, Becca. Fight for me."

She put forth the effort and slowly turned her head. Squinting against the bright lights, she struggled to pry open her eyes.

"You talk." Her words were rough, her throat parched. "More than a girl."

Darion laughed, his eyes glistening. He spoke to another person in the room, and then gripped Becca's hand tighter. "You had us scared there for a while."

"Me too." She closed her eyes again. "Is Liz okay?"

"She's alive." He must have come closer, because she could smell his warm breath. "You terrified me, Becca. I'm not sure if I should throttle you or just tell you how much I love you."

A weak smile tugged at her lips, while debilitating exhaustion threatened to drag her down. "Tired," was the only thing she managed to say. What she really wanted to say was "I love you too."

The next morning, tucked into a white bed in the med unit, Becca remained unconscious while Darion clung to her free hand.

"She'll be okay." He looked up, pushing Doc to agree with him.

Doc wrapped up the black blood pressure cuff. "Her blood pressure's better, but she's not out of the woods yet. We're not sure what Bael did to her."

Darion cringed at the reminder of Bael and what could have happened. At least he got a chance to tell her how he felt yesterday during the few seconds she was awake. Even if it was returned with an "I'm tired." He planned to give her hell for that soon.

Caleb burst through the door. "Rebecca?"

"She's out again," Darion said.

Caleb's face fell slightly. "But she woke up? Was coherent?"

"Briefly, a few times."

Caleb approached and sat at the foot of her bed. He laid a hand on her foot, as if making sure she was safe and whole.

Despite Darion's better judgment, jealousy reared its ugly head. He wouldn't have been able to keep her alive these past months without Caleb. He knew that, but he also knew the two friends had a bond that ran deep.

"She's said your name," Darion told him. "A few times."

"Really?" Caleb's brows raised in surprised.

"Yes. Nikki wasn't too happy about it." Darion lowered his voice, even though Nikki wasn't on shift.

Caleb shrugged. "We're friends."

"With who?" It wasn't Darion's business, but he couldn't help himself. Staring at the white walls of the med unit hadn't been good for his mental health.

"Both, I guess." Caleb watched Becca with an intensity that said something more than friends.

Darion couldn't blame Caleb if he was still in love with Becca. He just wanted to know what he was up against. Hard to compete against a damn saint.

"Obviously, I love Becca, but not like you think. As a kid, I was in love with her. She was my future." Caleb shifted slightly on the bed, keeping his eyes on her. "But when she left, things changed. I couldn't save her, wasn't there when she needed me. I still love her. She's the only piece of my old life I have left. She's changed so much and so have I, but in some ways we're the same. We still need each other."

"I never know whether to thank you or hate you," Darion muttered.

"She may care for me, but she loves you." Caleb looked up at him.

"I hope you're right."

Caleb didn't seem to mind Darion's irritable mood. "Did Andre say what happened?"

"Surprisingly, he isn't quite sure himself. At thirty years old, magic is pretty new, and the connection Becca and Elizabeth share isn't anything Andre has seen before." Darion hadn't even heard of the type of connection he held with Becca, but he wasn't going to bring that up now.

"So their connection helped Becca call Bael and survive?" Caleb asked.

"I don't think so. Bael was called because of Becca's sacrifice. Bael had tasted Becca's magic when she offered herself up to him. I'm not sure there has ever been such a willing sacrifice before. It was Andre who saved her, saved me too. He banished Bael, and then Doc brought her back from the dead. For a Mundane, he is very gifted." A dark dread of what could have happened hung in the recesses of his mind. Darion swallowed the knot in his throat.

"Why?" Caleb's initial relief that she was okay appeared to morph into fury at what could have happened. "It was a suicide mission, and she couldn't even tell us goodbye."

"We wouldn't have let her otherwise. Don't get me wrong. I'm furious at what she did. But if the roles were reversed, and Becca was the Soultorn, wouldn't you have done the same?" Darion watched Caleb, and the answer was obvious.

"Yeah."

"That's what you do for those you love."

Becca sat up in a white bed in the med unit, slowly eating a bowl of applesauce. She kept glancing over to Elizabeth in the neighboring bed and watching for every little movement. Becca scooped up another bite to eat.

The last time she had applesauce, she was a child, being fussed over by her mother. Now, instead she had Darion watching her like a hawk. It was her first morning awake, really awake, not wading through the dreamlike state of unconsciousness—such weird dreams. He glanced at her bandaged left arm again, his scowl deepening the lines in his face. Despite the pain meds, her arm ached fiercely.

"I'm okay," she told Darion again. "Really."

"Don't lie." Darion narrowed his eyes.

Becca swallowed another bite, knowing Darion had every right to be angry. If he did the same thing without telling her, she'd be beyond furious. She would understand, though, and hopefully he soon would too. She had not worried about dealing with the aftermath of her actions, but given that Elizabeth was still alive, she'd take the consequences.

"How are you feeling?" She changed the subject, worried about the tiredness in his eyes. Especially since he was still recovering from his gunshot wound.

He wore the loose-fitting cotton clothes of a patient, though he sat in the chair next to her bed instead of his own bed. "Fine, unless Doc and Nikki ask." He lowered his voice a bit. "Then I'm really sore, and warm on occasion."

She raised an eyebrow.

"That way I get to stay in these killer outfits." He motioned to the pale shirt.

Nikki, who had been cleaning, approached for the now-empty bowl on Becca's lap. "Are you done?"

"Sure. Thanks."

Nikki nodded and headed out of the room, probably back to the kitchen.

"What's up with her?" Becca watched the door swing shut.

Doc continued reading at his desk.

"Nothing that matters," Darion answered.

"It's not nothing."

"I said nothing that *matters*." He huffed in exaggeration. "She's upset that you endangered the community. And it didn't help that you said Caleb's name a couple times while you were out."

"I did?" Becca draped the blanket up around her. What else had she said while out? Embarrassment warmed her face.

"A few times." Darion's face showed nothing.

"I was having the weirdest dreams about my family." Becca couldn't shake off the dreams. They were of home, but home after she had left. And the conversations with her sister were so real. She tried to push them aside. "How is Caleb? I hope I didn't ruin anything between him and Nikki."

"He's good. He'll be here after dinner to check on you."

Becca wanted to give Darion an explanation. Not that she had to, but she wanted to. "It was these dreams. They were so vivid of my past, my home, my parents, Elizabeth, and Caleb too. I've never dreamed like that since..." She trailed off, unsure of how much she could say without sounding crazy.

Darion leaned forward. "Since when?"

It took Becca a few moments to answer as she slowly

pieced it together. Since at the cabin when she'd started training? No, it was before that. She glanced over at Elizabeth, lying unconscious. Doc had said it may take her a bit longer to wake up—if she did at all—due to the trauma.

"Becca?" Darion sat on the foot of her bed. "What are you thinking?"

She tried to straighten out her muddled thoughts. "I've had these dreams since my tattoo was taken off. There was so much going on, so I never gave a thought to them. But they seem connected to my sister. How could that be?"

"I'm not exactly sure. You two shared a blood bond that was created with old magic when you were young. Even Andre hasn't read much about it."

Becca only vaguely remembered the day Elizabeth hurt her arm on their tree house. Once the blood had started, Liz was so scared, crying nonstop. Becca had cut herself with a pocketknife and told her sister they could become blood sisters, trying to dry Liz's tears. It cheered her up for a bit, before their mother caught them. Becca realized that she saved her sister this time with a similar blood sacrifice.

"Blood bonds are powerful. Compelling another magician to do another's will can influence their thoughts, and more. That's how covens work. Blood oaths. That's why Andre is so against them in his community."

"Yeah." Becca was only half listening, watching her sister's pale and almost frozen form.

"What's wrong?"

She shushed him. "Give me a second."

She recalled how she shared a telepathic connection with Liz back at Ryma's when they were awaiting their fates. They'd spoken to each other then, so why not now? Maybe it was Elizabeth in her dreams this whole time. If Becca could reach her, maybe she could wake her.

Becca focused her magic, which was still weak, but

tried to project out to Elizabeth. Becca glanced at her still sister. When nothing happened, she told Darion, "I thought maybe I could wake her."

He reached for Becca's hand. "It doesn't mean you can't. Give it some time. It took me a while to get through to you, and she's been out for a while."

She gripped his hand, grateful for his touch. Emotions built in her chest as she realized how much she owed him. "Thank you, by the way, for saving my sorry hide."

"I recall a good tongue lashing I received a while ago, about not facing threats together. Remember?"

Becca gulped. The fight on the cliff side. She remembered.

"I promised you that I'd never leave you behind. That we fought together or not at all."

She nodded, knowing where this was going.

"Promise me you'll never do that again. We're in this together, okay?"

Becca wanted to argue that this was her fight for her sister, her battle to win. She didn't want him to get hurt. But he did, trying to save her.

"Promise," she said. "We fight together."

He leaned down, and his lips brushed against hers. The quick movement surprised her, giving her no time to react before he pulled back. She raised her fingers to her lips, an electric sensation still present from his touch.

"Good, now get some rest." He smiled that devilish smile of his that she loved.

Before she could agree, a scream pierced the air, sharp and frantic. Elizabeth, eyes wide open, shrieked as if the hounds of hell themselves were chasing her.

CHAPTER TWENTY-TWO

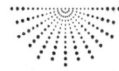

D oc raced over to calm Elizabeth down. Her screams tore at Becca. Against Doc's order to stay put, Becca and Darion went to Liz's side. Becca laid a hand on Liz's arm, but it was quickly thrown aside as she began thrashing around.

"Hold her," Doc yelled as he ran to grab a needle.

Darion and Becca pinned Liz's frail frame down.

Her screams continued, conveying a pain and fear that Becca never wanted to hear from her sister again.

Doc returned and injected something into her arm. Seconds ticked past, and then the fight slowly drained out of her. Her screams turned to moans. Soon, her eyes closed, and she sank into unconsciousness.

"What did you give her?" Becca gripped her limp hand. Her eyes burned with unshed tears.

"A sedative," Doc said between heavy breaths.

"What's happening to her? I thought Bael was gone."

"I don't know, honestly. I need to go see Andre. He wanted to know if anything happened. Maybe he'll have answers." After a few minutes to make sure Liz would remain unconscious, Doc left the unit.

Alone and both sitting next to Liz, Becca turned to Darion. "Do you have any ideas?"

Darion sat back in the chair. "I wish I had answers, but I don't."

That scared her most of all. The unknown was the hardest to battle. Becca climbed on the foot of Elizabeth's bed. Becca and Darion watched Liz silently until Doc came back with Andre and Jemi.

Great. She hadn't had the chance to apologize to Jemi for what happened before. People don't forget getting knocked out, and by Jemi's glare, it was fresh in her memory.

"Doc said Elizabeth had an episode," Andre said.

"That's a nice way to put it," Becca replied. "More like the hounds of hell were after her."

Andre nodded to Jemi, and she grabbed a chair and sat by Elizabeth's head.

"What's she going to do?" Alarms went off in Becca's mind at a variety of magical spells that could hurt her sister, all in the name of subduing her.

"I'm not going to bash her in the head, if that's what you're asking." Jemi gave a sickly smile and placed her hands on Elizabeth's scalp.

"She's searching her mind," Andre explained. "It shouldn't hurt."

"Shouldn't" didn't sound good. Trying to make peace with Jemi, Becca turned. "Look, Jemi, I'm sorry about that..."

The words fell on empty ears as Jemi's had already tuned her out.

No one spoke for a minute, waiting for Jemi. She finally opened her eyes.

"They were nightmares," she explained. "And with being cooped up with a demon for a few months, they're pretty bad. She's in there, but too exhausted to wake up. Like coma victims, she put herself into a guarded status to protect herself."

"We'll have to wait," Andre explained. "Doc—"

"Becca is connected to her subconsciously," Darion offered. "She could reach her if she knew how."

Everyone turned to Becca for confirmation.

She nodded. "Through our dreams."

Andre turned to his second-in-command. "Jemi—"

"No," Jemi said. "That girl knocked me out and left me to get devoured by Bael. I don't care if she makes nice with her sister."

"What?" Dread hung in Becca's stomach.

Andre turned to her. "Becca, you will be punished for your behavior. It's not okay to hurt others here. You will be assigned extra chores until I say so."

Becca nodded. The chores didn't bother her. She probably deserved them.

He continued, "As far as your training, your powers are similar to Jemi's. Where she can delve into people's mind, your powers can influence others, like the guard the other night. Jemi would be an invaluable teacher."

"I'm not going to train her. Lance is good enough." Jemi stood, sticking out her chin defiantly, her hair sticking up like a pixie. A very angry pixie.

It was the only time Becca had ever seen her contradict Andre.

"Maybe." Andre rubbed his bald head. Becca had seen that look of exasperation a time or two on her old boss, Nikko's, face. "Why don't you start with a scan of these two, and then I'll let you decide."

The word "scan" sank heavy and cold in the pit of

Becca's stomach. She remembered the last time Jemi scanned her.

"What are you talking about? A scan?" Darion stood facing Andre.

"I don't want her in my head," Becca protested. Jemi's anger radiated off of her, not that Becca blamed her, but she wasn't about to let her poke around in her mind.

"The attack on the community, the men you fought, it wasn't accidental," Andre explained. "I have wards to deter many. They broke them down and hid their magic from me. They had to have inside help. Someone sent them, and I want to know who."

"Doesn't help that one of them was your friend, and he got away," Jemi said.

"He's not a friend," Becca said and turned to Andre. "So this is how you do it? Instead of requiring blood oaths, you invade everyone's privacy constantly?"

"A little price to pay for safety."

"But a price, nevertheless." Becca narrowed her eyes.

"Everyone will be evaluated by Jemi. Becca, you can stay in here with your sister until the beds are needed by Doc. But I want you back working with Lance as soon as possible." Andre strode out.

The idea of letting Jemi get in Becca's mind made her insides turn cold. There definitely was a price.

CHAPTER TWENTY-THREE

Caleb left from visiting Becca in the med unit, and for the first time in days, he felt hope. Granted, his anger still simmered that she would be careless enough to almost kill herself without regard for him or Darion. But Caleb had known Becca since childhood, so her behavior should really stop surprising him at this point.

At least she'd survived. Every day she improved, his anger lessened. Her color had finally returned since her battle with Bael. Elizabeth was still unconscious, but there hadn't been a bad episode for days now. Even Jemi said things in Liz's mind were settling down.

Even though Andre, Leon, and many others were seething mad at the danger of Becca's actions, they still cared for Becca and Liz like family. After months on the run, things were finally coming around for them.

He headed down to get something for lunch. He was starting to believe that maybe things could work out here.

The energy inside the cafeteria was palpable. Pine cones and sprigs of evergreen hung on the cave walls. People placed strands of popcorn on a large pine tree in the center of the room, while others tied on red ribbons. A child stole a strand of popcorn and ran away in delight. The noise of children playing, others talking, some even humming a tune, created a blissful racket.

It was Christmas. Something Caleb thought he'd never see again like this. Memories of his mother rushed back. She would have loved it here, with the tree and decorations, and everyone would have loved her songs and sugar cookies. After weeks of fighting it, he realized this maybe was the closest thing to family he'd ever find.

"Merry Christmas." Nikki appeared next to him, her hand extended with a brown bag. "A peace offering."

"There's no need." There had been an awkwardness between them for several days, and it probably had a bit to do with Becca.

"Take it, stupid." Nikki smiled.

He opened the bag, and inside was an orange. A bright, beautiful orange. He brought it close to his nose and inhaled.

"You remembered." The citrus smell brought back a flood of memories, all happy ones. "Thank you."

"My dad gets one for everyone in the community." She folded the brown bag back together. "Again, I'm sorry. I know you care for Becca. I ..."

"We're just friends, Becca and I." A lot of history lay between Becca and himself, but he knew it was purely platonic. After spending over a month on the run with Darion and Becca, that much was obvious.

"No. It's more than that. I think I was jealous of her relationship with you." A flush colored her dark skin. "But don't worry. I'm good now. You don't have to worry."

Maybe it was the lightness in his heart, the memories of his mom, or the Christmas spirit, but he couldn't lie to her. He kept his eyes on the tree in front of him. "I'm the one that should apologize. You're not the only one that feels something between us, but I'm not sure I'm ready for it to be. Does that make sense?" He wasn't sure it made sense to him. He glanced at her out of the corner of his eye.

"Of course." Keeping her gaze straight ahead as well, she didn't give anything away.

He decided to change the subject. "Do you believe in Christmas?"

"What do you mean? The old white guy breaking into people's houses to deliver presents, or the young mother who claims to be a virgin?"

He couldn't help but laugh by her take on things. "Not a believer, then, I take it."

"My mom died when I was young, and I was raised in a cave by my father. Call me a skeptic."

"It's about hope," he explained.

"I guess I could see that. People want miracles or things to happen without having to work for them."

"Boy, you are a skeptic."

She didn't seem upset at the conversation though. "Why do you believe?"

"Because I know what it's like not to." He remembered the day he found his parents dead. The darkness and pain as his world had been ripped from him. "Finding this place, knowing you, it gives me hope. And I don't care if Santa's a fraud. I want to hope, to strive for something greater than me. This place does that. It inspires me. Maybe there is more to life than the madness outside these walls."

"So you're thinking of sticking around?" She turned towards him, the smell of oranges clinging to her.

He wasn't sure what was next for him, but he wasn't in a hurry to leave. "Well, if I left, who would Leon torture?"

The soft lines of her lips curled up into a beautiful smile. "True."

Becca sat near the top of her sister's bed, her hands placed on Liz's smooth blonde hair. She poured what power she had left into waking Liz up. Becca caught glimpses of Liz's dreams, similar to the ones that were haunting her at night —darkness, freezing barren landscapes, and disturbing voices. Despite the visions, nothing indicated that Liz was close to waking up. Becca slouched back in the chair, exhausted and frustrated with the lack of results.

"You need a break. Come on." Darion shuffled a deck of cards on the bed next to her.

"I know." She'd been working on getting through to Liz all afternoon.

"You don't have the strength to do much good right now. And it isn't a matter of magic," Darion explained. "I tried to wake you when you were out. Andre and Jemi tried to wake you, but it didn't work.. Liz needs rest. Her mind needs to recover at its own pace. Otherwise, she might start rambling about Caleb or something."

"You're not going to let me forget that, are you?" She glared at him.

"Not likely. Come on. Just play a hand." Darion dealt out the cards.

"If I can stay awake, I'll kick your butt." As tired as she was, she thought a distraction may be what she needed.

Doc sat at his desk and read an old western, not acting as though he were disturbed by them. She climbed on the white bed, folded her legs underneath her, and waited for Darion to finish dealing.

"What game are we playing? Poker?"

"Sure, what ya' betting?" He kept a straight face, but the glint in his eyes gave him away.

"How about an extra ration for the soap back in my bunk?"

"I already have soap."

"I may have some coins from the last city."

"Not interested." His intense gaze never left her eyes.

Heat burned her cheeks. "I'm not interested in strip poker if that's what you're inferring. 'Cause we'd have to invite Doc to play, out of courtesy of course, and I'm not dying to see what color underwear he wears."

"What about my underwear?" Doc peered over the top of his book.

"Becca wants to see you in it." Darion brought up the cards in his hands.

Becca grabbed the closest pillow to throw at him. "Nothing, Doc, only Darion acting juvenile."

"Glad to hear it. Life is getting way too serious lately." He lifted his book back up. "By the way, they're green boxers if you're curious."

"Nope. Not curious at all." Becca's face burned with embarrassment as she glared at Darion. "Just deal the cards."

"I can't believe you think so little of my moral standing." Darion dealt, the edges of his mouth turning up.

He was doing this for her, she realized. Distracted her, embarrassed her, and made her smile.

"Thanks," she told him.

He didn't ask for what.

Becca killed him in the first hand, and he demanded a rematch. By midway through the second hand, they had another visitor. Navina. She wore a tall green hat that kept slipping into her eyes.

"Hey, Navina," Becca welcomed. "Starting a new fashion style?"

"No. I'm an elf," she huffed. "Ya' know, Christmas and all today."

"Christmas?" Becca knew the holiday was approaching but hadn't kept track of the days lately.

"Yeah. Christmas. Don't you celebrate it?"

"When I was a kid." There wasn't much in the way of Christmas the past few years. She usually worked like every other day. "Guess I didn't realize what day it was. Why didn't you guys say anything?" Becca looked to Doc and Darion.

"Didn't seem like a great day to celebrate Christmas," Darion answered, glancing at Elizabeth.

"I brought you presents from Andre," Navina piped up.

"Yeah? Anything good?"

"You'll have to open it." She dropped a brown package on Becca's lap.

"Thanks." Becca opened the simple brown sack and retrieved an orange. She couldn't remember the last time she'd eaten one. She pressed it to her nose, and the clean, sweet smell filled her senses. Looking up, Darion was looking at his orange, his face lighting up with a grin. Maybe this really was Christmas after all.

"Thanks, Navina. They're great," he told the girl. "Want to play a game with us?"

"Nah, dinner is to start soon, then singing and hot chocolate. Are you guys coming?"

Becca looked at her sister, still prone in bed. Now she understood why Darion didn't tell her. She couldn't go enjoy herself while her sister was here, alone. "I'm not feeling quite up to that yet."

Navina's face fell a little. "Okay."

"I'll head down with you," Doc said. "I'll get a bite, then bring some back for you two."

"No rush. Enjoy yourself." She didn't want to ruin his night.

"If you start to starve or get bored, there are some nuts in the desk drawer." He shrugged on his jacket. "Better than strip poker in the winter." He winked at Becca.

"Oh, shut up." Becca looked for something to throw at Doc, but he was already heading out the door.

He held the door open for Navina as she asked, "What's strip poker?"

Becca and Darion both struggled to contain their laughter.

Doc quickly turned sheepish. "Nothing," he said, following the girl out the door.

"Poor Doc," Darion said.

"Wait till her mom hears," she said, imagining the scene. She shifted on the bed and accidentally knocked the cards off. They scattered on the floor.

"I'll get it." He slid off and gathered up the cards.

She got off the bed, feeling guilty that he was cleaning up her mess. "I'm sorry. I can help."

"Don't worry about it. I'm all done." He stood up, their faces mere inches apart.

Quiet filled the room as they realized, probably simultaneously, that Doc was gone. She watched Darion's features, so sharp and serious these past weeks, soften. The worry and ache absent.

"It's good to hear you laugh again." He reached for her hand and gently touched it. "I wasn't sure if I would ever hear that again."

"Me either." His touch settled her spirit and lit her nerve endings on fire.

"You scared me good back there, Becca."

"I'm sorry."

He pulled back slightly. "You're not." Before she could argue, he asked, "Would you do it again?"

She swallowed. "Yes, I would."

"Then no more sorrys. Even if you scared the hell out of me, I understand why you did it."

"Wait." She struggled to put into words how she felt. He'd gone to hell and back for her, and even though his past involvement with the coven had troubled her for some time, she was ready to move forward with him. Together.

"What's wrong?" He glanced at Liz.

She shook her head, trying to clear her head. "Nothing. I'm just …"

"It's okay." He nodded, the worried look disappearing from his face. He stepped closer, his body encompassing her view, her world, her everything. His touch still burned on her hand. He leaned towards her, slowly closing the distance between them.

As if irony was smiling at their timing, a frail voice spoke from behind. One that Becca would recognize anywhere and made her heart swell. Elizabeth. "Rebecca? Rebecca?"

CHAPTER TWENTY-FOUR

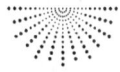

Peter stayed staring at the cheap bathroom sink longer than he should have. He didn't dare look in the scratched-up mirror; he quit that habit long ago. Bent over, he focused on his breath, trying to ignore the pain running up and down his arms as he waited for his pills to kick in. He couldn't help the anger that crept through him, high-lighting his pain.

He wanted to go back north and continue Nevada's treatments to heal his body. Since his last treatment, his hair had finally started growing back and now hit the top of his ears. If only it was long enough to hide his scars.

Instead, he was stuck down in this hell hole, some run down school in the city, working with a bunch of rejects. Arturo may be the head of this coven, but he was a drunk and ran a sloppy ship. Probably the reason why a rebel base was able to grow so large right under his nose.

The roughly twenty wizards Arturo gave him to work with, to train for an attack, didn't understand the meaning of work.

After another couple minutes, Peter's pills finally dulled

the pain to the constant droning he was used to. He pulled on his hood, the smooth black fabric dropping over his face.

He headed to the gymnasium, his head held high. The gray metal doors slammed open as he walked into the large room. No one dared to stare, not after the first guy had. The walls were an aged white, almost yellow in color with a large cat painted on one wall. The GO COUGARS painted on the other wall was barely visible.

Peter whistled loudly. "Line up," he hollered.

The men, who were playing basketball and lifting weights, paused and slowly started to move. Anger fueled Peter's magic. He pushed a simple spell out into the crowd that would cause pain. A weight clanged to the floor as the noises of surprise and agony echoed throughout the gymnasium. Several men took a knee. Two men stood strong, eyes trained on Peter. *At least they're not all useless.*

"I said line up." Peter's quiet voice carried through the now still gymnasium.

The men gathered together, lining up in front of Peter. Some men still had pain etched on their faces and pushed back against Peter's magic enough to make it to the line.

"Defensive magic will save your lives. Keep your walls up at all times, even around your friends." Peter approached a middle-aged man. His stomach protruded like a pregnant woman, and his soft features were topped off with a bushy beard and a balding head.

"Name," Peter demanded.

"Bud." He stared above Peter's head.

"Do I repulse you, Bud?"

The man glanced at Peter. "No."

Peter didn't have to use magic to see the untruth in his face.

"Don't lie." Peter attacked Bud instantly with a spell,

gradually crushing his airway. The idiot didn't even try to stop him. "Well, you disgust me. You're fat, lazy, and didn't even obey the command I just gave the group. Keep your guard up. You aren't worthy to house the demon I keep in my dog right now."

A phone buzzed in his pocket. The only person that had this number was Ryma.

Bud's eyes bulged as he tore at his throat. Peter released the spell, and the man collapsed on the floor. No one else moved.

"You are a waste of oxygen." He turned away from the men and answered his phone. "Yes."

"We need to act now," Ryma said on the other end of the phone.

Peter swallowed the expletive he wanted to use. If Ryma were here, he would have fed Bud to his demon. "These men are not ready," Peter explained. "Arturo does not run his coven with the same effectiveness as you do." That was an understatement.

"Regardless, they'll be enough. We're dealing with rogues that breed with Mundanes."

"Do you want me to keep you updated?" Peter wasn't going to make the same mistake twice.

"Yes. The only way I'll get my report is if you stay behind the lines."

"I'm glad I can be of use." There was a subtle blandness to Peter's response since he'd repeated the line more than once.

"I have not forgotten about you and your needs. Nevada is waiting to work on your scars."

"Thank you."

"Do not thank me yet. You still have a job to do," Ryma informed him. "There are some vermin that need to be chased out of the sewers."

Peter watched Bud finally get to his feet. "And I know who can be the cheese."

After sending Becca to bed, Darion watched Elizabeth sleep. Liz hadn't slept easy though. There were ramblings and a few moments of consciousness where she opened her eyes. She didn't stay awake for more than a minute or two.

He'd spent a lot of time with Elizabeth in the past months, mostly keeping Bael under control. As he watched the sisters sleep in the med unit, he saw the resemblance between them. It wasn't their coloring. Where Becca had fair skin with contrasting hair, Elizabeth had gold hair with freckles.

As they slept and battled their dreams, they clenched their jaws, and a similar determination etched into their brows. These two were fighters; no one else could have made it through what they had.

The lighting in the med unit began to brighten, signaling the start of the new day. Doc and Nikki appeared soon after for their morning shift. Becca rolled over and gradually sat up. Her eyes were still heavy. He wished she could have slept more.

"How's Elizabeth doing?" Doc hung his stethoscope around his neck. "Any more coherent?"

"A bit," Darion replied.

"She kept me up most the night rambling about a fire," Becca added.

Doc glanced at Darion.

Why does everyone look at me when the word "fire" is mentioned? "It could be the fires from Ryma's coven. Flashes of the past," Darion offered.

Nikki came over with a new IV bag. "She'll come around."

"I hope so." He wished he could be that optimistic, but he knew better than to promise things he couldn't deliver. "What happened to the prisoners they took alive?"

"Dead. Whoever he was bonded to shredded his mind once they realized he was taken prisoner. So sad." Doc shook his head in pity. Then his attention returned to Liz as he took her blood pressure and listened to her chest. "She seems to be improving since Bael's death."

"Demons tend to take a lot out of you." Becca rubbed her face, trying to wake up.

Doc finished setting up Liz's new IV bag and tucked the blanket around her thin frame.

Andre entered the med unit.

Doc greeted him. "Coming to check on your daughter or the patient?"

"Both." He squeezed Nikki's arm as he walked past her. Standing at the foot of Liz's bed, he pulled back the sheet and touched her ankle.

Becca watched him closely, worry tightening her mouth. Darion moved to stand next to her and took her hand. She squeezed it back.

"She's getting back her power," Andre finally said. "She'll get there."

"Her power?" Becca swung her legs over the bed, ready to jump.

Darion tightened his hold, hoping to calm her down. Could she be so oblivious as to not think her sister had magic? Magic ran in families, and given Becca's power, Elizabeth had to have it as well.

"Yes," Andre replied. "She has magic humming through her body just like you." He looked pleased, like he'd acquired another magician to join his community.

Becca must have been thinking the same thing, hence the annoyed expression on her face.

"I'm glad you got a little rest, Becca," he continued. "Lance will be expecting you in training today."

"Training? I need to stay here." Becca's point might have been better made if she hadn't just jumped out of bed.

Darion wondered why Andre was so eager to get Becca back to training.

"You are needed in training." Andre's deep voice took an edge. "We have clothed, fed, and cared for you and your sister. You have a debt to repay."

"A debt?" Color flooded Becca's face, her shoulders tensing. "How long do you deem this debt?"

Darion interrupted before she said something she'd regret. "Is this about the attack from earlier? Did Jemi find any information?"

The serious look on Andre's face told him he might've been right. Darion assumed Andre didn't have Jemi delving into people's mind unless there was a reason, and it may be more of a reason than Darion knew.

Andre's thin lips spoke more than he probably wanted them to. "Becca, Lance is waiting for you. Nikki will watch Elizabeth until you return."

"I can be with her," Darion offered, willing to ease Becca's annoyance which looked like it might explode any minute.

"No, I have another job for you. Please get dressed and meet me back at my office after breakfast." Andre strode out of the room, nodding at Doc and Nikki briefly.

Something was setting him on edge, and Darion wanted to find out what it was before it came back and bit him in the butt.

Pissed didn't begin to describe Becca's mood. She hadn't lived on her own for the last several years so now she could be ordered around by some guy with control issues. Andre quickly flipped from a man who acted kind and caring to just another petty dictator.

Unfortunately, she always paid her debts, and there was no denying she owed him for her sister's life, and for helping speed up her healing. Her arm where she'd cut herself still ached, but she'd regained full use. She wished payment wasn't so soon. With her disturbing dreams and her connection to Liz, Becca wanted to explore what was really happening between them.

Instead, Becca headed back to the dorm to get dressed. Thankfully no one was there to see the large bandage on her left arm. The rumors of her actions had probably already flown through the underground compound, but she wasn't ready to face up to them yet. After lacing her boots, she skipped breakfast and headed straight to the training room, hoping she could kick a few rounds in with the dummies before anyone showed up.

In the training room, Lance was alone, pulling some mats out of the closet. "Hey, girl. I didn't expect to see you up and around so soon." He tossed the training mats on the floor. Despite the cooler temps, he still wore only a black tank top and dark pants. His frame was thin in comparison to Leon and Caleb, but defined muscles still stood out on his arms. "How are you doing?"

Ignoring the question and his concerned look, Becca helped pull the mats. "Andre made it seem like you were expecting me."

"Then I probably was." He grinned. "Wanna spar until the others show up?"

The idea sounded great. No better way to prove she was okay than to jump back into things.

Becca stretched out her arms and legs. "With muscles or magic?"

"The fact that you asked that question raises serious doubts." Lance widened his stance and rubbed his closely shaven head. "It's always both." Then he winked.

She didn't know whether to laugh or punch him. Instead, she put up her guard mentally, and raced forward. After a couple steps, something tripped her up, and she flew forward, ending up on her back as Lance stood over her.

"How did you get through my defenses?" She didn't feel a single attack against her shield.

"I tugged up the edge of the mat. You tripped." His labored breaths must've been from the magic, because he hadn't moved a muscle. Moving physical things was difficult, especially if it wasn't your specialty. But that was why Lance was in charge of training. He could do magic in every concentration. Not enough to move an ocean or start a fire, but he could control many of the elements.

"You okay? Did I push too hard? I should have realized you were still injured." He stretched out a hand to help her up, and she wanted to slap that sympathy off his face.

She rolled to one side and swept his legs out from under him. She pounced on top of him and struck out at him, several times in quick succession, not giving him time to think. During the fight, she kept her shield in place, a constant barrier in the back of her mind. Using his weight, he rolled, pushed her off, and pinned her face down on the mat.

Down but not out, she closed her eyes and focused on her offensive powers. She crept into his mind and tried to influence him. His barriers were strong, but she remembered his advice and tried to sneak in, not barge in.

He quickly loosed his grip. "Was that crack from you? What's broken? Are you okay?"

As he lifted his weight off of her, she pulled her legs in and kicked out at his chest. It caught him off guard, and he fell backwards on his butt.

The shouts of others surrounded them. Becca realized that several people were watching their fight. She wiped the sweat out of her eyes and stood.

"I don't know what Andre was talking about recovery." Lance was already on his feet, not showing any signs of injury. "You're stronger every day I see you. Even without a demon."

"People use demons here?" Most magicians did, but she hadn't seen any sign of them. It was her favorite part about this community.

"Most people don't. None in training. You have to get permission from Andre. But Andre and a few others do. He buries the pentagram and demon in the mountainside. So at least it is safe for the rest of us." Lance rubbed his chest. "You sure you don't train with Leon?"

"I learned to fight in the city." Her thoughts turned to Nikko and her past jobs. "It was a lot easier without magic."

"In some ways. Most people usually rely on one or the other. Keep working on your powers, and you may surprise a few people."

Navina appeared at Becca's side. "I missed the fight. Are you guys going to go again?"

"Not now." He ruffled Navina's hair, ignoring her annoyed look. "We have work to do today."

Navina followed Lance into the crowd of people, her questions coming faster than he could answer.

Becca rolled her shoulders, working out the aches. It had been too long since she'd sparred, and her wrist throbbed in pain. Despite everyone's emphasis to work on her powers, she couldn't let her other skills fade. She spent the rest of practice making that happen.

CHAPTER TWENTY-FIVE

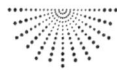

After breakfast, Darion returned to Andre's office as instructed. Andre was reading a letter at his desk and held up a finger for Darion to wait. While waiting, Darion thought about Becca and worried for whoever ended up on the opposite side of her bad mood. Becca didn't do well taking orders, even if they were in her best interest. This community might've been difficult for her to adjust to, but it was better than anything else out there.

Darion grew up with his parents in a coven. He knew Andre's community held a freedom little others had, and there was a protection in numbers here. If they stayed, Becca and Darion could have a future, if she still did want a future with him. Between Caleb and the chaos with Elizabeth, he wasn't sure where they stood. Their timing never quite worked.

Damn the timing. He wasn't giving up.

"Thank you for coming." Andre folded the letter and sealed it back into the envelope before looking up. "Have a seat."

"I didn't get the impression there was a choice. We

have a debt to pay." Darion didn't begrudge Andre, but wanted him to be forthcoming.

"I didn't want to play that card. Trust me. But Becca would have spent days there tending to her sister, when she needs to learn to protect herself."

"I agree with you on that, but then why do you have your own daughter there? She has powers, and her specialty isn't healing." Darion wasn't stupid. Andre wanted to protect his daughter, but that wasn't the smartest way.

At the mention of Nikki, Andre's firm features lost any decorum of civility. "She's my daughter, and it's my decision. This isn't a democracy."

Darion nodded and didn't blame him. He liked to push people, so he knew what to expect. It was those people who were always so damn happy and pleasant that when push came to shove, they scared the hell out of him. "What do you need from me?"

Andre stood, walked over to his library, and shelved a book, "I'm impressed by your ability with languages and magic. It's noteworthy. I am surprised Ryma let you get away."

"He didn't let me. I burned my way out."

Andre nodded. "I'd be a fool if I didn't utilize your power or try to convince you to stay to help protect our community and way of life."

Darion stayed quiet, not wanting to commit. He enjoyed the community, but wasn't sure what was going to happen to Becca and Elizabeth. He wouldn't plan a future that didn't include Becca.

"So I hope you decide to stay," Andre said.

"Do we have a choice?"

"Of course. I cannot force you to stay. If you choose to go, I will have to get a binding blood promise that you won't reveal our location. But it will be your choice." Andre leaned against his desk, watching Darion's response closely.

"We haven't discussed the future. Becca will wait and see what happens with her sister. But a word of advice." Darion leaned back in the chair. "If you push Becca, she'll shove back."

"I've come to see that." Andre chuckled. "So you ready to get to work?"

"Sure."

"First, with the books you have read in Greek and Latin, I want you to translate them and copy them in English. Word for word. We need to make these available to others."

"I agree." If possible, Darion would even love his own copies of the books.

"It will be painstaking."

"I know."

"Maybe someone can help."

Darion thought immediately of Becca. "Maybe."

"For the next task, you'll have to follow me."

Darion trailed Andre out of his office and into the tunnels. They turned down an unfamiliar path, away from the cafeteria and dormitories. The trail turned again deeper into the earth, and lights became scarce.

Andre picked up a lamp on the floor. "Will you?"

"Of course." With a wave of his hand, Darion created a simple flame in the lamp and held one above his own hand. The lights threw shadows against the dark, narrow path. The air felt stilted and damp down here.

"Are we headed to the dungeon or something? Please tell me you're keeping a dragon down here." As a child, Darion once saw a demon that resembled a dragon.

Andre turned around. "Dragons? Really?"

"A kid can dream, can't he?" It was on the top of Darion's Christmas list every year until he'd turned eight.

They turned into an open room, littered with a few piles of dirt.

"As you know, I created these tunnels and caves. It took decades, and while I can do much with my magic, metal is not one of my gifts." Andre dragged his hand across the wall, and it crumbled with ease. "I need to reinforce these walls, protect them physically and magically as well."

"Okay." Darion wasn't sure where Andre was going with this.

Andre turned back to him. "So how hot can your fire get?"

Becca stood in line for dinner, achy and tired from a long day of training. The pale-colored soup up ahead meant clam chowder again. They'd had it every day for the past three days. At least it was hot, and fresh. She'd swear it had snowed, but it was the ice cold water that slammed against the cave's walls. Even with two pairs of socks, leggings under her pants, and a few layers on top, the cold seeped through to her core.

Caleb joined her in line for food. "Wondered if I'd catch you here." They both had been busy with training.

He'd been a little distant with her since the incident with Elizabeth. She called it an incident; he'd said she tried to kill herself. He was hurt. She understood to some degree.

"Grabbing dinner to take down to Liz at the med unit." Becca had been able to wake her long enough to eat a few bites.

"Care if I join you?" He sounded chipper. Maybe he'd forgiven her.

"Sure." With this long line, she'd love the company.

"How's our pyro? What's he been up to?"

She mentally cringed. Not her favorite subject, especially with Caleb. "Doing something for Andre, I assume. Not sure. He stays pretty busy with Andre."

Her best friend stared at her, seeing more than she wanted him to. "Things not going great? I thought once I left our crowded living space, you'd work stuff out."

Becca kept her gaze on the neck of the man in front of her. "I'm not sure what's happening between us, but I don't feel like talking about it here."

Caleb laughed quietly. "I bet everyone in here knows more than you do about it. These caves are only so big."

"What?" Becca flashed him a worried look.

"Don't worry about it." He gave her a quick side hug. "It's obvious how the two of you feel about each other. I used to think it had to do with your magic, some type of connection I couldn't compete with. Just don't be an idiot."

Becca choked in surprise and covered it with a cough. "Thanks for that bit of sage advice. I'll try not to be an idiot." She was happy for Caleb's support, even if she had her own doubts.

Navina popped up behind her. "Mind if I cut in?"

Grateful for the distraction, Becca ignored the glare of the woman behind her. "Go ahead. How's training with Joshua going?"

Navina rolled her eyes. "He's a pushover. Easier than you on your first day."

"Ya' never know. Give him a chance to catch up."

The young girl grabbed a couple bowls. "Mom's working late. I gotta take some food down to the nursery."

"Tell her I said hi."

"Will do." Navina balanced the bowls and some rolls on a tray and headed off through the double doors.

Becca and Caleb grabbed their food and headed to the med unit. Liz slept soundly while Nikki cleaned Doc's desk. He must have already headed down to dinner.

"How's she been today?" Becca set the food down.

"Good." Nikki smiled at Caleb before turning back to Becca. "She had a little broth for lunch."

Elizabeth looked frail, sunken in. She needed more than broth and soup. They fed her intravenously as well. Doc planned on solids soon, hopefully very soon.

"We brought dinner," Caleb said.

"Thanks. I have to finish a couple things first." Nikki headed off to the back room.

Becca was glad to be done with their awkward flirting. She didn't begrudge whatever they felt towards each other, but she was not in the mood.

She placed the soup down next to Elizabeth. Her sister stirred slightly. "You hungry, sis?"

Elizabeth cracked open her eyes and made some noise in the affirmative.

With Caleb's help, they lifted the back side of the bed up and surrounded her with pillows. Elizabeth kept those green eyes open, though they still didn't have the clarity they used to have. Becca fed her slowly.

Caleb ate quickly, almost looking disappointed. He had guard duty on the beach tonight and had to be there by seven. It was the first night Leon had put him on the rotation, and he couldn't be late. She wished him well, and with one more glance at the back door, he left. Becca never said anything about his work with Leon, but it worried her.

With Caleb gone, Becca spoke to Elizabeth as she fed her. "I hope you like clam chowder. We never had seafood growing up, and now we live off the sea. Funny, huh? The large tuna are pretty good. Clams are still too slimy for me."

While feeding her sister, Becca's voice tightened, and guilt flooded over her. Had she done the right thing? The idea that Liz could be a vegetable the rest of her life haunted Becca constantly. Liz may never be herself again, and that meant Becca would still be responsible for killing her. She wondered if some part of Liz hated Becca for what she did.

"I'm sorry, Liz," she whispered.

Elizabeth's eyes widened, ringed with fear. "Fire." The word sounded hoarse and broken.

Any hope that Liz might've been responding to her fled. She'd been talking about fire for days. They all assumed she was remembering the fire when they escaped Ryma's estate.

Now, she clasped Becca's hand. It had an urgency and life Becca had never seen from her sister.

"Fire. Now." She kept repeating the same words, over and over, her voice rising.

Nikki rushed over to Becca's side. "Does she need something?"

"Not yet," Becca said. "I want to figure out what she is saying."

Liz continued to ramble. "Fire. Smokey, fire." She began turning as if she wanted out of bed.

"Hold on, Liz." Becca tried to restrain her.

"I'll get her meds." Nikki rushed to a cabinet.

Becca caught the faint smell of smoke in the air. Becca and Nikki turned to look at each other.

"You smell that?" Becca kept a hold on her panicked sister.

"Yes, but there can't be a fire in here," she said. "My father is a water mage, and we live next to the ocean. How could there be a fire?"

"We can discuss the improbability after we get out of

here." Becca grabbed an extra blanket to wrap her sister in. She would have to carry her. The beds were too wide to get through the halls quickly.

"Maybe someone started a fire in the training center, or Darion is working on a project. Could he have done this? This really shouldn't be happening." Despite Nikki's words of denial, she began packing needed supplies into a huge bag.

Screams carried through the tunnels. This was happening whether Nikki believed it or not.

Becca pulled Liz into her arms. She was lighter than expected. "Just please tell me you have a back door to this place."

CHAPTER TWENTY-SIX

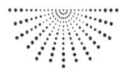

C aleb walked back and forth along the path leading up from the ocean, tightening his coat against the air. Its cold bite penetrated deep. He wondered if he'd ever get warm again. Maybe when summer came around. Until then, at least the cold kept him awake.

The loud crash of the waves blocked any other noise, so he continued to scan the cliff face. The moon shone bright, but shadows blended into the cliffside. He could make out the other guard, though, pacing back and forth on the mountainside. Ever since the last attack, Leon had added extra men to guard duty.

The wind picked up, and he braced against the side of the cliff. Small rocks and debris tumbled down, scattering dust on his head. Once the dirt settled, he scanned the darkness for any sign of others. He readied the rifle in his hand. Voices carried on the wind, so someone must've been above him. Leon had said they weren't expecting any visitors tonight.

Caleb stepped back into the shadows. Hushed, urgent

tones traveled down the cliff. With the noise of the ocean, they had to be close. He readied the rifle.

The wind screamed now, reverberating inside his mind. He shifted his feet to steady himself and glanced down at the ocean. The tide ran back out to sea at an alarming rate, exposing the wet sand below. Why would Andre open the lower entrances now?

Adrenaline raced through his veins. Wanting to notify the others, he considered giving a warning shot or lighting the flare in his pocket, but he didn't want to give away the element of surprise. He almost lowered his gun to run back down and warn the others, but didn't get the chance. Someone rounded the corner.

Protocol required visitors to announce themselves. Caleb initially decided to give this person a chance to explain why they were sneaking down the mountain in the middle of the night. But once the armed men rounded the corner, all sense of protocol and friendliness fled.

From the cover of darkness, Caleb shot the first man in the thigh. His conscience wouldn't let him kill the man outright, and they may have information.

That was a mistake. The wizard hollered out in pain, and with a wave of his hand, Caleb flew over the edge.

He tumbled down the cliffside, reaching out for something to grab. Rocks scratched and clawed at his body. Finally, he clung to a plant of some kind, a root possibly. His breath came out in heavy gasps as he grappled for better leverage.

His hands and body ached as he fought against gravity, but he was alive and nothing felt broken. Turning to look below, he saw people streaming onto the beach. Yelling, he tried to tell them to leave, to warn of the danger ahead, but the waves carried his voice away. No one could hear him.

The sandy floor lay a good forty feet below. He had to make it.

He half slid, half clawed his way down the cliffside. More shots rang out from above. Caleb glanced at the people on the beach, who scattered, trying to find cover. Could they not hear the shots? The smell of smoke drifted on the air, and he realized they were trapped. He let go of the cliff, fell, and rolled into the sand.

Luck was with him as he found his gun several feet away. Someone shouted his name. He hurried to the other people. Leon stood out in the crowd.

"Wizards coming down the cliff," he told Leon, almost crashing into him.

"And there's smoke in the caves. Where is that damn pyro when we need him? Or my brother?"

"They're dealing with the problem in there." Jemi stood next to Leon.

"We'll secure the beach, then. How many did you see?" Leon held a small automatic rifle that could pack a hell of a punch.

"I shot one, but there were at least three behind him. I didn't get a good look before they tossed me over."

Leon looked him over, his expression incredulous. "You must be a damn cat." He motioned to the other men near him. "Let's meet these bastards head-on."

"Yes, sir." This time there would be no warning shots. Caleb's stomach dropped as a familiar form raced towards them.

Buried deep in the earth with a pile of ore and a handkerchief covering his mouth, Darion melted the last metal plate in this section. Smoke billowed in large clouds, burning his eyes. As he finished the spell, he turned towards the cave's entrance to grab a gulp of air. Hot, sweaty, and tired, this was some of the hardest work he'd ever been asked to do that didn't involve a demon. He loved it.

"Not bad," he told himself.

Light steam with a touch of magic radiated off the thick metal wall, nothing too amazing but something that would cost a magician a small sacrifice to get through. Burnt metal assaulted his nose and throat. How did blacksmiths do it all day?

Done for the day, he grabbed his jacket. A layer of dirt or two covered him from head to toe, and he planned to wash up, grab some dinner, and find Becca. The idea of seeing her caused a smile to grow. With a lantern in one hand and thoughts of Becca floating around, he started back up to the main levels.

For the first time in a long time, thoughts of a future with Becca felt almost tangible. This community full of runaways might hold a place for them. Becca probably wouldn't admit it, but he had watched her grow here, making friends and maybe even trusting some of these people. He may not agree with everything Andre did, but this community may be the closest they got to a home. He would talk to Becca soon.

When he hit the main level, smoke permeated the air. At first, he worried something went wrong with his work, but the smell wasn't behind him and lacked the metal bite to it. He jogged towards the smell coming from the kitchens. Screams echoed in the distance, but he continued forward. Though the corridors were empty, he searched for any sign of Andre. He wouldn't let this place burn.

Darion covered his mouth with a handkerchief and tried to search for the source of the fire. Now in the kitchen, the smoke burned his eyes. Searching for a flame, he quickly realized this wasn't a normal fire. Someone was pumping smoke through the small air holes Andre used for ventilation. He pushed his magic out as far as he could, which would have been farther if he hadn't been working for the past several hours, but he didn't sense anything.

He headed toward the exit, scanning the door and rooms as he went along. His head started to spin, and he knew he had to get out. The other people must have already evacuated, probably onto the beach. His heart raced as he continued to search the rooms as he went. He prayed he wouldn't find anyone, but he'd feel better knowing for sure that Becca was safe.

Something caught his attention out of the corner of his eye. Navina.

"What are you doing? We have to go," he shouted. His head pounded from lack of clean air.

"I couldn't leave all of the cats to die." The young girl shoved another cat into a large duffel bag, their cries carrying through the canvas. "They were hiding in the training room."

He took the bag of cats from Navina and grabbed her arm. "We have to go now."

She began coughing as they hurried from the room. They collided with Andre in the hall.

"Have you cleared the rooms behind you?" he asked Darion.

"Yes. We have to get to the beach."

"Leon is handling the beach. We need to handle the problem on this end." Andre then looked down, realizing Navina was still there. "Child, hurry to the others."

Navina nodded, taking the bag from Darion before taking off.

Andre hurried back towards the kitchens. "They are using my vents to push in the smoke."

Darion tried to talk, but began coughing. He struggled to think clearly. He had a shield up, but for some reason, it wasn't working. Bent over coughing, tears streamed from his eyes.

"I'm sorry, I thought you were protected." Andre put a hand on his back and spoke a spell.

It felt as if a cold glass of water had been poured over his head, and a protective bubble floated around him. He sucked in the clean air, and his head cleared.

"We need to keep moving," Andre told him and continued forward.

Darion started up again. He kept coughing on and off, his lungs trying to rid themselves of the toxic fumes.

They hurried past the kitchen to the back of the compound.

"Do you feel them? The magicians doing this?" Andre obviously could.

"No." He shook his head, ashamed to admit how weak he was right now.

They passed the turn for the women's dorms, and Andre stopped, put his hand on the wall, and the world began to shake.

Darion reached for the wall for support. The floor trembled under his feet. Dust and rocks showered Andre, but he stood firm. It lasted for several minutes. Darion tried to use his magic to feel what was happening, but there was too much power swirling around. Whoever was above them was fighting back.

Finally, Andre stepped back, and the trembling stopped. "I can't get to them without drowning everyone else on the beach or tearing off half of the cliff face."

"The beach." Panic pushed through Darion. If these

people knew so much about the vents, they might know about the escape route.

"The beach." Andre nodded, and they broke out into a run.

Once Becca had tucked Elizabeth and Nikki into an alcove, far enough from the entrance that the wind carried the smoke away, she hurried to where she'd spotted Leon. He spoke to Caleb and Jemi with a gun in his hand. They were going to fight. Trapped on the beach, they had no other choice, and they needed Becca's help, whether they admitted it or not. She heard her name as she approached, and Leon glanced her way.

Caleb turned to her. "Is there any way I can convince you to stay behind? Watch over Elizabeth and the others?"

She didn't even bother answering that ridiculous question. She'd fought next to Caleb for the past two months, getting out of scraps and surviving the wild. No one would watch his back as well as she could, and he knew it.

"Can you follow orders?" Leon asked.

She squashed the urge to say, "only if they aren't stupid," because that wouldn't have helped her case. "Yes," she answered instead.

"How good are your shields?"

"All right. They're not my specialty."

"Yeah, thought so." He gave commands to the people surrounding them. Jemi and the majority of the other wizards stayed on the beach, focusing on strengthening their defenses. After handpicking several men to go with him, he turned to Becca. "Keep your shields high, and subdue all you can."

"Of course." She planned on focusing on defensive

magic. It took a lot of energy to influence a man, and with so many people around, it was hard to grasp a consciousness and hold on to it, especially without getting killed herself. Before they left, she had to ask, "Where's Darion?"

"Inside with Andre." Leon gave the group one more glance. "Let's head out."

Becca nodded and tried not to think of Darion, not that it worked. Illogical feelings that once again he'd chosen to go with Andre and leave her behind flitted in the back of her mind. They both had jobs to do, and worrying about something she couldn't control wouldn't help anyone. Darion would be safe, especially with Andre. Moving through the sand, she kept close to Caleb and focused on what she could do.

"You ready?" His arm brushed hers. It was a familiar comfort.

She nodded.

They kept a fast pace towards the cliffside. Several feet before they reached the start of the trail, Becca spotted them. There had to be ten to twenty of them scattered up the side of the mountain. A scream sounded behind them, followed by gunfire. Whoever these men were, they didn't need to get close to inflict harm.

"Don't look back," Leon ordered. "Just kill the bastards in front of us."

"Up there." Becca pointed up to a group of men trying to blend with the shadows. More shots echoed through the night.

Becca strengthened her magical shield, while Caleb and the other men took a knee and aimed. Gunfire rang in her ears. Reaching out with her magic, she prodded at the minds of the men. The first two were well protected. Before she could go any farther, someone attacked her shields. She focused on building up her walls. Sweat gathered at her temples by the time Leon issued the next order.

With a single command, they were up and rushing to the cliff side. Leon had removed his magazine and reloaded in one fluid movement. With the power of a bull, he charged up the steep trail. When they approached the first attacker, Leon had him on the ground in less than a minute. The next soldier was tossed over the side, and the party continued up the switchbacks. The next attacker didn't have any chance to figure out Leon's unique gift before he flew over the edge. Unfortunately on the next turn where the path widened, a small group waited for them.

Shots flew as Leon continued to charge with Caleb right behind him. Becca, knife in one hand, followed after. Caleb tackled a nearby man, and the next one in line came after her. He attacked her shield, but she easily defended herself and swung out at him.

Her knife sliced along his forearm, and she turned to avoid his punch. Before she could strike out again, someone grabbed her from behind. She slammed her knife into his leg, and he threw her into the wall. Her shield shattered, and the night spun around her. Not waiting for her vision to clear, she ducked low and reached out to the minds around her. She instantly recognized Leon and Caleb, but it would be hard to differentiate the others. Off to the side where the path narrowed, she glimpsed a wizard in the shadows focused on a man howling in pain. Keeping low, she rushed him and kicked out his knee. He crumpled to the ground.

Someone or something struck at her from behind. Pain reverberated down her back, and she lashed out. Her attacker stumbled near the edge of the cliff and grabbed

Becca's arm. She struggled to break free, but he remained locked onto her.

A shot rang out behind her, striking the man in the chest. He began to pull her backwards over the cliff.

Let go. She drove the thought with her mind. *Let go!*

Finally, he released his grip. The momentum dragged him over the edge. She scraped the side of the cliff to find purchase. His screams carried into the oblivion below. She pulled herself up and crouched down, trying to steady her breath. There weren't many men left standing.

Caleb appeared and offered Becca a hand. "You all right?"

"Yeah." She stood up and shook out her hands. "Do you have another knife?"

"You always loved your blades." Caleb's casual tone told her the immediate threat was diffused.

"I can take your gun if you want," she said sarcastically.

"You know I'm the better aim." He handed over the knife, and they joined the others.

Leon motioned with his hand, and they continued up the path. Near the back of the group, Becca faced less conflict on the trail but stepped over several dead attackers on the way up.

"Spread out to make sure we're not missing anyone," Leon told the group as they climbed over the ridge.

Becca tried pushing her magic out to sense anyone. Unless they were under a great shield, she sensed nothing. Becca sucked in a lungful of cold air and stared into the night sky. A good mile or two off, someone stood on the cliff's edge, jacket flapping in the wind. She blinked and he was gone.

"We need to head back and check on the others," Leon told them.

They began the fast run back. Flashlights pointed on the ground lit the path. The corpses along the way haunted Becca. So pointless. Why would someone light a fire and attack them on a cliff? Was this connected to the previous attack when they left for town? This wasn't a big enough force to win.

"Leon, did you see this?" Becca stopped the group and bent over one of the injured men whose shirt was torn open. His chest was tattooed, a partially done pentagram with a unique symbol inscribed inside. She'd seen these before in some of the cities. It marked those indentured to the coven, magicians and Mundanes alike.

"Yeah. It's the nearby city's coven, Arturo's. Didn't think he was stupid enough to start this. Marco," he said to the man in the front of the lines, "pick up the pace."

Becca looked once more at the top of the cliff, searching for the cloaked observer. Maybe she imagined it? Whatever this was, it didn't feel finished.

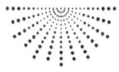

CHAPTER TWENTY-SEVEN

Back on the beach, Becca found Elizabeth asleep on Nikki's lap. "Is she okay?"

"Yeah. She was up for a while mumbling but crashed again when the gunshots stopped."

Becca needed to get her sister back inside. The cold ocean breeze assaulted them as if angry it was being controlled by Andre. The cave appeared clear of smoke. Hopefully they could go back in.

"Thanks for watching her." Becca kneeled beside Liz.

"They are directing people back in. Let's get her in the med unit." Nikki gently lifted Liz up.

A couple guys helped carry Liz back inside. Becca searched for Darion to make sure he was okay. An odd stench still hung in the cave's tunnels, but there was no sign of smoke or Darion.

Back in the med unit, Becca tucked Liz into bed, her skin icy to touch.

"I'll grab a couple more blankets." Nikki went to the cabinets. "It'll take her a bit to warm up."

"Maybe I can help?" Darion entered the room, his face covered with dirt and soot, but no blood.

Becca turned at the sound of his voice and gripped him into a tight embrace. He was whole, safe, and with her. After a second, her rational brain caught up with her and realized the scene she'd created. He was with Andre during the fight, chose to be with Andre, and she shouldn't worry. He probably didn't.

She stepped back and avoided his gaze. "You're okay. I didn't see you on the beach."

"Yeah, I was working with Andre. You all right?" He looked her up and down as if searching for injuries.

"Yeah."

He grabbed onto the metal bed frame. "Let me warm things up a bit before I go take a shower." It didn't take long before she could feel the warmth radiating off of her sister's bed.

"You're a great heater." Nikki placed a couple blankets on Liz.

"One of my many parlor tricks."

"So did Andre figure out what happened? Or who started the fire?" Becca remembered the lone figure on the cliff's edge, and the gnawing sensation in her gut grew.

"Someone was pumping smoke through the air vents in the kitchen. Andre stopped them, but they took off." Darion rubbed his face, streaking the dirt.

Becca probably looked the same. She felt grimy and exhausted. "We got most of them on the beach."

"What?" Darion cocked his head to the side. Evidently, he hadn't heard of the fight on the beach.

"It was a trap. They smoked everyone out and attacked the beach."

His lips formed a grim line, and his face darkened as Becca briefed him on what had happened outside.

"He didn't tell me." Darion's voice tightened with anger.

Becca gave a brief exhale. It now made sense why Darion never made it to the beach. And as much as they could have used them, Darion was probably more useful in dealing with the fire.

"Andre needed you," she told Darion. "They were easily outnumbered. It didn't make sense really. They should have been able to sense us. Instead, they walked into a slaughter." Becca glanced at Nikki, but she busied herself in the cabinets.

Darion said nothing. His exhaustion etched into his dark eyes.

Nikki came over to check Elizabeth's vitals. "Have you told him about Elizabeth?"

"What?" Darion looked between the two of them.

Nikki didn't give Becca a chance to answer. "Her premonition. She'd been speaking about smoke for days and warned us before we smelled the smoke. She may be a seer." She tucked the blankets around Liz. "Her blood pressure is good. She's warming up."

Elizabeth's color was returning, and the pressure in Becca's chest lessened slightly. Though she couldn't wrap her mind around the fact that her sister may be a seer.

"I need to talk with Andre." Darion stood, fists clenched.

"I'm coming with you." She turned to Nikki. "Can you watch her?"

Nikki nodded. "I'll have an easier time with Elizabeth than you will with my dad. Good luck."

They headed out into the tunnels. Even though it was still the middle of the night, people littered the halls: security, magicians, and Mundanes. It would take a while before people felt comfortable sleeping.

Darion walked close to her and spoke in a low voice laced with fury. "Andre had no right to keep the attack on the beach from me."

"He needed you."

"No, he didn't, and it was not his call to make." Warmth emanated off of him as his anger grew. "He's blind if he thinks my reinforcements are going to stop what's coming."

Once they arrived at Andre's office, Darion banged on the door. "He knows we're here and probably not happy." Darion waited stone-faced.

During the silence, Becca wondered if this happy community was as good as it appeared. Every family held secrets, and Andre had more than his share. If Ryma knew Becca and Darion were here, he wouldn't stop until he saw their dead bodies. Her stomach sank at the idea that they were putting this community in danger. It didn't help that they hadn't asked to come here. Not that she regretted the decision. She couldn't have saved Liz without Andre's help. No family came without its drama.

Jemi finally opened the door. "Come in."

They walked in. Andre paced by the bookshelf while Leon stood with his arms crossed on the other side of the room. He didn't look happy. Jemi took a spot near Andre.

"When are you planning to evacuate?" Darion glared at Andre.

Andre kept pacing. "What evacuation?"

"The evacuation to save everyone's lives when Ryma comes back with reinforcements."

"I'm not afraid of Ryma." Andre brushed away the concern with his hand.

"You should be. He has over a hundred magicians in his coven."

"Are you done?" Leon stepped forward. "We're wasting time."

Andre stopped and looked at the both of them. "We're more concerned about how Ryma knows about this place. If we have a spy, then it's pointless to run."

Jemi sat on the edge of the desk. "We didn't have a problem until you three came here, especially after your little trip to the city."

"You guys dragged us here, remember?" Becca snapped. "The whole kidnapping and whatnot. And we're running from Ryma, not informing him. You searched our minds. Or was all that just for fun?" She remembered the invasive combing of her memories that left a sick feeling crawling along her skin.

Jemi's icy lips turned up into a sneer.

"If that is true, then it means we may have had an informer for some time. Ryma let us be until this group arrived." Andre stared off into space as if trying to entangle Ryma's intentions.

"So we throw them to the wolves and be done with it," Jemi offered with a flick of her hand.

Andre frowned. "You know better."

"I thought Jemi could search everyone for answers," Becca pushed. "Don't you know who is keeping secrets or has a past?"

Silence settled in the room as anger shot from Jemi's eyes.

"It's not an exact science," Andre explained. "We have over a hundred people here, many Mundane."

"And no one is tied to you?" Darion asked, though they both knew the answer.

"I'm not stooping to create a coven. I won't."

Hence the problem, Becca thought. How to help control and protect a people while keeping them free of magic? That was why the cities were cesspools for demons, Soultorns, and bloody magicians.

"My sister is a seer, I think," Becca said, changing the subject. "She'd been talking about the smoke for almost two days before it happened."

"Really?" Andre's face lifted in surprise.

Jemi sneered, doubt evident on her face. "I can look around her mind and see what I find."

"I'm not letting you pick and pry around my sister's head because you can't do your job and find a spy among your people."

Jemi's face turned red, and she looked at Andre for a decision.

"I have a better connection with my sister," Becca said to Andre. "We share dreams. I can help her more than a stranger."

"Truly?" Andre leaned against the chair.

"She can do it," Darion said. "There's a connection between them I can't explain."

"Old magic," Andre said. "Lately most magicians focus on collecting mass power, but people forget the strength in old magic."

"Andre," Jemi said. "We can't chance this to beginners. If you want to stay, we have to be prepared."

"And have an exit plan," Leon said. "I won't agree to any plan that doesn't leave us a back door."

"To run like wild dogs, living as scavengers," Andre practically spit. "You can have your exit plan, Leon. Darion, you'll work defense with me. Jemi, work with Becca and her sister, and keep searching for our culprit. They could be anyone not born here, or who spent time in the cities. Leon, we'll need to go to the city again for supplies and to listen to the rumors. If they're going to attack again, they will need men, more than before. And they'll probably pay them greatly to go to their deaths."

Images of the dead men flashed through Becca's mind. She'd long ago learned to bury regret and guilt for her actions. Their deaths were caused by their own hands. She'd fought in self-defense. They all had. But the anger of whoever sent those men to fight, to die, burned in her gut.

Leon must have felt the same as his arms tightened, ready to fight. "I don't want to leave you short on men."

"Me either. But we need the information. Hopefully Elizabeth can help. Or Jemi, but there is no guarantee."

The weight of the task ahead lay heavy among them. Andre planned on taking on a coven. Granted, she wasn't sure if Ryma himself would come down here. If he did, they would all pay. Her heart went out to Navina and the other young magicians who would be forced into servitude or imprisonment. They could never beat him.

Should she stay with a sinking ship, or flee? Maybe this was the time to run, but this was the closest to a community she'd ever known. The one hope she'd found that maybe humanity could right itself. She couldn't let Ryma tear it apart.

Darion reached for her hand, a warm comfort in the darkness of her mind.

Andre must have sensed her thoughts. "None of our tasks are easy. Necessary, yes, but not easy. A life of freedom never is."

CHAPTER TWENTY-EIGHT

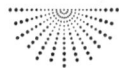

Becca spent the next day trying to search her sister's mind to no avail. Elizabeth slept most of the day, which should have made it easier for Becca to connect to Liz's subconscious, but Becca sensed nothing. Doc and Nikki reminded Becca that Elizabeth needed sleep to heal. Through the night, Becca caught glimpses of Liz's dreams, but the brief pictures didn't make sense.

After fruitlessly spending another early morning with Liz, Becca headed down to training with Lance in hopes of finding some help, and also because Andre wanted her to train more with Lance and Jemi. Becca would pick Lance first in hopes to avoid the latter. Inside the training room, she spotted Navina, who was busy rolling her eyes at her partner.

Lance approached in his usual fitted athletic gear. "About time you strolled in here. You're supposed to do some mind work down here, not that I have time to help." Dark circles and a three-day beard covered his face. The recent attack must've been putting extra pressure on everyone.

Becca shifted from one foot to another and tugged the wool cap she got this morning over the tips of her ears. "I'll stay out of your way."

"Not unless you want to spend the morning with cats." He grinned at her.

"Is controlling others a specialty of yours?" Becca often wondered since Lance appeared competent in most areas of magic.

"Not really. I'm a jack of all trades, dearie. It's not about who has the most strength to move a mountain, but who is clever enough to manipulate what they got."

She often thought of people as focused in one or two branches of magic, and forgot that most competent magicians excelled in all mediums.

"So, do I get to dive into your crazy mind?" She was curious on how she'd be working.

He flinched back ever so slightly, and then gave a short laugh. "Nah, I'll have you working with the twins today." He hollered across the room to the guys in the back and then turned to her. "They're working on their elemental magic. You can practice screwing with their brains. Not much harm can be done there." He walked off.

Apprehension and fear struck her mute for a minute. What had she become? What used to repulse her she now found herself embracing. This was for the greater good, she justified. The ounce of fear, hiding in the recesses of her mind, said otherwise.

The rest of the morning passed in a blur. After a late lunch, she headed back to the med unit and found Jemi.

If Becca thought Lance was on edge, Jemi was worse, snipping and correcting her every step of the way. In this world, though, teachers didn't have the luxury of patience.

In ripped jeans and a brown coat that doubled her size, Jemi perched in Doc's chair. "Don't force your way in like a battering ram. Find your center, connect your magic, and then seep into her unconsciousness. When people feel threatened, they build more walls to force you out."

Becca shook out her hands and tried again, placing her palms on either side of Elizabeth's head. This time, Becca tried to relax and reached out to her sister. The connection they had was so strong before the demon Bael had possessed Liz. Now, any connection took a lot of energy on her part. When she'd dared to mention it, Jemi wasn't sure if it would return or not.

"I'm seeing glimpses," Becca whispered. "A forest."

"Don't tell me," Jemi instructed. "Just move towards it. Focus on the connection."

Becca didn't recognize the forest. Large leaves and vines painted the trees bright green. She tried to follow her sister, who hurried ahead. Pictures of death, of fire and blood flashed amongst the trees, but the images fled too fast to really understand. The cold air played with Liz's long unbound golden hair, the hospital gown billowing around her. The harder Becca ran towards her, the faster Liz went.

"Wait," Becca yelled to her sister. "Why won't you wait?"

She finally stopped and turned to face Becca. The light gown hung on Liz's thin frame. She appeared troubled by something Becca could not see.

"What's wrong?" Becca stepped slowly towards her, a hand out.

"Everybody dies." The words came out in a whisper, haunting and clear. Then Liz turned and sprinted away.

A scream filled Becca's mind. Her eyes snapped open to the Elizabeth on the bed, frantic and yelling.

Nikki hurried over to help restrain her.

"What did you do to her?" Jemi helped hold down Liz's ankles.

The accusation stabbed at Becca. "You're okay, Elizabeth," Becca murmured to her over and over. It took several minutes until she calmed down.

"It was only a dream," Becca told Liz as well as herself. "We're okay. We'll be okay." She would do whatever she had to to make sure they would be okay.

After several minutes, Elizabeth began to settle down. Her breaths quieted, though that frightened look in her eyes didn't disappear.

"Want some soup?" Nikki offered.

Elizabeth nodded. She hadn't used many words since she'd awoken from Bael but enough to communicate.

Nikki left to get soup from a thermos on Doc's desk, and Jemi moved closer to Liz.

"Did you see something?" Jemi asked.

Liz's eyes widened, and she shot Becca a nervous look.

"I'll tell her. Don't worry." Becca leaned down to hug her sister tightly. "Love you," she whispered in her ear.

"Love you." Elizabeth's grip tightened before letting go.

Becca blinked back the tears gathering in her eyes. It was the first time Elizabeth had said that since Bael. And for one moment, all the pain and suffering she'd gone through to save her sister was worth it, and she'd do it again in a heartbeat. That was why she had to talk to Jemi and Andre. They needed to run and now.

"I'll be back later tonight. Okay?"

Elizabeth nodded and Nikki returned with the soup.

"Thanks again," Becca told her and headed out into the hall. She needed to find Andre.

Jemi stepped in front of her. "Where are you going?"

"To see Andre. We need to tell him what happened."

"Tell me first."

"We can't waste time," Becca explained, but Jemi didn't move. Becca stepped around her and continued on the path. She kept her defenses up in case Jemi wanted to stop her magically, but she didn't. She followed close on Becca's heels, complaining about overeager girls in hysterics. Becca ignored her.

The door opened at Jemi's touch, and they found Andre in his office, poring over books. Those damn books that he thought held all the answers.

"We need to evacuate." Becca's heart pounded against her chest with Liz's panic fresh in her mind. "Everyone. Get out of here as soon as we can."

"What did you see?" He placed the bookmark in his book, but did not close it.

She described the dream in the foreign forest. "We all die. We have to run. Now." She stepped in front of the desk. How could he remain so calm?

"Please sit down, Becca." Andre motioned to the chair across from the table.

Jemi sat in its pair already.

"No thanks." Becca couldn't calm the blood racing in her veins.

He closed his book and sat on the edge of his table. "I can't move everyone out during the winter because of these glimpses. We need more. If we have a battle, there will be death, *that* I'm not naive about. But we need specifics if we are to protect ourselves. Leaving, we could get attacked in the same forest she was describing. I'll not run like a chicken with my head cut off. Not with women and children in the middle of winter." He leaned forward. "I need you to get more from her. I need information I can use."

Becca's temper flared, but she had to admit he made

sense. How could she make her sister relive it again when it had upset her so much the first time? This was a different kind of hell Becca was forcing on Liz, and Becca dreaded the necessity of the task ahead.

"I told you, you were jumping the gun." Jemi stood, signaling the end of the meeting. "We'll meet back there tomorrow afternoon. She'll need to rest tonight."

Becca nodded and left the room. Her legs felt like rubber carrying her through the tunnels as her mind raced. Though the visions weren't clear, death was evident. Becca knew Andre had saved her sister. He was the reason they were both alive, but now he asked for both of their lives. Becca didn't owe him that.

They could leave. Run away with Darion and Caleb. It would be easier now that Liz was better. She remembered the smile on Caleb's face last week at dinner when he'd talked with Nikki. Would he even want to leave? Putting one foot in front of the other, Becca continued through the tunnels, thoughts spinning through her mind, and she wasn't sure which ones to trust.

CHAPTER TWENTY-NINE

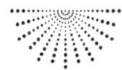

As soon as Doc came back, Nikki told him about Elizabeth's episode. He said he'd watch over the now sleeping girl, and Nikki excused herself, heading straight for her father's office.

She raised her hand to knock when the door opened by itself, her father sitting at his desk. She hated that little trick.

Alone, he stared at papers scattered on the desk in front of him. After a long minute, he lifted his head. His eyes were dark and heavy. She'd seen it before, as if the weight of the world was his alone to bear.

"What did you decide?"

It took him a moment to figure out what she was talking about.

"Oh, you must have been there with Elizabeth." He nodded absently. "We need more information before we decide."

"Decide what?" she demanded.

"Please, sit down."

She'd outgrown rolling her eyes. Instead, Nikki perched

at the edge of the chair. He often told her to "please sit down" every time a lecture came her way. Being a single parent, her father gave more than enough lectures for *two* parents.

"War is coming," he started.

"So it's true. The girl is a seer?" Seers were rare, like true healers. Elizabeth would be worth a great deal.

"Probably. I'm not completely sure. We can't rely on her yet. She's too unstable." He took a sip of his tea. "But the last attacks were well planned. They're testing us, if you would. There will be another, and it will be worse."

"You have to let me fight." The familiar argument tumbled out of her mouth without thought.

"You know why I can't." The pain in his eyes was still there after all these years. "Plus, you are a great healer."

"I'm a glorified nurse. That's all."

"Don't underestimate—"

Frustration built inside her. The dirt around her feet stirred, and she didn't bother to contain her magic. "Stop. Please. We both know this is about Mom."

She'd said it. They hadn't spoken about her in years. And watching his countenance fall, she wished she hadn't now. No. They needed to talk about it. It had been too long.

Her mother died ten years ago. Appendicitis, painful and traumatic. He'd searched out a doctor since then, not a magical healer but a medical doctor. Nikki had been assigned to work with Doc as a healer since she fifteen. At first, she found it interesting, but now she knew the assignment was to keep her from more dangerous tasks.

"Nikki." His voice was steady and controlled. "I can't have this conversation now."

"Then use me. I'm a witch. You can feel my power. I'm

not as weak as you think." Pushing out her magic, the papers shuffled on his desk.

He stood abruptly. His cup tipped over, and he stilled everything on his desk. Liquid froze in the air while the papers lifted, suspended.

"I have never once thought you weak. But we will need healers, now more than ever. You're assigned to your post, like everyone else here. Do it." With a wave of his hand, his desk slowly returned to proper order. He spoke like a god, his word law.

Her face burned in frustration. "No."

His eyes, angry and piercing, flashed towards her.

She stood, hands clenched. They trembled with everything that had been unsaid for so many years. "You can't order everyone to the lives you think they should have in here. There is more to this world than you."

A myriad of emotions flicker on his face in no more than a second—pain, anger, hurt.

Too angry to regret her words, she lifted her chin, daring him to reply. This was the first time she'd ever spoken to him like that. It was liberating and terrifying all at the same time.

"Nikki, please sit—"

"Don't." She heard her own voice, loud but breaking. "I'm done sitting."

She stormed out. She knew had the power to stop her. He didn't.

Caleb had spent the day in training, more tactical work against magicians. Leon's immunity against magic had taught him a lot in fighting magicians over the years. And Caleb soaked up every second of it.

The sun set early today behind a cloudy sky. When they were dismissed, Leon called for him. Though his legs protested, he jogged over. Caleb loved training, the rush of the waves, of actually doing something. After the past few months of feeling helpless at the hands of the magicians, he was learning how to fight them, to protect freedom for Mundanes and magicians alike. There was hope, and it was more than he could have dreamed of.

"I have a job for you," Leon told him.

"Yes, sir."

Leon hesitated for a moment, which was completely unlike him.

"What?"

"When giving an assignment, it's usually an order. No questions asked."

"I understand," Caleb replied. Leon was a brilliant soldier; he trusted him.

"This is an exception. You can turn it down." His eyes were weary.

Caleb nodded slowly, an uneasiness settling in his bones. "What is it?"

"Report to my brother in his office. He will give you the details." Leon watched Caleb for a moment as if looking past him. "You're a great soldier." He paused for a moment. "Dismissed."

Caleb turned and headed towards Andre's office, while his brain swam with thoughts, worries, and wild guesses about what that cryptic message meant. Why did Leon's dismissal feel like a goodbye? It wasn't like they needed a human sacrifice for a demon. They couldn't be that crazy. Right?

His steps quickened. The sooner he got there, the quicker he would know. The damp walls inside the cave felt closer than normal as he navigated them.

He stopped in front of Andre's door. He didn't knock. Shouting traveled through the door. Nikki.

Caleb stepped back, knowing this was a family moment that he didn't want to interrupt. He was torn for a moment, not sure of where he should hide.

Before he could decide, Nikki barged out of the room and ran straight into his chest. The door slammed behind her.

Surprise and embarrassment flashed across her face as she hastily wiped at her eyes.

Words froze midair. What could he say?

"You heard all that, huh?" she said.

"Sorry. I would have left, but I'm waiting for..." He paused for a moment, unsure how much he was supposed to tell her. "A new assignment."

"What? Where is he sending you now?"

He shrugged.

Her eyes were rimmed red and full of emotion. He fought the urge to hug her, comfort her, somehow tell her it would be all right. He couldn't send her any more mixed messages though. Her gaze traveled down the hall, but her thoughts appeared more distant than that.

"I better head in. You okay?" He stepped towards the door.

Her attention snapped back to Caleb. "Yeah, I just may be." She nodded as if agreeing with herself.

An uncomfortable sense of worry hung over him as he watched her walk away. He shook his head, clearing his thoughts for the task in front of him, and knocked on the door.

"Enter." Andre's voice carried through the door.

Inside, he was shelving books, his back to Caleb. He took a seat and waited.

Andre finished and took his place behind the desk. His

composure revealed nothing, but he couldn't hide the sadness in his eyes. "Leon says you have more than proven yourself in training lately. One of the best in class."

"Thank you." It felt good to be complimented, but Caleb's wariness remained.

"Your excellence in fighting, surviving city life, all while still being a Mundane, has made you one of the few, in fact one of the *only* people Leon feels comfortable recommending for this assignment."

"What assignment is that?"

"I want you to head back to the city and infiltrate the army gathering to attack us."

Caleb tried to swallow, but it got stuck in his throat. He coughed several times, not sure what to think. Andre wasn't an idiot. Why would he think Caleb could do this?

"I see your surprise. But don't underestimate yourself. You are a hunter and survivor. You have skills that come from living in a world where you are fair game."

"But a spy?"

"We need to know what they are planning." Andre leaned forward on his elbows. "They have the advantage. Someone here is leaking information, and we know nothing." Anger shone in his dark eyes, a passion to protect those he loved.

"How do I get the information back to you?"

"Magic. I will give you the stones you will need to communicate to us. They will carry your message through the air and back to the sea here." He leaned back in his chair. "Will you do it?"

Caleb tried to think this through. Could he do this? Lie constantly, pretend to be someone he wasn't?

At his continued silence, Andre kept on going. "There have been visions of a slaughter. I can't guarantee your safety. There will be war, and many will die. I'm humbly asking for your help in hopes the casualties are not ours, because if we lose, then this way of life is over."

For some reason, Caleb thought of his own father. His parents and the way of life they tried to have outside of the coven with their family. They hadn't had a warning, or an army of soldiers to help them. They'd had no one and were murdered. He realized his whole life had been leading to this fight. Fighting against their magic, and their control. He couldn't walk away now, or ever.

"Yes."

Relief washed over Andre's face. "Good. You'll leave tonight."

Becca found her sister sound asleep and the training rooms empty, so she wandered the halls. An uneasiness settled in her bones, creating a restless feeling she couldn't shake. Avoiding dinner and any sense of small talk, she found herself drawn to the back of the compound, where Darion said he worked. She grabbed a nearby torch off the wall and continued down the darkened path.

She lost track of how long the path carried on for, but continued until she smelled something burning. "Darion?" After the last fire, worry crept into her voice.

"Becca?" Darion called out. "Is that you?"

"Yeah." She paused, listening for where his voice came from. "Where are you?"

A light burned bright around the corner, and Darion appeared, his hair disheveled and his face flushed. He wore a gray undershirt, jeans set low, and a flannel tied around his hips. This relaxed look was new for him, and she loved it. Back in the city, he was always put together. He looked better here. This life suited him. Maybe he wouldn't want to leave either. They had started a life here, all of them. What was that life worth?

"Hey, Bec, good to see you."

"You busy?"

He shrugged. "I'm creating my own furnace. Come see."

"Furnace?" Intrigued by the offer, she followed.

They hadn't been able to spend much time alone in a cave with tons of people. They had separate dorms for good reasons, showers and whatnot, but she missed Darion and his messy hair every morning. She realized how badly she wanted him in her life and couldn't imagine a future without him.

She followed him into the room where metal snaked up the walls. Steam hung heavy in the room.

"This is impressive. You've been busy." She peeled off her jacket and scarf.

"Yeah. I've never used my magic this way. It's exhausting and exhilarating all at the same time." His face flushed with a warmth and pride she hadn't seen for a long time. "Let's take a seat. I'm due for a break."

They moved farther into the room where the metal had already cooled and sat down. He had water and some other supplies.

"So this is where Andre has you holed up?" She tried to keep the bitterness out of her voice.

"Until my energy wears out, then I head up to his library to finish my translations."

"What is this for?"

"It's an escape route. Or will be. This portion will be closed off soon, and another entrance created from the beach. He wants it hidden by magic, which is harder than it sounds, but Andre's strength is impressive." He reached over and touched her hand softly.

It sent a warmth through her skin, of magic and something else. She wondered if this was normal for him, an electric current coursing through anyone else he may touch. Or was this something more? Her insides fluttered recklessly.

"What brought you down here?" he asked.

The jumble of thoughts and worries tongue-tied her for a minute, then she started from the beginning. "Liz had a vision."

His head snapped up. "What was it?"

She described the vision, and her conversation with Andre. Darion remained silent for a moment, his eyes focused on their hands.

"I can see his point," he started, and her heart sank. "He has to consider moving over a hundred people in the winter. I'm not sure running may even be possible with this many people."

He might've had a point, but... Did it matter either way? Was what Liz showed Becca inevitable or only a warning? Becca wondered if her fighting would lead to that foreign forest or if staying would. Knowing the future could be just as damning sometimes as not.

"Do you really think we need to leave?" he asked.

"I can't sit here and do nothing, waiting for the slaughter."

"This room I'm creating can hide people, protect them from the rages of magic and Mother Nature. You will be safe. I'll make sure of that." He swallowed as his hand tightened around hers. "But if you really want to leave, then we can leave. I'll talk to Andre tonight."

"I thought you were committed to Andre and this community."

"I'm committed to you." His warm hand encompassed hers, sending a tingle up her arms. His open face showed feelings that she hadn't seen for some time. "That is if you'll have me. I know you've had a lot to process with your magic, your sister, and your past, even with Caleb. I didn't want to press you. But this has always been for you, for us."

Surprise, bliss, and pure, utter contentment almost overwhelmed her. While something had always remained between Becca and Darion, she'd been telling herself his priorities were elsewhere. He felt so distant at times, only their magic bringing them together. She wanted her future to include him, no doubt, but she knew this was more than about what she wanted.

He thrived here, working with Andre, using his magic in a way that didn't bloody his hands. And if she was honest with herself, for the first time in a long time, she felt safe here, like she belonged. Maybe staying wasn't sacrificing her family, but fighting for them instead.

His anxious gaze searched her face while she thought. "Becca?"

Decision made, a feeling of rightness settled in. "Let's stay and fight."

The edge of his mouth lifted up slightly, though his eyes remained worried. "You sure?"

"Definitely." She pulled him into a hug and buried her face in his chest. Surprisingly, a sense of security came over her, even in the face of what threatened them. She was home in all the ways that counted.

He ran his hand up and down her back. "I've missed you, Bec."

His warm palm unraveled the tension she'd been holding for so long, and she sank into his body. It felt like forever since they'd had time alone, to lose herself in his touch. His thoughts must have mirrored her own, for as she lifted her face, he quickly found her mouth.

The heat in his lips ignited a passion free from restraints. Though his touch might've been boiling, the sizzling warmth growing deep in her stomach was more than that.

He drew her onto his lap, and she wrapped her arms around him. Her kisses held a hunger she thought would never be satiated. A small moan escaped his lips, and her grip tightened.

Her worries outside this room melted. For this moment, it was only Darion. And it was more than enough.

The temperature rose, and she lifted her mouth for a breath, gasping slightly. His lips moved down her neck, and he helped her out of her jacket. The warmth, radiating off him, struck her to her core. As heady emotions rolled through her body, settling in her stomach, she buried her fingers in his hair. His hands grasped her hips as if he would never let go and kissed her deeply. Lost in his kiss, she ached for everything she missed when they were apart. How could they be so close, and yet it wasn't close enough?

Against her desires, he pulled back and watched her closely as if memorizing her face. She admired his careless hair and parted lips, their taste leaving her craving more.

"Becca."

She looked up, his dark eyes burning with his own need.

"I've missed you. Missed us."

"Me too." She placed a hand on his chest and took a breath as emotions boiled near the surface. "I needed to tell you something. Something that has been threatening to burst out, and I'm afraid I'll scream it in the cafeteria or something."

This got his attention. His eyebrows shot up. "What?"

When she hesitated, he kissed her one more quick time, as if he couldn't wait for her answer.

Foreheads pressed together, she said, "I love you, too."

He froze, his hand resting on the nape of her neck.

"I do," she continued, unable to stop. "I love you. I've wanted to tell you, but there was never a good time."

His lips widened into that slanted smile she adored. His face brightened into something she'd never really seen before. He drew her close, his breath a warm tickle on her cheek. "You know how I feel. I love every last stubborn inch of you."

Heat blossomed inside of her, and she wasn't sure she could contain it all. Pressing up against him, she tried to show him how she really felt.

Someone cleared their throat behind them.

Becca jumped off his lap, pulling down her shirt, and hit her head against the wall. She swore and rubbed the sore spot on her scalp.

It was Caleb, face red and eyes glued to the floor. "Sorry to interrupt."

Darion gave her a regretful look before standing up and smoothing out his clothes. "What's up?"

Becca yanked out her hair tie and redid her rumpled ponytail, avoiding Caleb's gaze as her cheeks warmed with embarrassment. Not that Caleb didn't know they were together. It was just... It wasn't a position she cared to have anyone catch her in. Especially with a guy she had a history with. Even though they were only friends now, she didn't want him to catch her making out. He didn't seem to enjoy it much either.

"I-I'm heading out," Caleb said. "I wanted to say goodbye, but couldn't find Becca so thought I'd try here. Sorry." He stammered over his words.

The only thing Becca heard was "heading out," and

she forgot about her embarrassment. "Where are you going?"

"Andre has an assignment for me."

"What assignment?" Darion asked. "I haven't heard of anything."

"You can't leave now." Becca reached out as if she could stop him. "Liz had a vision, one of death and war. We need to stick together."

Caleb took her hand, but didn't speak right away. Something wasn't right. This didn't feel like a supply run, but a goodbye.

"What is the assignment?" Becca narrowed her eyes, demanding an answer.

His gaze darted to the side. "Collecting information on any potential upcoming attack."

"What? That's dangerous. Who's going with you?" Becca would have continued with her tirade of questions and concerns, but Caleb stopped her with a raised hand.

"You know it makes sense. We need info, and you two are needed here to build up our defenses. Please don't make this hard." Caleb dropped his hand and stepped back.

His sober eyes quieted Becca for a moment. She didn't want to hurt him, only protect him. How could she do that if they separated?

"You don't have to go," she said.

His eyes glimmered with understanding and peace. "I do. Just like you do."

Darion pulled something out of his pocket. "I've been making a few amulets down here. This metal wall here is a type of huge amulet, actually." Three large silver stones gleamed in his hand. "They won't work miracles but can save you in a pinch against minor spells." He placed them in Caleb's palm. "Be careful."

The bond they'd forged these last few months on the run wasn't easily broken. Caleb turned to Becca, and she hugged him. She couldn't say goodbye to him. Never in a million years. Caleb might not tell her what his specific assignment was, but she'd find out where he was going and hunt him to the ends of the earth if she had to. She'd done it once before.

"I'm glad you two finally straightened things out," he whispered into her hair and kissed the top of her head. "Be safe."

Why couldn't she be cool and collected like Darion? She knew the risks, and they both had lost so much. She knew every goodbye could be the last. Her heart ached at the idea of not having Caleb with her again.

"Don't make me come after you," she said.

"And face your wrath? Never."

Tears blurred her vision. If this wasn't a goodbye, why did every part of her feel like it was?

CHAPTER THIRTY

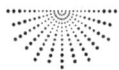

Peter tried to relax as the magic poured down his face. He had a drink and pills to numb the pain, but the sensation of someone prying off his skin didn't settle well.

Despite the unnerving pain, he held still in his suite while Nevada worked on his face. Thankfully, Ryma sent Nevada down early. He arrived last night and resided in one of the rooms near Peter. These rooms were better equipped than the rest of the coven's. He wondered how Arturo would explain his poor housekeeping to Ryma. Arturo wasn't fit to run this coven, and Peter planned on showing Ryma why *he* was.

The magic slowly withdrew from his face.

"That's all I can do for now." Nevada slumped into the chair next to him, grabbing his own drink. He wore tight slacks and a large wrinkled shirt. Sloppy. His hair grew like an unkempt bush.

"You need more demons. Your limitations are pathetic," Peter chided him. Anyone serving Ryma should be suited to the station, for the coven's sake.

Nevada shrugged, finished his drink in one large swallow, and headed to the liquor cabinet. "Look in the mirror. It's not as great as my illusions, but I have only so much to work with."

"Shut it." Peter snapped at the insult. He didn't want an illusion that could be torn from him. He wanted his face whole and perfect when he killed Darion.

The pale, puckered skin of Peter's face had faded, looking much better. Completely smooth, his forehead and cheeks showed no sign of scars. Yet, part of his burned features still peeked out, reminding him of the nightmare that had been his life for the past several months.

"Your eyebrows should start growing back soon." Nevada filled up his glass one more time. "I'm heading to my rooms."

"Don't be late tonight." Peter wanted to have a plan in place before Ryma's arrival. "And be sober."

Nevada shrugged and took another drink.

"Nevada," Peter said. "I'm sick of your insubordination. We have a job to do. Don't half-ass it, or I'll take care of you on behalf of Ryma."

Nevada tilted his head back and laughed. Peter wanted to kill him on the spot. He stepped towards him, gathering his magic.

"You can't kill me. How would you get your pretty little face back?"

Peter itched to wipe off that sarcastic grin. "And what about when you're finished?"

"You forget that I'm an indentured servant, and my death doesn't mean as much to me as it may to you." He turned, swaying slightly, then continued out the door.

As much as Peter wanted to punish him, it was true. He did need him, not only for his face, but Nevada played an important role in the upcoming attack. These rebels were stronger than he'd thought, and Peter wanted to prove to Ryma that given the right tools, he could wipe them out. Arturo used his magic in this city to get fat and be lazy. He was a waste of magic. Peter would be more.

The stakes were high, professionally and personally, and Ryma was due by the end of the week. If everything went smoothly, they would flush out the rebels, Peter would replace Arturo as coven leader here, and his personal debt with Darion would be repaid.

Caleb finally climbed out of the switchbacks and stood on the top of the cliff, stretching out his back. The nocturnal sounds welcomed him as he breathed in the scent of trees and soil. The scattered clouds and high moon gave him barely enough light to see, but not be easily spotted. The anxiety about the task in front of him lessened slightly as he started on the trail.

Out here, he could think more clearly and try to figure out how to complete Andre's assignment. This was his element, the forest. He grew up in it, hunting and fishing. He could spend the rest of his days out here, and one day he would, but he had to make it safe first.

A twig snapped behind him. He spun, crouched low, and notched the bow that had been on his back.

It couldn't be.

He stood slowly, lowering his weapon. "Nikki?"

In a dark-hooded camouflaged jacket, she ducked her head and approached. She blended perfectly into the darkness of the night. It was the noise that alerted him.

"What are you doing here? What's wrong?"

"Nothing. I'm to accompany you." She adjusted the straps on her bag, not meeting his eyes.

"Really? After the fight with your dad, I'm to assume

he sent you with me?" Doubt laced Caleb's voice. Did she really think he was so stupid?

"He didn't want me to come necessarily, but Leon did. You need me. Those stones he gave you are tricky to use. Magic helps."

"They'll eat you alive. You can't come."

"They need me. If they're recruiting for a war, they'll want a witch. I can even pass as a healer. And it makes more sense if we come together, as a couple." She set her jaw as if preparing for a fight. "I'm not going back."

"Yes, you are." He could deal with the fact if he died fighting, but not her.

"Then I'll sneak out and go on my own, but I'd be safer if we stuck together."

He turned his back to her and ran a hand through his hair. "Why are you being so stubborn? First your father asks the impossible, and then you ask to jump on board. You're going to get us both killed."

"I'm not trying to get anyone killed. I can help. Really. I have squelched my abilities for so long, trying to be something for my father that I'm not. I have gone on supply runs and worked with my uncle before. I can do this."

This didn't ease the fear in his gut. Part of him knew she shouldn't be out here, but he knew she was stubborn enough to go without him.

"I'm not going back, Caleb." She repeated herself as if sensing his thoughts.

He eyed her thin frame, hoping she was stronger than she appeared. "Did Leon really train you?"

"First time a boy asked me out, Leon taught me how to fight. He wanted me to learn how to protect myself. But don't worry. With my powers, I don't allow anyone that close unless it's by choice." Her dark steel eyes were serious and determined, and if she was anything like her father, he didn't have a choice.

He nodded once and turned into the forest. "You need to lighten your step. Be wary of where you walk."

"I can use magic if we need."

"Being detected as a magician out here can be as bad as a Mundane. Better to lie low where possible."

She softened her step.

What was he doing taking her into the lion's den? If anyone discovered who she was, everyone in those caves would pay. He was stupid and crazy to agree to this. Maybe, but sometimes stupid and crazy paid off. At least that was his hope.

Becca and Darion went to dinner late. A quiet worry settled over both of them. Becca couldn't help to be troubled with Caleb out there alone. No magic against a whole army. His only chance was to blend in.

Navina and her family were still in the cafeteria. Becca sat across from them. She could count on Navina to keep the conversation going.

"So you think Lance will let me fight?" the girl asked out of the blue.

Alarm flashed on her mother's face. Thomas hollered in agreement, though at two years old, he had no clue what his sister had said.

"He better not," Navina's mother, Bree, replied.

Knowing Navina's willful personality, Becca added, "Maybe you can be on protection duty. Your mother may need help protecting the kids, *if* there is another attack." There was no official declaration that there was going to be another attack, but most everyone could figure out they were vulnerable here. And Andre's preparations were not hidden.

"Not backup again." Her head lowered.

"You're not fighting yet." Bree, her eyes full of emotion, laid an arm on her daughter's shoulder.

"You could always help make amulets," Darion offered. "If you give them to the Mundanes for help, it'll be your magic that saves them."

"Amulets? I don't know how to make those."

"I can help teach you. There's fire involved."

"Fire?" Bree again looked nervous.

"He's a pyro, Mom. It's cool." Navina's curiosity peeked through her excited eyes.

"Cool, huh?" Bree shook her head slightly. "If it keeps her out of trouble, I'm okay with it."

"He's the safest person to be around when fire's involved," Becca said, trying to reassure her.

"I better get going, but I'll teach you soon, Navina." Darion squeezed Becca's leg under the table in parting.

A warmth spread through her body. She grabbed his hand, not quite ready to let go. She didn't look forward to spending the night chatting with the women in the bunk room. They were nice, but didn't understand the worry knotting in her stomach about Caleb.

"Wanna come with me?" Darion must have noticed her reluctance. "I'm translating ancient text for Andre. Not exciting but—"

"Good enough for me," she quickly agreed. "I don't think I can sleep anyway."

Navina started to ask if she could come, too, but Bree cut her short. There were chores to be done. They said their goodbyes and walked to Andre's offices.

"So how long have you been doing this? I thought you stopped after we found the spell for Liz," Becca said.

"He wants me to translate the books into English. So they're available to more people. I guess all those useless lessons as a child actually paid off." He reached for her hand again.

The welcomed warmth helped steer off the chill in the tunnels. Becca had been busy between training and working with Elizabeth. Once at the office, he put his hand to the door, and it opened with a click.

"He trusts you with his office?" Becca couldn't believe he'd earned that level of trust that quick.

"Just his books. There are so many wards in this place, I worry that I may trip over something."

As they entered the office, Andre was putting on his coat as if leaving. "Good evening, Darion. Becca." He nodded in acknowledgement.

"I brought Becca," Darion said, "to help with the writing."

"That's fine. I didn't get to read last night's notes. Did you make any progress with the new book?"

"Yes, some interesting material on dimensions."

"More than one?" Becca couldn't hide her surprise. She'd always assumed the demons came from some other realm, dimension, or plain hell itself. "What does that mean? More demons?"

"My findings aren't conclusive," Andre answered. "But it's definitely worth exploring."

A cold dread poured down Becca's back. "Why would you want more demons in this world? You rarely use any as is." One aspect she loved about this community was the absence of those nightmarish creatures.

Andre cocked a brow. "What gave you that idea?"

"There are no Soultorns here. I've never seen a pet demon." Becca remembered Lance telling her about Andre's demons, but she'd never seen them.

Dirt and rocks crumbled and fell off the wall. Becca shifted backwards, grabbing onto a chair. A sinking feeling in her gut told her she shouldn't have brought this up. On the other hand, part of her wanted to know who Andre really was. Dust rose in the air, and Andre smothered it with a hand. Sections of the wall cleared, showing small concave prisons, each containing its own demon. Inside were the salt outlines of small pentagrams.

Andre didn't move, the demons still at his back, and his face showed nothing. "I detest demons as much as you do, but when it comes to protecting my people, I do what I must. I don't care to look at them, so I bury them in the walls."

"Convenient," Darion said.

Creepy was more like it.

"Is that why you want to learn about other dimensions, to find more demons, more power?" Was that the wisest course of action? More demons in this world would tip the scales against Mundanes even more.

"Possibly. But who knows what is out there?" Andre finished buttoning his coat to leave.

Someone knocked on the door. Andre opened it and greeted one of the guards. He had a youthful appearance with blond hair and sweat collecting on his brow.

"What is it?" Andre asked.

The guard glanced tentatively at Becca and Darion. "It's Nikki."

Surprise or maybe panic stole all the noise in the room. The guard's gaze skittered nervously around.

"Go on, son." Andre spoke calmly, but Becca could feel a power radiating off him.

She glanced at the row of demons still exposed and realized how much power flowed through him.

"She's missing. Doc asked us to look for her. I can't find

her inside, and Leon wanted me to ask you to meet him outside."

Andre didn't speak. He covered the demons, putting them back into their dark prisons, and then left, dust stirring in his wake.

CHAPTER THIRTY-ONE

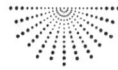

Andre had never found the cave walls so confining. He'd grown up here, creating this world with his own hands. Now, he considered tearing it all to pieces to find his daughter.

He pushed out his magic, trying to sense Nikki's. She and Leon were the only people he could sense like this, presumably due to their genetic bonds. Leon's magic pulsed on the beach, but there was no sign of Nikki anywhere.

He plucked a nearby stone from the wall and gripped it in his hand. He struggled to maintain his composure as he continued out to the beach. There was no sense in starting a panic, not with the threat of war already so close.

The evening sky and salty breeze greeted him. The moon hid behind scattered clouds, and Andre prayed those clouds would hide his daughter from danger tonight as well.

Leon stood staring out at the beach, hands clasped behind his back.

"Where is she?" Andre demanded. He wanted to force

his magic on his brother, to force him to look at him. But despite Andre's power, he couldn't force his brother to do anything. "How could she be gone?"

"Your daughter, like you, is quite capable of anything."

He dreaded the response to his next question as he could almost guess the answer. "Where did she go?"

Leon slowly turned. "I don't know for certain. She checked out a pack and said she was getting it for an assignment you gave her. They had no reason to doubt her. She left shortly after Caleb did."

"She left." A heavy weight pressed on his chest, and the waves rose behind him. People often marveled at his strength and magic, but his power was nothing if he lost her.

"Calm yourself. I don't have time for a swim."

Andre closed his eyes and calmed the current behind him. Leon was right. He had to think rationally.

"Why would she go with him?" Echoes of their earlier argument surfaced.

"The only thing I can think of is her relationship with Caleb."

"What relationship? I didn't know Nikki was seeing anyone." Andre fisted his trembling hands.

"It's not what you think." Leon shook his head. "I would have known otherwise. But she favored him. Maybe that was enough?"

Andre turned from Leon, rubbing his head and recalling their final words to each other. "I did this."

"What?"

He had to face what had happened. "We got in a fight. She wants to fight, to train. I refused. She left to prove me wrong."

Leon took a deep breath. "Great time to rebel. Couldn't she just get a tattoo or something?"

Andre glared at Leon. He'd always watched over his niece, helping to take care of her since Andre's wife had passed. But it wasn't the same as having your own daughter. "We need to find Caleb. I only sent him off a few hours ago. He couldn't have gone far. I struggle to see why he'd agree to take her."

"Caleb is a good man..." Leon looked up at his brother's face. "But your daughter is stubborn. He would have brought her back if he could have."

"Or they're both dead."

"I can leave right away. I have my bag ready. They only have a couple hours head start."

"Maybe..." *Unless Caleb covered his tracks and Nikki's magic, then they could hide from magic or men.* Andre didn't add his true thoughts, for Leon already knew the enormity of what was at stake.

How could Andre send his brother, the best warrior and military strategist, to find his daughter when their whole community was under the threat of attack? Andre couldn't even go. The children. They would be defenseless without them. He took a deep breath, trying to calm his racing mind, and tried to figure out a way to save her. He had nothing.

"We can't go." He spoke so softly because he didn't want to believe it himself. "We are their only defense."

For the first time, he felt weak, like maybe he wouldn't be enough to save everyone. *Being a leader is making the hard choices* was something his father had often said to him. There wasn't a harder choice than this.

"We can send others though. I have a few men at the ready, if needed," Leon offered.

"Can we spare them?"

Leon hesitated. "We will make do."

"Send them. Have them watch for approaching forces as well, and then return to report."

Leon called a guard over to give instructions while Andre moved to the sea, watching the dark waves. The energy they created soothed him. He could feel the waves travel on forever. Leon returned to his side.

"Are we insane, brother? Can we really make this stand?" Andre asked his brother, not his military commander. "Maybe we should run and hide."

"They would find us," Leon replied. "And we would never rest again."

"We will evacuate the women and children. They will be protected, and the Mundanes are easier to hide."

"With Becca and Darion, magically we're stronger than ever before."

Dread hung heavy in Andre's stomach. "It's nothing to the power of the coven."

"I know. The coven may be strong, but are they smart? They haven't had to fight much. Their parents won their wars for them. They're cocky. And we've been training for years. Who knows?"

Andre almost laughed. "Who knows? Is that your official position?"

Leon looked at him, his face serious, but his eyes full of emotion. "Any time I approach a fight, I ask myself is this worth dying for. Because no matter how much I train, death hangs over me, watching and waiting for its turn to snatch me."

Andre had no idea Leon thought so much about his death, but it didn't surprise him.

Leon turned forward again, letting his words carry on the wind. "Everything we do here, striving to live, to make a new world... Maybe grabbing those kids triggered all of this, but this fight has been years in the making. And this is one fight I'm ready to die for."

Anger, fear and frustration built in Andre as he gathered magic and released it into the ocean. Waves rose and fell far out at sea, crashing with a ferocious beauty. "I understand what you're saying, brother, but I'm not sure if I'm ready for you to die just yet."

"We don't always get a say." Leon's answer was barely audible, his words stolen by the wind and carried out to sea.

Becca rubbed a cramp out of her hand then sipped her warm tea. It was getting late. Darion placed the ancient text they had been working on back on the bookshelf.

Unease tightened her stomach as she thought about what they had been translating. The book spoke about the first man who opened the demon dimension, Lazario, and the temples and old magic from the south. Her skin crawled while imaging a world full of demons.

"Do you think this wise?" She motioned to the pages in front of her. "Translating this into English to give others more power?"

"Those in real power already know all of this. We're trying to give the rest a chance." He gave a wide yawn.

"But does it matter right now? Maybe we all should focus on preparing for an attack."

He didn't answer.

Exhaustion weighed down her limbs, but she wasn't ready to leave Darion yet. She was grateful. These past several hours were the longest she'd spent alone with him since arriving at the compound.

"I think it matters, especially with the threat of Ryma.

We need to have copies that are protected." Darion slumped back into his chair. "I've been meaning to talk to you about your training with the other magicians. Do you have any idea who could leak information to Ryma?"

Becca flipped through those she could recall, but there were several people she'd never even worked with. "I don't know, really. I'm not the epitome of a social butterfly."

"True," he said with a smile. "I think Andre puts too much trust in Jemi, and they are both too close to these people. Get a list of everyone tomorrow, and we'll see what we can find."

"I know I can't sense power well yet, but most of the people in there aren't very strong. There are a few, but—"

Darion leaned forward. "Remember when your magic first flared?"

"Yes." How could she forget? They were trying to save Caleb and at the mercy of a powerful Soultorn. Its fiery death still haunted her.

"People can hide their magic. Conceal their powers. You need to push them."

She blinked, unsure she was hearing this correctly. "So fight everyone, piss them off, and get them to show me all their magic? Sounds like a fun day."

He stood and grabbed her hand, pulling her out of her chair and into his arms. The mix of sweat, smoke, and mint from his tea mingled in the air. She worried if she fell into his arms, she wouldn't have the energy to pry herself free. But his face, mere inches away, drew her in.

"You don't have to distract me. I agree it needs to be done."

"Maybe *you're* distracting me." He leaned in to nuzzle her neck.

"I'm not looking forward to Andre catching us."

He stepped back, but didn't release her hand. She

followed him out into the now dim corridor, his hand tight around hers. As they walked through the nearly empty halls, neither of them spoke. Becca clung to his hand and considered the task ahead. She'd work on it after she slept.

In front of her door, she turned and wrapped her arms around him. "Goodnight." She hated saying it, hated leaving.

He leaned forward and placed a light kiss on her lips. "Love you," he said simply and then turned back down the dark hall.

Her chest ached as he walked away, not only for his touch but for the future. Life had finally started coming together for them all, and now Ryma threatened to take it all away from her. *Suck it up*. She knew better than to fret on the future. The present held more than enough troubles, and she had work to do.

A dim light shone from the bathroom while the rest of the bunk room occupants slept. She changed into warm sweats and used the bathroom before heading into bed. Her head hit the pillow with thoughts of what they spent the night translating. Images of temples, foreign countries, and demons mingles into her dreams.

"I'm almost done," Nevada told Peter as he worked on his face. "I should be able to finish up tomorrow."

Pain seared Peter's skin, but he bolted up at Nevada's words. "No. Finish it tonight."

"I know you want to look your best for Ryma tomorrow, but my demons and powers are drained. Even I have my limits." Nevada brushed his palms against his jeans.

Ryma was coming tonight, a battle planned for the morrow. He wasn't bringing any of the elite from the coven. The older generation hated to dirty their hands anymore. Ryma would be enough of an army to easily take the rebels.

Peter wanted to find Darion, to see the surprise on his face when he saw his unscathed face. Then he'd laugh as he killed him. Easy enough.

Peter didn't care about Nevada's weakening power. This needed to be finished tonight. He reiterated his previous comment with a push of magic. "No. You will finish tonight."

"Even I can't get water from rocks. I have nothing left." He shrugged his shoulders in defeat.

"Jose." Peter called his newly formed Soultorn to his side, a Hispanic fellow with a mousy face. Not his first choice, but necessary nevertheless. "Fetch me one of the new hires from outside."

Unreadable emotions flashed in Nevada's gaze.

Peter ignored them. "I'll feed your demon, and then you can continue."

"Willing to do anything for a pretty face?" Nevada's cockiness reappeared. "Tomorrow isn't a beauty contest."

Peter pushed his magic forward and shoved Nevada against the wall using an invisible hand to tighten around his throat. Nevada's defenses were gone since he'd exhausted his power healing Peter. Which made it easy to knock the idiot down a peg or three.

"You don't understand anything." Peter slowly stood on his feet and walked towards him. Nevada didn't struggle, though his breath came out in harsh gasps. "Finish a job for once in your life."

His Soultorn returned, an unconscious man hanging over his shoulder.

"Now feed your demon, or I'll feed you to mine."

CHAPTER THIRTY-TWO

One of the last ones to wake, Becca stumbled out of bed exhausted, haunted and troubled by her dreams. The haunted images remained etched in her memory even while she struggled to discern reality from nightmare.

She dug around the shared closet to find a clean shirt and the jeans she'd worn yesterday. Once she found a brush, she ran it through her hair and then wove the strands into a braid to keep it out of the way during training.

With no time for breakfast, she grabbed a coffee and briefly searched for Darion in the cafeteria. No luck. Rubbing her arms, her thoughts went back to yesterday in the caves. She didn't let herself dwell too long on Darion. Today she had a job to do.

Inside the training center, the warm smell of bodies already permeated the air. People worked together in small groups.

"Ready to get to work?" Lance greeted her with his usual jovial expression, obviously feeling better.

"Yeah, I was wondering if I could work with some new people today?" She hoped it didn't sound too forward

"Why? The kid bugging you?" He referred to Navina.

"No. I want to try my powers out on different types of magicians, especially with what's going on."

He looked over at the others who were training, quiet for a minute. "You're right. We should mix things up a bit more. Leon stopped by earlier and took a few people, but there are enough left."

He turned and called everyone over to explain the new training schedule for the day. A few soft moans and eye rolls spread throughout the group at his schedule explanation—short fights, rotating partners each time, creating a perfect opportunity to learn different opening strategies. The complaints mostly came from the large group of teen boys in the back.

The morning flew by in an exhausting blur. Becca found she was often surprised by others' power. Each time, they pushed her in different ways. Elizabeth had consumed most of her waking moments, but now, Becca would be fighting side by side with these people. They all depended on each other to live or die.

She started working with one of the boys, Steve, a lanky boy whose powers were still emerging. His stand-offish attitude fled, and a determined scowl tightened his face. It didn't last long.

While keeping her magical protections in place, Becca took him down in a few moves and then locked on to his mind. She couldn't sense much—rage dominated his emotions like a storm at sea. Probably from being beaten so easily.

Lance called the fight, and she offered him a hand up. "Good fight, Steve."

"Don't mess with my mind." He pushed aside her hand.

"If we get attacked by a coven, they'll fight any way they can," she reasoned, but understood his anger. The idea of being mentally controlled or prodded sickened her, but they all would end up doing a lot more if called upon. This would be war.

Steve mumbled to his friends. She had to agree with him. Guilt gnawed at her. A year ago, she'd have said the same thing. Now with what was at stake, she couldn't think about it.

Thankfully not all were put off by her mental ability. Navina had grown lately, her strength challenging Becca, pushing her more than the others. She had even quickly picked up the self-defense moves Becca had taught her. They both sat panting on the mat after their match.

"You're improving," Becca told her.

"Not as quick as you," she replied.

"I have several years to make up for."

"True."

"Hey, was that a knock on my age?" At twenty-four, she'd never considered herself old.

Navina started to laugh and then headed off to her next match. "So sensitive."

Becca talked to Abbey briefly, a fifty-year-old woman who was abused by a coven. Lance said she wasn't fit to serve as she wasn't mentally all there. The woman was kind, with a round face and short copper hair. Becca couldn't help but think it could all be a hoax. Maybe the crazy lady act was a cover.

After talking to her, if it was a hoax, it was a hell of a hoax. She asked Abbey if she could take a look in her mind since she was still learning her control.

Abbey answered, "Stewart always takes the dog out. So go right ahead."

Becca had never touched a mind like hers. Abbey had power, but it was random, scattered like her mind was. She was open to any suggestion, and that alarmed Becca.

Becca thanked Abbey and headed to the cafeteria for a quick bite to eat. She felt depleted after working with so many different people, and wasn't sure how she would pull it together to work with Jemi and her sister.

For the first time, she understood the temptation to have a demon. How easy would it be to pull from another source and keep going? She shuddered at the idea.

The sun, high in the sky, finally appeared from behind the clouds. The cold chill from sleeping in the forest finally began to leave as Caleb watched the trader's warehouse in the distance. He glanced at Nikki, and a wave of uneasiness settled over him. Was he really taking her in there?

"Is there any way I can talk you out of this?" he tried again.

A seething look answered for her. Her bright eyes and smooth, clean hair would stand out in a second. She wasn't a warrior.

"You need to disguise yourself better. Here, let me help." He dug into the dirt and approached Nikki.

She laughed nervously and stepped back. "You're putting dirt on me?"

"We're supposed to have lived out in the wild alone. You need more dirt under your nails, and in your hair."

She held up her hands. "I can do it myself."

"Okay. Try to cover up to. Maybe a scarf or something. Hide..." How could he put it? Try not to look pretty or some thug may try to rape you? Maybe she needed to be scared.

"I get it." She took off her scarf and unbound her full hair. After grabbing a handful of twigs and leaves, she rubbed it through her hair. "I want you to know how long this will take to get out of my hair. Hours."

Caleb smiled then turned to his gear. No one in the wild would have a pack as clean as his. He left his bow alone though. No matter how dirty you got, you always took care of your weapons. He rubbed some dirt into his neck and hair, which needed to be cut, then tucked it under his cap. Hopefully his hair and the beard he'd started would help his disguise as well. No one should recognize him. Besides, he'd never even met Ryma. He only went to his estate once, and that was as a servant. Nothing worth noting.

After a few minutes, they both looked in desperate need of a bath.

"Ready?" she asked.

"No. But let's go. Hopefully it's not too late."

As they approached the warehouse, a small group left the building. One of the larger guys watched Nikki with too much interest. Caleb kept a good grip on his bow, and itched to use it. Finally, the group climbed into a beat-up truck and took off.

Caleb let his breath go, thankful that didn't turn into a confrontation. He didn't miss this life, the worry and mistrust around every corner. It reaffirmed his purpose though. It was a basic human right to live free.

They pushed through the front door to find it was just as Leon had told him. Random junk, tools, and even some weapons littered large old tables. Large guards with automatic weapons clustered around the exit.

Nikki stayed at his side as they meandered through the aisles. "Not much magic in here," she muttered quietly.

"They have big enough bullets to make up for it." Caleb wasn't sure what made him more nervous: magicians or trigger-happy thugs.

"I could put up a shield to protect us, but I don't want to give anything away." She picked up a can of soup.

They'd discussed on the way in what to pose as, so now they were a couple. She was a weak witch, and he a Mundane who could fight. As a pair, they should work.

"Let's go buy dinner." She held up the can proudly.

"I could kill us something better than that."

"But this holds a chance of botulism." Her full lips turned up into the perfect smile.

"Don't smile." He headed to the checkout. He didn't mean to snap at her, but worry coiled tight in his stomach.

"Any coin or barter?" the woman at the counter asked. Her life was summed up on her battered face. Trailing down her cheek was a scar she tried to cover with her dark curly hair. A man with a large rifle stood behind her.

"Coin." Caleb retrieved two silver pieces, and the woman snatched them both before he could argue the price. He started to say something, but out of the corner of his eye, he watched the man's hands tighten on the barrel of the rifle.

"I'm looking for work." He spoke to the man. "Anything around here?" Andre assumed if they were preparing a battle, there would be need of soldiers or mercenaries that magicians could use as their front lines or for demon fodder. Either way, they needed information or a way in.

"Information comes at a cost like anything else," the woman replied.

"Two pieces?" He reached into his pocket.

The woman narrowed her eyes.

"I can give you three, but then I will really need to find work soon."

She held out her hand, waiting for payment. He noticed for the first time that she was missing a small finger. A cold chill sank deep into him. It was probably a sacrifice, a common thing for magicians and desperate, wannabe magicians.

He dropped the coins in her hand.

"A small army is gathered maybe five miles north of here, by the big lake. They came by recruiting mercs this morning. Be there by nightfall." She dropped the coins in her drawer and slammed it shut.

That was it. Her lips pursed in a tight line, signaling the end to the transaction.

He nodded, and then headed out with Nikki.

"An army, so close." Nikki rubbed her arms.

"We should make it, if we hurry. But you need to contact your father, especially while the wind is going strong." He didn't understand everything about the stones, but he remembered the message traveled on the wind.

"What?" She straightened, her defenses bristling.

"Didn't you hear? If we have to be there tonight, then this battle is starting a lot sooner then he thinks."

The problems Nikki had with her dad didn't matter now. They had to warn them. Hopefully the city would hold more answers. They couldn't stop an army, but maybe they could find something to help.

CHAPTER THIRTY-THREE

"Don't push. Pull." Jemi's annoyance with Becca was evident. "Coax out the information. The more they fight and resist, the harder it is."

"Liz isn't fighting," Becca pointed out.

Her sister's eyes flashed in recognition of her name.

Becca combed her hair back. "Hey, sis, you still doing okay?"

Elizabeth squeezed her hand. She had become more and more aware of those around her. She still had terrible nightmares and was confused a lot, but there was progress. That bit of progress gave Becca hope that this may all be worth it.

"I know she isn't trying to fight, but subconsciously, it's a different game. Like pushing a flame towards a person, they naturally flinch. We're the flame, and she's still blocking you."

"I don't want to hurt her." Becca remembered Jemi's force when she'd searched Becca's mind.

"It's not physical pain, like burning your hand. This type of magic is different than other forms where you push your power towards its destination. It's like the night that you convinced the man to go to the cafeteria." Jemi scowled, her blunt reminder of the evening Becca had knocked her out and almost got herself killed.

Guilt pricked Becca's conscious.

"The guard was probably a little hungry already," Jemi continued. "So, convincing him of something that part of him wanted anyways wasn't much of a stretch. Don't force. Ease yourself into their minds."

"Maybe I'm better at putting ideas into someone's mind than taking them out like you."

"Probably, but you have a connection to your sister. Use it."

That was true. Becca had been able to communicate telepathically with Liz at one point before she was possessed. And even while a demon had resided inside her sister, they'd shared dreams, glimpses, sometimes of the hell Liz was going through. Becca still had the dreams, but she was unable to tell what was a vision or random flashes from her own mind. If only they could re-forge their connection, maybe she could help pull Liz out of this.

One of Leon's men entered the med unit. "Andre's called a meeting for all combat forces out at the shore room while tides are low."

"When?" Jemi asked.

"In ten."

"Thanks for the advance notice," she snapped back.

"I'm just the messenger." He hurried out the door.

Becca stood to leave. "We better head out. Could Caleb have already sent information?"

Jemi raised her hand. "Try one more time."

"Really?"

Jemi nodded in the direction of Liz.

"Okay." With a deep breath, Becca sat back down,

trying to push Caleb, the meeting, the imminent attack, everything out of her mind.

Placing both of her hands on her sister's head, she leaned over Liz. "You ready to try again?"

Liz nodded slightly and closed her eyes.

"Try to pull her out with a good memory," Jemi coached. "Something you both enjoy. Make a connection."

"Got it. Good memory." Closing her eyes, Becca thoughts traveled to years ago, before the magic, the demons, her uncle, back with her parents when their homestead was their world, and it was enough.

She focused on her breath and magic, the slight humming sensation located deep within. Instead of projecting her magic, she let it fill her up, encompassing her body. A tingling sensation traveled over her skin, and she focused on one of her favorite memories—swimming. Every summer, the two girls would put on shorts and a tank top and run to the river.

Elizabeth would inch into the water, slowly adjusting to the temperature, while Becca would find her favorite tree trunk to climb up and jump in. Becca remembered one summer, when the sun hadn't completely erased the chill in the air and Liz struggled to enter the water past her knees. Becca climbed into a tree, and with a huge leap, cannonballed next to Liz.

She'd screamed loud enough for Becca to hear it under the water. She hurried to the surface and swam over to apologize before their mother came and made the girls get out. While Becca stood in front of her apologizing, Liz, who had a wad of mud hiding behind her back, smeared it down Becca's face.

When the cold sludge had hit, Becca gasped in surprise, barely able to see past the mud dripping down her face. Then both girls erupted in fits of laughter, splashing and playing in the chilly river until their fingers turned blue.

You deserved that. Elizabeth spoke, clear as a bell in Becca's mind.

Elizabeth! Becca's thoughts jumbled as she tried asking her sister a million questions all at once, which confused both of them. She concentrated, forcing aside the celebration in her heart until she could slow her pulse.

I've missed you, Becca started. *Are you okay?*

Yes, I think. Things are different. Harder to think. Hard to make sense of everything.

It's okay. It'll take time. I'm here for you.

A warm happiness emanated from Elizabeth. It was more of a feeling than a thought, but it fled as soon as it came.

I have bad dreams. A coldness crept into Elizabeth's voice.

Becca swallowed, wishing she could do more to protect her sister than just talk to her. How could she fight against dreams though? *I know. Can you tell me about them?*

Liz flinched, fear thick in her mind.

Maybe I can help, if you show me.

They weren't put into words, but pictures: flashes of snow, waves out of control, and those foreign trees with leaves bigger than her head and vines over ten feet long. Gunfire exploded all around. Men shouted and their screams tore at Becca's sanity. Two men fought in the distance. Becca recognized several of Leon's men on the ground as she struggled to take everything in. An unfamiliar man ran off, dodging unseen obstacles, and went straight through a tree. Becca blinked, unsure she'd seen that right, but the man had disappeared.

The vision continued, the sounds of battle creating a cacophony of hell itself. A scream pierced the air, and Becca turned towards the cry only to pull up short when she saw herself. There, in a small clearing, she held Andre's limp body on her lap.

Becca dropped her hands, and her eyes flashed open to the med unit. She knocked the chair over and scooted back to the wall. *That couldn't be real.*

It's what I see. Elizabeth's voice rang in Becca's mind, mixed with sadness and confusion.

Becca placed a hand on her temple, realizing somehow they were still connected without touching. "No," she whispered.

If Andre fell, then they were all doomed. No one stood a chance of escape without him.

Jemi kneeled down next to her. "What is it?" She reached out to Becca.

Becca pushed her hand away. "Give me a minute."

The horrors remained etched in her mind. Was this real? Could this be a nightmare? Not with the ocean. Granted, Elizabeth had lived next to the ocean for over a month, but she'd never seen it with her own eyes. Becca couldn't believe Liz could create that detail of pain and destruction on her own.

"We have a meeting to go to." Jemi stood up, the scowl that constantly painted her face back in place.

Becca nodded and stood up to return to Elizabeth, whose eyes were still closed. Her face was peaceful.

Becca hated to leave her sister's side, especially after what she'd seen. "Are you going to be okay here alone?" She brushed back a piece of her sister's hair.

"Doc's in the other room. He'll help her if she needs anything." Jemi shrugged on a jacket.

Elizabeth barely opened her eyes then closed them. *I'm tired.*

Sleep, then. I love you, sis. Becca leaned down and kissed her forehead.

Jemi pushed out the door, not waiting for Becca, which was for the best. Becca wasn't ready to talk to her about what she'd seen. She needed to figure out a way to stop this fight they couldn't win.

The sun had begun its steady decline behind the trees when Caleb first heard the small army. The smell of bodies and campfire reached them, warning them of what was to come.

"It's almost funny that you complain more about the smell than the fact we may not survive the next twenty-four hours." Caleb watched Nikki pull up her scarf to cover her mouth and nose.

She shot him a disgusted look. "Why *almost* funny?"

"We're both walking into that." He focused on the path, watching out for guards.

"I wish we were heading to the city instead."

"It smells bad in the city."

Nikki huddled into her jacket as the wind picked up. "I know, but I've never been to the city. Just read old tales about running water, toilets, and movies."

"I've seen a movie once, when I was little. Exciting for a kid, but depressing now."

"How so?"

"It's a reminder of the world that once was, what could have been with magic, not the hell that was created."

Caleb noticed a man ahead smoking a cigarette and then turned to Nikki. He leaned in close, enjoying the combination of saltwater and pine clinging to her skin. "Is there any way I can still talk you out of this?"

She shot him an angry look. "You've lived with us for a couple weeks. This is my whole world at stake."

"Okay." He strengthened his resolve, and they continued forward. "Hello," he called out to the guard.

Startled, the man dropped his cigarette and leveled the gun at Caleb's chest. "Who goes there?"

Caleb lifted his hands to show they were empty. "Just looking for work. Heard you're hiring soldiers."

The man studied them as they approached. Then, with a sigh, he lowered the gun and picked up his smoke. "They close the books at dark. You better hurry up." He motioned to a dirt path, his gaze on Nikki.

Caleb's gaze flicked to her, but she ignored the man and continued forward, walking into hell without a backward glance. He admired her courage as he stayed by her side and scanned the campsite. Dark-colored tents hid among the trees, and raucous noise carried through the forest. They must've been drinking themselves into oblivion, not that Caleb could blame them.

The trail opened up to a clearing where an older man sat behind a desk. A small lantern perched next to him, glowing with witch light. "Hurry up," his deep voiced boomed. "I'm starving and likely to eat the next person who pisses me off."

The man's dark eyes barely showed any light. For a moment Caleb thought him a Soultorn and worried the man's threat was real. But as they moved closer, the man's old eyes glinted white, just enough to be human. Not that it made him any less dangerous.

"Do you have any special skills when you kill anybody? Or just another tool?" the man asked.

Caleb lifted the bow off of his back. "I'm a pretty good shot."

"Really." Doubt filled the man's voice. "Everyone says he's a good shot. It won't get you more money."

"May I?" Caleb lifted the bow, pulled an arrow from his quiver, and took aim.

The man nodded and reached for a small flask. He waved Caleb on while lifting it up for a drink.

Caleb released the arrow. It sailed straight and true, rising up high to a wide tree a good hundred yards away, and buried dead center.

The man gave a mumbled acknowledgement and turned back to the paperwork. "Names."

They both gave him their names, changing the last names.

"You get a fourth of your money today, the rest after the work is done."

Smart, Caleb thought, since they wouldn't have to pay most of these guys.

"Mess hall is by the lake. Watch the gators, and sleep wherever you can find a spot. You're responsible for your own weapons." The man set down his pen and looked again at Caleb's arrow. "You're going to wish you had that tomorrow."

As if on cue, the arrow reversed direction out of the tree. It floated down, then turned and headed tip first towards Caleb. He glanced at Nikki, but she focused on something in the distance. His heart raced inside his chest at the thought of being at these magicians' mercy, especially since they could control the one weapon at his disposal. As the arrow sailed towards him, he held his ground. They wouldn't kill him. They needed him. Right? The tip stopped an inch from his face. Nikki let out a breath at his side.

"What do we have here?" A cloaked figure stepped out of the shadows. "Someone that can actually fight?" The figure was not large, and his voice held some youth to it.

"He can shoot at least, sir." The aged man stood straight as he addressed the figure.

"Better than half the losers we saw today. They all think we have an unlimited supply of bullets. Put him with my team."

"Yes, sir." The man scribbled something on the paper at his desk.

"And who are you?" Caleb had to ask. They had to have as much information as possible.

"The man who determines whether you'll live or die." The bottom half of his face stuck out through the robes. It was pale and flawless like a child's. "Report by five thirty in the morning for logistics."

"We will." Caleb picked up his arrow that now lay at his feet.

"We?" The hooded man turned back. "I only agreed on you. What can your friend offer me? I felt a bit of magic, but nothing of worth."

"I'm a healer," Nikki said.

"We work as a team," Caleb added. "Her minor magic helps with my aim and protects us both."

"Work as one, get paid as one," the man barked from the table.

"Not so fast." The hooded man approached Nikki.

Nikki lifted her chin and didn't move under inspection.

His cloak fell from his head, revealing perfectly pale skin with a tinge of pink as if recently scrubbed clean. It stood out against his dark clothes and the falling night sky. His sharp features reminded Caleb of a mannequin, almost too perfect and unnatural. The young man's pale blond hair was worn short and pushed to one side. He slowly licked his lips as he watched Nikki, as if deciding whether to bed her or eat her.

"We don't need this." Caleb pulled Nikki's hand, wanting to get her away from the disturbing male.

Nikki didn't move, and before Caleb could pick her up and throw her over his shoulder, the man spoke. "I'm Peter. And you'll both be on my team, but not together. She has better things to do then guard your worthless hide."

Caleb began to protest, but Nikki squeezed his hand. "We'll do it," she replied.

Peter lifted a hand and gently laid it on Nikki's face. "I think you have more potential than you want to share. You'll do fine." He turned on his heel and left.

Caleb ground his teeth together, regretting not tying Nikki to a tree somewhere safe.

"I hope you weren't wooed by that baby face," Caleb whispered once Peter was out of earshot.

She glared at him.

He had to joke or otherwise he would throw her over his shoulder and run. He knew a predator when he saw one.

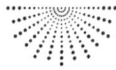

CHAPTER THIRTY-FOUR

B ecca ran down the hall, shoving her hands into old mittens and ignoring the looks from others. She opened the training center door next to Leon's office. Similar to where she worked with Lance, its only difference was the back of the room opened to the sandy beach. Waves lapped in the distance, sending a blast of frigid air over the group collected there.

Leon spoke to the group, with Andre, Jemi, and Lance at his side.

Becca tugged discretely on Andre's sleeve. "I need to talk to you."

Leon stopped talking, and everyone turned to her. The close to forty faces felt like four hundred as their attention bore down on her. Darion stepped forward, but Becca shook her head. They'd talk later; she needed Andre first.

Becca ignored the looks and kept her voice low. "Liz had another vision."

Andre glanced at Jemi.

Jemi shrugged. "Ask her."

"I need to talk to you alone." Becca stood her ground, not willing to be silenced.

"All right. I'll give you one minute. We don't have time to waste." Andre walked away from the group.

Becca followed, and they moved several feet away out of earshot. Leon continued speaking, giving instructions.

"This better be good." Andre turned to face her. "We're preparing for war."

War. The vision was true. It had come to this. "Is Caleb all right?"

"If you'd come to the meeting on time, you would have heard. Caleb and Nikki infiltrated the coven's ranks. They plan to attack in the morning."

"So soon?" Dread coiled in her stomach. "Nikki?"

Irritation irked his expression. "What was the vision about?"

"Yes. The vision." She had to focus, but everything was happening so fast. She relayed the beginning of her vision, trying to describe in detail as much as possible, hoping it would help. Then she got to the part about Andre. She swallowed, unsure how to tell someone they would die. Could they change it?

His gaze remained focused on her. "What else, Becca?"

There was no easy way to say it. "You die, sir. I watch you die, fighting Ryma."

Andre showed no response, his face chiseled stone. Even his eyes remained hard and locked onto her. When he spoke, his voice was low and serious. "If you speak a word of this to anyone, I will force you into unconsciousness until I release you or my powers are gone. Do you understand me?"

Her voice stuck in her throat. He wouldn't—he *couldn't* —be walking to his own death and expect her to not say a word. She wanted to protest, but his power washed over her and a chill traveled down her spine. It wasn't a threat, but a promise that he would follow through. He waited for a reply.

She found her voice after a minute. "These people need you. With you dead, there is nothing left for them, nowhere to run."

His eyes softened a bit. "We can't outrun these forces. I'd rather fight them on my own turf, the waves at my back, than any other way."

"But we could regroup, attack again—"

He held up his hand. "I've gone through every scenario hundreds of times. This was going to happen. We'll evacuate those that can't fight, hide them behind spells, and keep them safe. The rest will fight. Ryma won't find those hidden, and our deaths will satiate his desire. The question is, do you want to fight or be unconscious, another burden for this community to bear?"

How could Becca say no? She glanced at the group in front of Leon, gathering to fight. Did they know they were all walking towards their funerals? Ryma wouldn't let any of them walk away. She remembered the vision, her cradling this man in his last hour. Did she even have a choice, or was it made for her? It didn't matter.

"I'll fight," she said.

"Good. Watch your tongue around the others. I don't make idle threats."

They rejoined the others, and she stood next to Darion. They were going to fight, and they may die, but hopefully they would take as many magicians with them as possible.

When Leon finished speaking to Lance and his group, he turned to Andre. "Anything else?"

"Stick to the plan." His words were a direct stab at Becca. "But everyone be prepared for illusions, possibly a rain forest. Team leaders, please prepare your teams."

Illusions? It made sense that those large leaves and vines were an illusion, especially with the man running through a tree. How would they do that?

Darion leaned in. "You're with me and Leon's team. We have to evacuate the kids and then pull up the rear in the fight. Liz will be part of the evacuated."

Liz. Bittersweet sorrow flooded Becca. She was grateful that she could see her sister to safety but worried at leaving her alone in this world.

Leon dismissed everyone and gathered his ten-man team. Becca recognized most of them. Marcus, who was injured on their last mission, stood next to Leon, no sign of visible injury.

Once the others were gone, Leon addressed the team. "If Caleb and Nikki's information is correct, they'll be here early tomorrow, and we will need to be evacuated before dawn. That means we have to move all these people, plus provisions to sustain them for a week, at least. I have everyone's assignments. There is no time to waste."

Caleb breathed in the smell of pine from Nikki's hair and relaxed into the warmth of her body. The sky held a deep blue of predawn, but the camp was waking. He hated to disturb her easy breathing, so he let her sleep a little longer. Pink from the cold colored her nose and cheeks. The rest of her light brown skin was hidden away under her hat and scarf. He didn't mean to end up in this position, lying so close to her, but now, he couldn't find the desire to move.

Last night, he made a makeshift tent with a tarp and ropes from his pack. With the raucous laughter of drunken men drifting through the camp, Caleb didn't want her to leave his sight. She sent a message to her father of the upcoming attack, and then they both spent some time mingling among the men. Caleb didn't enjoy their crude comments and how they leered at Nikki, but the more he knew the men, the easier he could take them down. The noise had finally settled down, and they'd returned to their tent.

She didn't comment when he held on to her jacket as they lay on their makeshift dirt beds, but instead grabbed his hand, both of them quietly fighting the dread of the coming morning. Even as he slept, he kept a hand on her, the other on the knife at his side. He didn't sleep hard. Every little sound kept him from a deep sleep. As the night wore on, somehow she ended up in his arms. For her safety, he told himself, though he knew it wasn't only that. He didn't want to dwell on what might have been. Not today.

As the sky lightened, he imagined the awkward conversation between them once she woke, and he decided he better get up. He gently extracted himself from the warmth of her body. He grabbed a drink from his canteen and then headed outside their tent to take care of his human needs.

By the time he returned, she was sitting up.

"Morning." He held out the canteen.

She took it with a nod but didn't drink, staring at the dirt.

"What?"

"I can't believe this is all happening."

He kneeled by her. "There is still time to leave, if you want."

"No, there's not. We're more powerful where we are." She took a drink from the canteen.

They packed up and stashed their bags in a bush, only keeping the necessities on hand. Neither of them could stomach much for breakfast, so they headed to meet Peter and their team. The old man from the night before stood in the middle of camp and directed people to their correct teams.

Peter's pale blond hair stood out among the rest. He was surrounded by several large guys. Security, Caleb assumed, and on closer inspection, three of them Soultorns. Their dark eyes sickened him. If he killed them all now, it would be doing them a favor.

"Problem?" Peter asked.

"No." Caleb stared him straight in the eyes, burying the desire to kill Peter and smoothing out his features. "Ready to go."

"We'll be front and center. You, boy, will be in the treetop firing out ahead. Ryma, our high priest, will be joining us today and stationed in the back." He turned to Nikki. "He has an illusionist with him, and your job is to lend him your energy if needed."

Caleb started to object, but Peter ignored Caleb and spoke to Nikki. "I thought with your power in healing that lending power would be second nature. Since you assist your archer here." Peter's impatient tone rubbed Caleb the wrong way.

"Of course." Nikki nodded.

"And here he is, our Nevada." Obvious disdain painted every one of Peter's words.

The thin man with short bushy hair didn't even bother to reply. He had caramel skin, soft features that looked worn, and an emptiness in his sunken eyes.

"Nevada and the girl will wait for Ryma and his team. The rest with me." Peter strode off, the Soultorns and few other men falling in behind him.

Caleb turned to Nikki, his feet leaden. He thought they would get to stay to together. Staying in the back would be safer for her, but not with Ryma. There was nothing he could do without endangering her further.

Go, she mouthed and turned around.

Caleb smothered his emotions and the fear threatening to ignite. They had a job to do, and he had to do it well, for her.

Nikki hoped no one could hear her heart beating wildly in her chest. Turning away from Caleb hurt more than she'd thought it would. The idea that she would never see him again burned, bringing hot tears to press against the back of her eyes. She didn't have a choice. If he thought she wanted to pull out, he probably would have tried, and it would have killed them both. She wasn't going to let this be goodbye.

"You okay, sweetheart?" Nevada leaned over to glimpse her face.

"Fine," she replied, blinking to clear her eyes. Doubt filled her mind. Maybe she should have forced Caleb to go back after they found the camp. Even though she was pretty sure that wasn't an option. Her father would be furious but grateful to see her. Thankfully, the stones her father gave Caleb only worked one way, so she didn't have to listen to her father's anger, or worse, his goodbyes.

She pushed aside her self-doubt. There wasn't time for it. She turned to face Nevada. "So, we're working together."

He tipped his head from side to side as if trying to read past her words. He would have been attractive if not for his hollow cheeks and tired eyes.

"What is your particular talent, dear? You don't feel

like much of a healer. Granted, I haven't come across a healer in years. But you do have power."

She shivered slightly at how much he could read off her. "Mostly defensive. But I can heal, only in more traditional ways." Her father had trained her extensively in defensive magic, but she had more of her father's magic in her than her father wanted to admit. With her experience, she was competent in most types of magic.

"I'd keep that Mundane stuff to yourself," he warned as he leaned in closer. "It's not looked well upon here."

"That's fine. The idiots can bleed to death." She kept her voice light and sarcastic. "So you're the illusionist."

"Yep. I'm not much of a fighter, more of a designer, I'd say. That's why they're keeping me alive anyways." He ran a hand through his short black hair, and it turned a sparkling shade of gold.

She'd never met an illusionist and was amazed at his sleight of hand. Unfortunately, she knew his magic extended beyond fun party tricks.

Power pulsed behind her as Nevada's face fell, blank and empty. She turned to find what only could've been the coven leader and high priest. He approached, surrounded by Soultorns and magicians on either side. Power radiated off him. His strength was evident, easily as strong as her father. But the similarities ended there.

A long scar marked his light skin, starting from his forehead down his jaw. His hair was buzzed short, as well as his beard. She quickly lowered her eyes before he could read more than she wanted him to. She might've been strong, but she needed to focus on how much she let him see.

"Are we ready?" he addressed Nevada.

"Peter's just finishing up his inspirational talk." Nevada motioned behind them where Peter addressed a large group of men.

Ryma turned his attention to Nikki, his power pressing up against her. Instead of fighting back like most witches would, she let him in, showing him what he wanted to see —a frightened girl looking to make an extra buck.

"Who's this?" Ryma asked.

"Peter found her to help me."

Ryma nodded, and his eyes searched for something beyond her physical appearance.

"Better keep this one on a tight leash. If you step out of line, I'll feed you to Kia here." He motioned to the Soultorn that had the body of a blond Viking.

"I won't."

"Not if you want to live. Trust me, I hunt down my enemies quite well." He had a glimmer in his eyes as if he were enjoying himself.

She lowered her gaze and raised her guard. She believed him. So she'd have to kill him on the first try.

CHAPTER THIRTY-FIVE

Seawater washed over Becca's boots as the evacuation party made their way along the shore. Becca and Darion positioned themselves on each side of Elizabeth, helping her navigate the path.

The morning sun had yet to show itself, and the cold breeze off the water chilled them to the bone. The hiding spot was a couple miles down the beach, but this group composed mostly of children and women kept a steady pace. Darion had completed the project with Andre late last night, and once sealed inside, the only exit would lie below sea level.

Another wave curled up the shore and sent a light spray of water over them. Several children squealed and were quickly quieted by their caregivers.

Becca couldn't help but think of the stories her mother had told her of the prophets of old parting the sea. Maybe they were magicians in disguise? Her mother would have called that blasphemy, but this was the same woman who put a hand of Mary tattoo on Becca's back, blocking her magic since birth, so Becca thought the jury was still out.

Mom? Liz spoke to Becca in her mind, and a feeling of longing surged into her. Becca and Darion were on both sides of Liz, helping her walk, though her feet rarely touched the ground.

"Yeah, I miss her too," Becca told her sister.

Liz managed a sad smile. Becca needed to learn how to block or protect her sister from Becca's darker thoughts or worries.

Darion watched the exchange between the sisters. "I take it you established your connection with Liz again."

"Yeah." Part of Becca worried about the connection. How many of her thoughts were subconsciously traveling to her sister? Becca had been consumed with her own worries to much lately to focus on their connection.

"Less talk, more moving," Leon barked from the rear.

Navina, who walked in front of them with her mother and younger brother, turned around and smirked at Becca.

She made a weird face in return. Out of the corner of her eye, she caught Darion smiling at her. She loved that smile that rose up on one side. It hurt a little to think about the day ahead, and not knowing for sure if she'd see it again.

The sun peaked over the horizon, bright and clear by the time they arrived at their destination. Because of the small opening, Darion carried Liz through, and Becca followed. The narrow opening traveled up at a steep incline for ten to twenty feet, before opening into a large gathering area.

"Andre has been busy." Becca moved to the side and helped lower Liz to the ground.

After giving Liz some water, Darion took a long drink and handed the canteen to Becca. "It's been here for a while. He wanted it for an expansion when more people joined him, but he slowly turned it into a hideout, adding the magical protection more recently."

Darion left to help the other men unpack supplies, and Becca tended to Liz. For as large of a group as they had, it all went very smoothly. Even the children helped out in carrying bedding and food.

Leon stood in the middle of the great room with hands behind his back and waited for everyone to settle down. Greg, who Becca had seen often working with Jemi and Leon, stood behind him. He had close-cut brown hair, peppered with gray, but his thick, muscular body didn't reveal any weakness of his age.

Once everyone arrived, the main gathering area was cramped.

Leon cleared his throat. "There are three exits to this place. One is the beach, which will be submerged soon by the tide. One exit will head to the top. My team's going to leave that way, and we'll magically close up that entrance, securing your location. Lastly, there's a small exit through your latrine area. It's not an easy exit. It was made that way on purpose. But those who have lived underground for years should find no problems navigating it. It travels for a couple more miles to another coast. Greg will be in charge here. He has a shortwave radio to stay in contact with me. His word goes. Listen to him. He knows what he's doing."

Greg, arms clasped behind him in a familiar military way, gave a small nod. "Thank you. We will be fine." He might not have been overly friendly, but his quiet strength helped build her confidence in the man.

"Any questions, please consult Greg. Okay, team, let's head out."

Already? Becca hadn't realized she'd have to say goodbye to her sister so soon. She helped Liz sit down next to Doc.

"I'll take good care of her." Light red stubble covered his tired face.

Becca found comfort in his kind eyes. He'd been a constant through her whole stay here. How could she thank him? "Doc, I—"

"I know. Thank me by coming back."

"I will."

"Liz." Becca turned to her sister and pushed her hair out of her face. She stirred under her hand and opened her eyes. "I love you."

Darion's hand touched her back.

Becca turned to him. "I know. I'm coming."

"No." He shook his head, worry heavy on his face. "Leon ordered you to stay and help protect these people."

Becca straightened. "What are you talking about? Of course I'm coming. You need me."

"We don't have time for this, Becca." His voice tightened. "Please, don't make this difficult."

Difficult? "Then why spring this on me at the last minute? We said we'd stick together. Fight together." Her voice rose, echoing in the large room.

Some of the others gave them space and others stared. She didn't care.

Leon marched over to them. "Cut the dramatics. We're all soldiers fighting to save the most lives possible. Andre said you were powerful and wanted you here. We expect you to help Greg and keep these people alive. No one has an easy task, but we're all expected to do it."

Andre had done this on purpose. He was the only other person who knew about Liz's vision. Did he really think Becca could protect all these people or help them after he dies?

She gulped down her pride at being left out, but for

once trusted that maybe he knew what he was doing. "Okay."

Darion squeezed her hand, and a wave of magic surged through her. "I'll see you soon."

She nodded, not trusting her voice. And they were gone, disappearing into the darkness of the cave.

"Okay, people. Let's get to work." Greg barked out orders to start organizing everyone.

Becca stayed with Doc and helped him arrange his gear in a small room near the front of the cave. They set up a cot for her sister and headed back to the great room where they left her with a couple of women for company. When Doc picked up Liz's light frame, she released an unearthly scream.

Becca cringed at the ungodly noise, and then turned to her sister and Doc. He, along with everyone in the great room, appeared unfazed.

"You okay?" Doc watched her wearily.

"It's Liz." Becca placed a hand to her pounding head.

Becca. Liz's voice reverberated in her mind. *They are going to be attacked. Darion and the others, when they leave the cave.*

"Greg," Becca called. This couldn't be happening already.

Thankfully still in the main room, he appeared at her side. "What is it?"

"Darion and the others, they're walking into a trap. I gotta warn them."

He grabbed for his radio. She didn't wait for his answer but took off down the cave. She grabbed a nearby torch with witch light and hurried to the back where she'd seen them disappear.

Someone shouted behind her, but she couldn't make it out. It didn't matter. Between one step and the next, something exploded up ahead. Falling to the floor, she covered her head as the blast washed over her. Her witch light vanished as a light layer of dust and dirt traveled over her. They had just sealed off the path and their fates along with it.

She pounded on the ground, the hard stone cutting into her fist. Angry tears burned her eyes. Dammit! How could they have left her behind? First Caleb and now Darion. She wiped her face and stood. Did this mean she couldn't change Liz's vision? Liz saw her in the battle, so there had to be a way.

Becca stood, dusted off her clothes, and pushed her hair out of her face. No use in looking crazy. Greg waited for her in the main room. Anger radiated off his whole body.

Are you okay? Liz was perched up on one elbow, eyes following Becca closely.

Yes, I'm fine. Just going to talk to Greg, Becca replied.

"Becca." Liz's voice rang out loud, a demanding voice Becca hadn't heard for some time. Liz was returning to her old self, piece by piece.

Becca stopped to stare at her sister. "Yes?"

Liz spoke in her mind again. *You need to go. You need to kill Ryma. He has so many people trapped, like I was. Let them all go.*

Was this a vision or advice? It didn't matter. Becca's gut told her the same thing.

I will, Becca reassured her and turned to Greg. "A word, please."

They walked to the cave opening for privacy. The waves crashed against the stone higher and higher, sealing them in. Her only way out was disappearing with every passing second.

"You can't go running off," Greg started. He must have read her intentions. "You'll get yourself killed."

"More will die if I don't."

His brow furrowed in doubt.

"My sister is a seer. Did you know that?"

"I heard, but I also heard she was still not in her right mind."

She ignored the insult and possible truth. "She's becoming clearer every day. She predicted the fire and has been seeing glimpses of this battle for days now. We share a bond, and I've seen it too."

Greg remained impassive, not giving her anything to work with.

Becca took a deep breath and hoped that if Andre learned what she was about to do, he wouldn't drown her. "Andre's going to die if I don't get out there."

Greg raised a brow. "That's hard to believe."

"I already told him. He was willing to sacrifice himself. But he doesn't realize if we lose him, we lose the war. I need to get back to the beach. I have to help him." That statement might not have been a hundred percent correct but she'd do what she had to do.

"And what about these kids and families that I'm responsible for? Your sister?"

He was right. They needed a chance to escape.

"I'm bonded to my sister, and she's a seer. If a retreat is needed, she'll give you a head start before they can get to you. And we can communicate faster than any radio."

His silence told her he was considering it.

"My sister's here. I'll make it back and will help with the retreat if needed. But if I don't go, Ryma wins."

"Okay." He nodded. "I hope you know how to swim."

She turned to the frigid water and dreaded what lay ahead.

"If what you say is true, you better hurry."

He was right. She didn't think, just jumped.

~

Walking to the battle amid the hundreds of men and magic, Nikki struggled not to be overwhelmed. It was unlike anything she'd ever experienced before. She concentrated on the shield she'd built for herself and Nevada, and made sure it was secure.

Positioned in the rear of the group, Nevada was supposed to work illusions on the fight scene, not be involved in the actual fight.

"You okay there?" Nevada walked next to her with a genuinely friendly demeanor that surprised her.

"Sure."

"Not every day you get to watch a battle this size."

His jovial words didn't help the unease in her gut.

"Why are you here? Surely your boyfriend there would make enough money for the both of you. Would he really chance your life too?"

"He's not my boyfriend." She wasn't sure what was between them, but last night proved there was something. "But no, he's not happy I'm here."

"Then why are you here?"

"Money." She kept her gaze straight ahead.

"Sure."

Ryma motioned to the group, and the men split into several factions. Ryma led his group of men to the coast, while the blond wizard continued straight into the woods. Nevada and Nikki stuck to the center, not moving much. Nevada had to cover as much area as possible.

She scanned the area, wondering how much damage she could do. Taking out Nevada might have helped, but that wasn't going to be an easy task, either, and it would attract a lot of unwanted attention.

Nevada spoke to the Soultorn at his side, a teenage boy

with dark hair. Its hungry gaze unnerved her, and she wondered about the poor boy trapped inside, a prisoner in his own body. She knew there was no help for the boy. Liz wouldn't have survived if not for Becca's insane behavior.

"Does it bother you?" Nevada must have noticed her gaze.

She couldn't answer that. "Why are *you* here?"

He laughed as if acknowledging her abrupt change of subject. "I don't have a choice, unfortunately. I'm blood bound to the bastard that's running this whole show. I just do what I'm told. Speaking of which..." He stopped and placed a hand to his head. "The show must go on." He closed his eyes and began to speak a steady stream of Latin. Before her eyes, the forest began to morph. Vines trailed down from the trees, large enough for her to climb. Trees grew up out of nowhere and others disappeared. His hands moved like a maestro conducting a great orchestra. A masterpiece in this case. It was quite a show. She worried how her family would fight it.

Darion's group didn't even make it a half mile before he heard others. Leon motioned to the men to stop, and they complied, taking cover through the forest. Early morning rays filtered through the trees, and birds flittered above. A perfect, picturesque morning. Which is when the shots began to ring out.

Darion dropped to the floor and focused on his magic. Heat radiated off the weapons in the men's hands, and while many were protected by magical shields, there were a few left unprotected. Making sure he focused on the correct weapons, Darion ignited the bullets still in their chambers, and explosions rang out through the forest, followed by the screams of pain.

Leon barked orders to his men as they fanned out through the forest. Before Darion could follow the others forward, someone attacked. Their magic crushed Darion's defenses, and he buckled under the pressure. Darion pushed back but struggled to draw a breath. He tried to fight, but it didn't matter what spells he tried. Needlelike pain spread throughout his body.

Leon appeared at his side and crouched low. "Where is it coming from?"

Darion pointed in the direction of the spell and dragged himself up against a tree. His body screamed in protest. Leon stayed low, running through the forest and dodging behind trees. Darion bit his lip to hold in the pain and prayed Leon would make it. In a last-ditch effort, Darion started a small brushfire near the source of the spell. He hoped the distraction would give Leon the advantage.

The pain vanished, and Darion's body sagged with relief. It took another second before he felt steady. This wasn't Ryma's main force. It couldn't be, or Darion would have been dead already.

He didn't feel much magic among the remaining men. Leon's men fought hard, and without their leader, probably the one that Leon killed, the others fell quickly. Leon's men had been fighting together for years, and it showed.

Darion did what he could. Thankfully the morning frost kept the ground damp, so it helped control the small blazes he set to prevent others from escaping.

Leon moved swiftly and precisely, a power in his own accord. Before these weak magicians realized that Leon's mind and body couldn't be directly affected by magic, he had taken them down. He used a knife, as it was harder to magically manipulate, like Darion blowing up guns. Leon's team worked together smoothly, and soon all the threats were neutralized. Darion didn't sense any magic nearby.

"All clear," Leon said. "Regroup and let's move out before their friends come."

Darion moved next to Leon who stood over the magician who had almost killed Darion.

Leon frowned at the body. "Why would they send Arturo unarmed out here?"

"No idea." Darion had never met Arturo before. Still, empathy rose. The man was another of Ryma's tools, now dead, and Ryma would never blink an eye over his loss. "This fight was too easy. This couldn't be the attack we were waiting for."

"No. They were probably covering the escape route. It disturbs me that they knew about it." Leon wiped his knife off on his pants. "And trust me. Where I was standing, it wasn't easy. We have four wounded men that we'll have to leave behind."

"Better than burying them." Darion remembered all too well what was at stake for them.

"True." Leon turned to the others, giving orders for the injured. "Let's move out."

The group continued carefully through the forest. Darion kept his shields high, but didn't feel anything for another couple miles.

The magic reached them subtly at first. A man ran into a tree. He swore quietly. Then another man tripped. Darion walked directly behind Leon, so it took him a minute longer to see it. He figured it out, though, when Leon walked directly through a huge bush, not a sound or scratch on him.

"Leon," Darion called.

Leon turned and walked back through the bush with no reaction.

"The illusions. They're starting," Darion told him.

The shadow of an animal appeared overhead. Some type of monkey. Darion blinked a couple times, and the brown monkey stared at him with those beady black eyes.

Unless Ryma had the whole coven with him, the only magician Darion knew who could perform this kind of magic was his friend Nevada. If Ryma had Nevada bound to him, then this fight just got a hell of a lot worse. Not only for Darion, but for his friend tied to the man Darion needed to kill.

"Those that have amulets or any protective tokens, make sure to use them." Leon, not seeing any of this, watched his men, their gaze traveling to the forest growing up around them. "Just when I thought fighting damn wizards couldn't get any weirder."

CHAPTER THIRTY-SIX

The water felt like frozen spikes stabbing at Becca as she swam through the waves. The current wanted to drag her out, pulling at her heavy clothes as each wave pounded her. Her heavy feet kicked and struggled against the tide. All feeling in her hands had fled.

The next wave crashed her into the cliffside, and she grabbed onto it with everything she had. She scratched her fingers along the wall, trying to find a grip before the next wave hit. Her legs slipped, and her muscles screamed in protest as she struggled to gain her footing. Crawling along the cliff face took less energy than swimming. With images from Liz's visions floating through her mind, she worried she'd be too late.

Time moved slowly. She concentrated on moving one hand, then one foot, then the other, holding tight before the next wave crashed over her. Her left grip faltered repeatedly as the wound on her wrist ached. Saltwater assaulted her senses, burning her nose and eyes as she shivered against the cold.

It could have been hours or minutes, but at last an

opening came into view. It was the training center entrance. It would be faster to go there and run to the other exit by Andre's office.

She entered the training room, finally finding her footing up the cave walls. Shivers coursed through her body as she moved into the training center. The same one she'd met with Andre less than a day ago.

Someone must have forgotten to turn out the small witch light near the entrance of the room, but it gave her a dim enough light to find her way. Next to a row of lockers, extra jackets and sweaters hung on hooks on the wall. Her jacket was already lost to the ocean, but she ripped off her shirt and put on a snug jacket. It was something.

As she headed towards the door, something caught her eye. Or someone. "Lance?"

Sitting over a silver bowl on the ground, his gaze flashed up. Gone was his usually lighthearted expression and replaced with disgust. His dark eyes were sunk in with lack of sleep, and he clenched a knife tightly in one hand.

"What are you doing here?" Despite her uneasy feeling, she stepped towards him. "Hasn't the fighting begun?"

"Probably, but I've done enough." He lifted the knife in both hands, pointing it at himself.

Without thinking, Becca tackled him. The bowl scattered as she knocked him backwards. They grappled on the ground, each struggling for the upper hand.

Lance ended up on top, pinning her arms on the ground. At least the knife was out of his hands. But he was a wizard. He didn't always need a knife.

"What the hell are you doing?" She grunted. Was he possessed? She spoke a simple spell, strengthening her magical shield, though she didn't feel any attack.

"Why couldn't you leave me alone?" His face flushed red in the dim light, desperation lacing his words.

"What's going on? Why aren't you at the fight?" She remembered the bowl and the practice of scurrying. Some magicians used water to communicate, to see the future or other things.

Shame washed over his face, and he lowered his eyes.

"It was you. Wasn't it? You've been talking to Ryma." The betrayal cut Becca deep, especially when she thought about Navina and the kids who trusted him.

Anger flared in his eyes, and his grip on her wrist tightened. "I didn't have a choice."

"Everyone has a choice," she spit at him. "Yours was to be a coward and traitor to the people who took you in."

"No. I didn't have a choice." His face softened a touch as if he wanted her to understand. "I'm blood bound to Ryma. Forced to cooperate. The only way to escape is to kill myself." He dropped her hands and scooted back. "Go ahead and do it."

Becca rolled over and grabbed at his knife in case he attacked again. He remained still, and his eyes turned to pleading. "Please."

He couldn't be serious. She couldn't kill Lance. Yes, he betrayed all of them, but... She didn't want his blood on her hands. The stains and memories already haunted her. He deserved a trial, to stand in front of Andre and these people and be held accountable.

"I've tried to fight it, but I can't. Death is the only way I'll be free."

"Maybe. How did you do it? How did you trick Jemi?" Becca remembered the uncomfortable sensation of Jemi searching her own mind.

"Ryma helped me. I'm pretty good at most magic. That's why I was the teacher." He gave a sick laugh. "But that included defensive magic as well. I had been here for so long, I wasn't much of a suspect. Anyways, Jemi and I were a couple for a while. She doesn't like to go digging around in my head."

"Ryma knew about this place for years and did nothing?" She found that hard to believe.

"He'd rather know where the rogues were collecting and keep tabs on them. Andre wasn't a threat. I tried to hold back as much as I could from Ryma. I swear."

Becca said nothing. If he was looking for absolution, he was looking in the wrong spot. She had none. He'd put her whole family in danger. She couldn't forgive him for those lives that would be lost today.

She stepped towards him with the knife in her hand. And to his credit, he didn't flinch.

"Put down your shields," she ordered.

He watched her closely. "I have none up."

It wasn't hard for her to invade his mind and render him unconscious. She pushed power behind the spell to keep him out for some time. Then she grabbed rope out of the closet and hogtied him in a rough, quick manner. He might've deserved to die, but she'd killed enough in defense to know it would hurt her more than it would hurt him. Andre could deal with him. And given the battle about to start, she was sure he'd find some takers later.

Caleb rubbed his hands together, bringing warmth into them. He needed his hands to work his bow, his best tool yet. Peter had sent him up ahead to position himself in a large tree. It took him a bit to climb, but soon he reached a high spot overlooking the forest. He'd made camp in a nice notch of branches.

Thankfully, he made it up before the forest changed. Branches morphed, and dark green leaves sprouted all around him. The change almost unsettled him, but he closed his eyes and held on to his branch. Then he remembered the necklace given to him by Darion. Caleb draped the amulet over his head, and slowly the forest morphed back to normal. The amulet warmed against his chest. *One hell of a parlor trick.*

Down below, Peter sent out a group of soldiers. Ryma's group headed towards the coast, and the others swung around wide. It looked like they planned to surround the rebels.

Nikki stayed next to Nevada near the back, and Peter strode straight forward with great confidence, meeting his opponent head-on. Granted, he had about a hundred men on either side of him, and a couple Soultorns next to him. He didn't have a reason to be scared.

Caleb moved slightly, getting better aim at Peter's group. Ahead, maybe fifty feet in front of Peter, Leon's group approached. They were walking straight towards Peter. Caleb's heart raced as he fought the urge to shout out a warning. He couldn't give away his position just yet. Or could he? He knew better than to waste a shot on Peter or Ryma. Their shields would protect against bullets and arrows. He had to wait until they were weak. Then maybe he would have a chance.

Caleb aimed carefully and let the shot fly. It stuck into a tree inches from Darion's head. He flinched, then gazed to the trees. Warnings were hollered. A single gun fired into the air. It had begun.

Rebels appeared from the east, springing into action, their battle cries echoing throughout the trees. From his bird's-eye view, he could tell the battle started long before the forces reached each other. Random rebels fell to their knees, writhing in agony. Shots rang out, but due to the scarcity of ammunition, there were few and far between the cries of pain. Caleb went into action, retrieving arrows from the full quivers on his back.

He took aim at the Ryma's men with guns first. After being at camp with them, he realized those without magic carried the most weapons, not completely unlike himself. The mercenaries went down easily. Caleb didn't think; he just shot, over and over.

The rebels continued to fall by the handfuls, and desperation crept into Caleb's mind. He didn't have enough arrows to take out all of Ryma's army. He'd have to go down there and make every shot count.

He hurried down the tree to get closer to the battle and at the bottom found Leon fighting one of the Soultorns. Leon kicked the man away, which gave Caleb a clear shot. The arrow met its mark in the Soultorn's chest. Leon didn't look surprised as he walked over and cut the Soultorn's throat. Leaving injured men around in a fight gave magicians and the Soultorns possible fuel for their dark magic.

Leon's men fought hard, but many still ended up on the ground, incapacitated. Several struggled with the illusions, trying to fight around invisible objects.

Caleb dropped low in the tree to get a better advantage with his shot and found Peter fighting Darion. They faced each other at least ten feet apart. Even to the Mundane eye, the sparks and magic between them were visible. Darion fell to his knees, struggling to stay upright. It was obvious he was outmatched.

Even though Caleb knew it probably wouldn't meet its mark, he let his arrow fly straight for Peter as a possible distraction if nothing else. It flew straight until a foot before its target. It froze and dropped to the ground. Peter glared in his direction.

A flash of pain struck Caleb's mind, disorientating him, and some force yanked him from the tree.

"You've grown weaker." Peter approached Darion. Peter's face shone a pristine white; all traces of the scars had vanished.

You'd be weak, too, if you were protecting more than yourself. Sweat dripped down Darion's face as he now focused all of his power to fighting Peter, but Darion's magic weakened by the second. He knelt in the dirt, clenching his hands against the oncoming assault of magic.

Darion had been trying to protect the other men, especially Leon. Being immune to magic made Leon their best weapon, and possibly their only chance at killing Ryma. Out of the corner of Darion's vision, Leon fought with another Soultorn nearby.

But now, Peter was out for blood. The eagerness for revenge was painted clearly on his face.

Darion's heart burned like it wanted to burst. He pushed aside his fear, and replaced it with a bravado he knew annoyed Peter. "If you were getting a new face, you should have asked for an upgrade."

Peter's jaw tightened. "Why you love fighting with these Mundanes is beyond me. So pathetic." He turned to a man next to him.

Bullets unloaded towards Leon and the Soultorn who were twisted together in a violent embrace. Darion forced the gun to explode in the soldier's hand, but it was too late. Both the Soultorn and Leon appeared to be hit as they fell apart. Leon knelt on the ground. A shot appeared to have pierced his thigh as the blood gathered on his pants.

Relieved that the shot wasn't worse, Darion acted fast. He lit the brush near Peter, and fire roared high into the air. It provided Darion cover for a few moments. By the time he got to Leon, the Soultorn was dead on the ground with a knife in the middle of his throat.

"Can you move?" Darion asked.

Leon grunted and Darion helped him up. Leon was still strong on his feet, but couldn't put much pressure on his leg without bleeding out.

"Cauterize the wound for me," Leon ordered.

Darion did a quick double take. Burning the wound would stop the bleeding, but it would hurt like hell. This was Leon though.

"Yes, sir." Darion quickly burned the wound.

Leon yelled with the pain, but kept standing, his grip tight on the tree. "Let's go get that bastard."

"My pleasure." Darion turned back to the flames but couldn't find Peter. He wouldn't have left. Peter wouldn't rest until Darion was dead. His stomach tightened with an uneasy fear. He'd rather fight the enemy he could see than the one he couldn't.

Caleb lay on the damp ground, struggling to breathe. The pain in his mind had left, but his body ached from the fall. He couldn't stay down. Shots rang out, people swearing, screaming—a cacophony of pain and injury surrounded him.

He rolled over and scrambled to his knees. Thankfully his bow was in one piece, the arrows nearby. He wouldn't have long before Peter finished him.

With one more shot to make, he kept low and sprinted back to where Nikki and Nevada stood. The sounds of battle echoed through the forest, but near the back, there wasn't much fighting. That would make his job easier. Scanning the area, it didn't take him long to find Nikki.

Once she noticed him, she nodded and stepped aside, giving him a clear shot to Nevada. Caleb released the arrow and sent a prayer that Nikki removed any shields. At the last moment, Nevada must have sensed it approaching. A shocked look crossed his face, and he tried to avoid it. He didn't move fast enough, though, and the arrow struck his shoulder. He collapsed and so did the illusions surrounding him.

Caleb didn't have time to celebrate. He sent the next arrow through the throat of the Soultorn. Shouts rose up around him as the illusions lifted. With both of the men on the ground, Nikki should be safe.

Screams sounded behind him. Nikki waved him off and he agreed. He had work to do. He couldn't wait around for a thank-you note.

CHAPTER THIRTY-SEVEN

Becca hurried through the caves to the exit near the battle. The barren tunnels full of memories of these people motivated her. If there was ever a chance at civilization actually becoming civil, this was it. They deserved so much more.

Still shivering from her wet pants and shoes, she slowed down as she neared the exit and waded through a good foot of water. The waves crashed on the path ahead. She'd have to time it precisely.

As soon as the tide rushed back, she sprinted. The path was rocky, which helped her secure her footing. She kept an eye on the water, but instead of drawing back again, the waves remained low. It could only mean a couple of things: somehow Andre knew she was on the path, or that he was too weak to control the water. She hurried, a sinking feeling that it was the second option. Her legs burned as she ran up the switchbacks, but she couldn't let herself stop. She tried to ignore the nagging part of her mind that told her she was fulfilling the vision her sister saw, that it was too late to help.

Bodies littered the trail, carnage of the war ahead. At a quick glance, they didn't look familiar. One broken body was wedged between the jagged rocks of the cliff.

As she neared the top, the sounds of battle grew: screams of pain, shouts of angry spells, and gunfire mingled with the faint smell of smoke. The thought of Darion pushed her faster. Legs burning, she finished the climb, steadied her magic, and pulled herself up over the edge.

A bitter taste flooded her mouth at the sight of the bloodbath in front of her.

Nikki ignored her conscience as Nevada screamed. She not only lowered her shield but attacked his personal shield and his Soultorn, so that Caleb would have a clean shot. It was the first person she purposely hurt. Pushing back the guilt, she grabbed his arm as he staggered to the ground.

"Try to stay still," she said.

"Easy for you. You don't have an arrow in you." He knelt on the ground and gritted his teeth.

"I'll protect us." She placed a shield around her and Nevada, but left out his Soultorn who lay dying mere feet away.

"I thought you were already doing that. Remember you were supposed to be protecting me," he snapped.

She grabbed a bandage from her pack to stop the blood and glanced at the forest. The vines and oversized trees vanished. The familiar forest helped settle her nerves. A glimmer of hope grew. Now, maybe her people had a chance.

Nevada's painful moan brought her back to nursing mode, and she put some gauze around the wound. Pausing, she realized that was all she could do. If she removed the arrow and tended to his wounds, he'd replace the illusion. She didn't know what she would do if the others came back to investigate.

She worried he would use the Soultorn's death to help heal himself. She wasn't going to impart undue harm, but if it was between him and her family, there was no real choice. The pool of blood continued to grow though.

Nevada winced. "What are you waiting for? You're the healer. Take care of this."

She lowered her eyes. "I'm sorry, Nevada. I can't."

He stared at her for a minute as if trying to solve a puzzle. "Who are you?"

She laid a hand on his chest, letting her power course through him. Already weak from the illusion, the arrow in his shoulder impeded his power. It would only take a slight push to stop his heart before the others came back. But could she kill a man?

"These are my people Ryma is killing," she said.

He tightened his jaw as he tried to push against her power to no avail. "Of course he is killing for no reason. Ryma is a psychotic power-hungry wizard."

"So stop working for him. Help save my family." She couldn't fathom Nevada wanting to work for someone like that. For the little time she'd known this man, she knew he danced to his own tune.

"Then I am dead." His chest rose with a heavy breath. Those large eyes weren't scared but accepting of his fate in a haunting way. "Either way, by your hand or his, I'm dead. At least this may be easier."

"Not if Ryma dies first."

"You can't stand against him. Sorry, princess, but he's as strong as a demon straight from hell."

"You haven't met my father. He can move mountains. Literally." She sent a prayer his way, hoping she was right.

～

Overwhelmed, Becca searched for those she knew scattered in the combat. There were flashes of recognition, but she couldn't see Darion or Caleb. She couldn't afford distractions, so she focused on finding Andre.

She closed her eyes briefly. A huge power surge pulsed to her right with enough magic to push her over, if she let it. Andre. She strengthened her shield against magical attacks and took off, swerving through the trees. She picked up a couple knives from a dead man lying face down on the ground, praying it wasn't anyone she knew.

Becca skidded to a stop. There they were: Andre and Ryma over twenty feet apart. Their power was like an oppressive heat pressing down on everyone. Electric sparks traveled between them as they used everything around them at their beck and call.

Andre uprooted a nearby tree that must have been fifteen feet tall and wide. He tossed it at Ryma, who quickly stopped it and then sent what had to be a Soultorn onto the tree. The man or demon jumped on the tree, maneuvering it with an inhuman skill, and headed straight for Andre.

Andre stopped the Soultorn a foot away, forcing him to the ground. While Andre dealt with that, Ryma's other soldiers surrounded Andre and Jemi, who protected his back. Was that all who was left?

Jemi fought hard, reaching forward to slice a man straight across his stomach. Her fierceness shone through her small frame. Magic radiated off her, paralyzing some until she could cut them through. But the soldiers kept coming, pushing Jemi back. One of Leon's men fell next to Jemi. She didn't have time to spare him a second glance as she fought the next man.

Becca sprinted towards her. A man turned and swung out at Becca. She slid to the ground and turned, slicing the back of his knees. He hollered and crashed to the ground. A demon would never cry out like that.

Jemi whipped around, gun in hand, and cut off his scream with a bullet. "What are you doing here?" She turned to meet the next assailant.

Becca reached out to a man headed towards her, hoping to take control of his brain. He was protected, but she tried anyway, then threw her knife straight at him in hopes of a distraction.

She never saw if it met its mark as another person struck her with magic. She fought off the physical attack in front of her, while people came at her with knives and guns. In the midst of chaos, she struggled to stay afloat. Fighting what felt like an endless onslaught. No time to think, just fight.

As she turned to take on the next assailant, something exploded. A weightless feeling carried her away. The roaring in her ears blocked out all conscious thought.

Silence permeated the forest for a moment as every person, tree, and blade of grass was forced down in a wave of deafening power.

A buzzing noise filled her brain as she pried open her eyes and struggled to her feet. What was that? Bodies littered the ground around her, a few moaning in pain. She searched among the injured.

Jemi.

Becca crawled towards her. Blood painted the front of her shirt. It looked like a gunshot. Numbness traveled down Becca's arm as she checked for a pulse. Nothing.

Anger, rage, and regret boiled inside of Becca, which helped her to rise to her feet.

A man nearby stumbled to his feet, one of Ryma's men. Becca grabbed Jemi's gun and shot him. She didn't feel a thing.

Her fury had turned to numbness as her body moved through the motions, almost disjointed from her mind. It knew what it had to do to survive.

"That was for you," Becca told Jemi.

She searched for Andre. He lay on the floor merely feet away, unconscious.

"No." The word came out as a whisper. It couldn't be over.

She dropped next to Andre. His eyes were bloodshot, searching for something unseen, and blood dripped from his nose. He was alive, but not for long.

"Run," he managed to whisper. "Get them out."

"They'll be taken care of." She'd already defied his orders once, so he may not find her words comforting, but she wasn't giving up.

Placing a hand on Andre, she lifted her gaze to find Ryma. He stood alone in the midst of a smooth, dusty circle, no stone or blade of grass visible. The explosion must have emanated from him. A bold move, killing some of your own people to eliminate your enemy, but to Ryma, people were expendable.

With the gun in her hand, she steadied her shields and walked towards him. She remembered Jemi's words when it came to her power. *"Don't shove your way into someone's mind. Slide in the back door. Give them something they want to believe."*

The scar on his shaven head stood out, pulling awkwardly as he grinned at her.

Becca lifted the weapon and fired. It did nothing. She

continued firing, emptying the magazine and tossing it aside.

Shouts sprang up in the forest behind her. Somewhere nearby, a fire burned.

Focusing on her magic, she didn't attack at first but spoke to him in his mind. *Can you imagine the Soultorn this leader would make? You could raise Lucifer himself with this man.*

"You think you can tempt me so easily." He smirked. "Not everyone comes back like your sister."

The blaze grew, blocking off the others from Becca. The fire pushed towards Ryma as if Darion was controlling it, but it didn't reach the magician. Grateful for Darion, she pushed out the thought of him. She couldn't let herself get distracted.

Then with a wave of Ryma's hand, the flames grew. "Trust me. I can take the heat more than you."

She continued to focus on his mental shields, to convince him he needed Andre alive more than dead. If she could keep Andre alive, and give him time, they may have a chance.

In a flash, the world around her changed. Then the heat of the flames pressed down on her. Sand covered the ground as far as she could see. The other people disappeared, and only Ryma stood in front of her, his clothes billowing around him.

"You want in my head, little girl?" His chagrined smile tightened. "Well, let's have a little trip, shall we?"

He assaulted her mind with a speed and viciousness that left her no time to prepare a defense. She fell back onto the forest floor. Her body was frozen as memories flashed in front of her. Her parents burning house. The disgust of her uncle's heavy hand. Her escape from Ryma's estate. Her encounter with Bael.

"Interesting." His voice curled around her mind. "You

freed your sister and met Bael. Quite a task for such a novice. And she's a seer. Lovely."

Becca built wall after wall in her mind, trying to block the image of her sister. Her frail frame hiding in the caves. *No, not her!* But his penetrating gaze pierced through her defenses, seeing everything.

"Take me," she pleaded. "A willing sacrifice must be worth something."

"I'll take them all for the grief you have caused me." He stood directly in front of her. His hand cupped her cheek. "And when we're done, you will be willing."

The images he sent her next were of his own creation. The torture of her and those she loved threatened to break her sanity's last straw. Had she come to this field only to let Ryma kill them all?

You're not alone. Her sister's voice pushed through the hell Ryma had created for her. At the same moment, Becca registered the smell of smoke, of Darion.

He won't touch us, Becca. You won't let him.

Becca embraced the rush of power, Liz's power flowing through her.

Becca didn't bother fighting his touch or the images he pushed at her. Embracing the demented images and leaning into his touch, she pushed down her repulsion and gave in to her fears. She focused her power to crawling into his sick mind and destroying any physical shields he had. Counting on that smell of smoke, that hope from Darion and the others to do the rest.

Ryma's head jerked suddenly, and his arms tightened around Becca. An arrow pierced straight through his throat.

Though his death appeared imminent, he somehow kept hold of Becca, blocking her sight of the world around them. He mouthed something, and strangled sounds of a dying man escaped his bloodied lips. Becca's world morphed into something unnatural as darkness gathered at the corners of her vision. Something or someone continued to pull her under to an abyss devoid of life.

Becca couldn't have said how much time had passed when she heard her name, over and over. At first, she couldn't tell where it came from or who was speaking. Warmth seeped into her body, and she realized just how cold she'd been. Someone held her, grasped onto her as if she may float away. Soon, she recognized the voice, the heat, the body: Darion.

"Stay with me, Bec," Darion said. He then spoke in a different language. The pain in his voice struck her.

Ryma's visions echoed in her mind, and she clung to Darion, her rock, her base. Liz's presence also guided her away from the ghost of Ryma. Their magic seeped into her soul and helped gather those pieces of herself that threatened to shatter completely.

Becca slowly regained consciousness cradled in Darion's arms. Smoke and ash permeated everything.

"Is it over?" she croaked, blinking to clear her eyes.

He kissed her forehead and then leaned back slightly. "Yeah, Bec, He's dead." Tears stained his soot-covered face, and a smile shone through the tragedy. "It's over."

She thought she'd be elated that they'd won, that Ryma was dead, but something in the pit of her stomach couldn't celebrate when so many lay dead and injured.

CHAPTER 38

Gratitude hung heavy in Becca's heart as she helped tend to the injured and collect the dead. Twenty-eight. That was the number of people from their community dead. Freedom shouldn't come at a such a steep price, but it always did.

The only silver lining: Andre wasn't one of them. Weakened from his battle with Ryma, he couldn't walk on his own, but it didn't stop him from tending to his people. Andre relied on others and used what power he could to draw back the ocean.

In the afternoon light, Nikki, Doc, Caleb, and several others moved the injured to the med unit. The children, women, and others returned from the hideout and began moving back into the cave. Wrapped in a heavy blanket, Liz refused to go back inside, but remained on the beach with Becca.

Andre also refused to go back in the caves, demanding he stay until the dead were taken care of. Perched on a raised rock, he remained on the shore watching over the dead. His gaze rarely strayed from their bodies.

Darion, with a few other magicians, worked on restoring as many of the shields to the compound as they could. In the end, they knew they couldn't stay. Everyone knew it, even though no one said it. Too many got away, including Peter, and that meant another force would come.

As the sun finished setting, Elizabeth leaned into Becca as they both sat on the damp sand waiting for the graveside service. Becca kissed the top of Liz's head and felt almost guilty in her happiness. There was so much loss today, but Becca didn't have to part with her loved ones.

Leon approached, limping heavily on a makeshift crutch.

"Should you be up on that?" Becca asked.

Leon brushed off her worry. "I'm fine. It went straight through. I came to tell you, there's a meeting in Andre's office tonight at nine. Be there. And bring Darion." He didn't wait for her reply, but turned around and went back to work.

The burials turned out not to be burials at all. They didn't bury their dead, concealing their bones for scavengers or magicians to find later. They sent them out to sea, aflame like the Vikings of old.

Twenty-eight rafts sailed out to sea that afternoon. Jemi's petite form that always had so much life and strength now looked small and still. If it wasn't for Jemi, Becca wouldn't be alive. They may not have always got along, but she owed Jemi her life. It was one debt she'd never get a chance to repay.

Lance also had a wooden raft that carried his lifeless body. Somehow, he'd broken free of her bindings and took his own life. It broke her heart to know he had hidden such heavy secrets behind his fun-loving personality. As their rafts drifted out to sea, silent tears slid down Becca's cheeks.

Standing on the beach near Leon, Darion reached out a hand and set the bodies ablaze. Beautiful flames of life that carried to the great beyond. Everyone watched the light sailing into the darkness until the flames disappeared. Then they slowly filed back into their caves, their home that would never feel the same again.

In the medical unit, Nikki directed Becca to place Liz in a bed in the back. The room buzzed with injured people, and Nikki had more than enough help. There were even some new faces.

Becca wasn't surprised to find Nevada in one of the nearby beds, though he looked drastically different from the last time she'd met him. Gone was his grandeur; now it was replaced with pain and curiosity as he watched everyone around him. Caleb caught her up on what had happened.

Becca motioned Nikki aside. "Caleb told me what you did with Nevada. I'm glad you saved him. You saved a lot of lives with what you did." Nikki had proven herself in more ways than one.

"I didn't do any more than anyone else." Nikki's eyes showed great pain. "Even less than what some gave."

"True…" Becca had barely gotten to know these people. Nikki had grown up with some of those who'd given their lives in this fight. "Thank you."

"Thank you for saving my father." They clasped hands, forging something that neither would soon forget.

Becca nodded and walked out the door. Her body felt numb from the events of the day, and her mind spun, wondering what came next for all these people. Months ago, she couldn't have cared, but now…Well, maybe she should make a dent in the debt she owed Jemi.

Mostly everyone headed to their rooms, but a few sat in the cafeteria drinking coffee. In the bunk room, the majority of the women were asleep. Becca found solitude in the shower, and finally allowed herself to break down in the freezing water. While tears slid down her cheeks, she scrubbed off the dirt, dried blood, and Ryma's stench. His touch and control of her mind scarred her more than any other physical wound she had received. Her body began shivering, and finally the cold drove her out.

While she dried off and put on clean clothes—sweats were the only thing left in the extra closet—her mind began to churn. What did the future hold for them? Searching for a new home? Hiding from the next threat? As much as she finally felt at home here with these people, she was tired of hiding.

After sneaking some dried fruit from the cafeteria, she headed to Andre's office. The large room felt cramped with the big men—Andre, Leon, Greg, Seth, and Caleb—but there was still one missing. Jemi's presence would be greatly missed. She'd pushed Becca and many others to grow, to make them stronger. Jemi had helped her to survive.

Becca stood next to Darion near the bookshelves and leaned into his shoulder. One of the antique books lay on the counter, and she traced a finger down the spine. These books helped Andre only so much, but it wasn't enough. An empty silence settled on the group as everyone focused on Andre, sitting at his desk. He held an old compass in his hands.

He cleared his throat. "Jemi gave this to me as a present last Christmas."

No one spoke. His words floated to the ground. Darion squeezed Becca's hand, and she leaned against him.

Andre twirled the compass in his hands. "She was trying to convince me to leave, to find a new shelter where we'd be safe. She even suggested the islands. But it took her death and the death of our family members to convince me." He looked up now, a dark strength returning to his eyes. "We can't stay here. It's not safe. Others will come for us. The word will spread to maybe even Lazaro himself. Any coven not bound to his people he'll view as a threat."

"Let everyone rest tonight, and we'll begin evacuation plans tomorrow," Leon said. "We have prepared for this."

"We should fight," Darion interjected. "We could take over the city, have our own protections. You're strong enough to run it how you wish. We never found Peter's body. I know he won't give up."

Andre shook his head. "Maybe, but I will not bow down to Lazaro, and we're not an army. These people are my family, and we're just trying to survive in peace." He turned to Becca and Darion, the pain still evident on his face. "I invited both of you to ask you to help Leon in preparations. We lost many good magicians, and we will need everyone for this move forward."

Darion looked to Becca. She knew he was more than ready to help Leon, but he waited for her reply. He mouthed the word she was thinking: *Together.*

Andre turned to Becca, awaiting her answer.

"Yes, I will help, but Darion has a point. They're never going to leave you alone." The thoughts from Becca's shower had collected into an idea as she'd watched Andre grieve.

"I'm not—" Andre started.

"Wait. Hear me out." They'd invited Becca and Darion for their skill. They had survived in the city and in the coven. Despite Andre's grief, he had to see all the options.

With a heavy sigh, he nodded. "Okay."

"We're not safe here. You're right. I don't think the city is safe, either, not for anyone. We'll never be safe. We can run and hide, but someone will find us or hear of us. Especially if you continue to take in people, which is what your community is all about."

"Then what do you propose?" Andre asked.

"We close the portal."

Andre dropped the compass on the desk, confusion creasing his features. The loud clang echoed through the room as all eyes turned to her.

"Is that even possible?" Leon asked.

"I don't know, but I got the idea from your books," she told Andre. "The one Darion was translating. It talks of how the dimension was opened. Introducing magic and demons into our world through the temples of old in the south. If it can be opened, why can't it be closed?"

Murmurs of surprise and disbelief filled the room.

Becca let go of Darion's hand and stepped towards Andre. "You say knowledge is important. Well, why not start at the source. Darion and I can travel to the southern countries. He's fluent in enough languages to get by. It may be the only chance of returning this world to what it once was."

"There's no guarantee that's even possible," Darion said.

"We're getting pretty good at the impossible. Look at Elizabeth."

"That almost killed you."

"But it was worth it." She didn't back down. She couldn't. "If we have the smallest chance of ending this, we have to try."

"There is much we don't know about magic," Andre said, his voice silencing the others. "We've only been taught what they want us to know, only what Lazaro brought back with him thirty years ago. There may be answers."

"Or just a wild-goose chase and death by the natives." Darion crossed his arms, bristling at the suggestion.

Becca couldn't fathom why he was against it. "We've faced worse. Together." She stepped towards him, wanting to reach out to him.

"And your sister? This will be dangerous."

"She can stay here with Caleb and help us communicate with the others."

He didn't reply, but his angry posture told her this wasn't over between them.

Couldn't he understand she had to end this? It wasn't just about keeping her sister and friends alive. This was the only way groups like this community could live. It would even the footing once again for everyone.

"You've definitely given us an option to consider. Let us sleep on it tonight, and we'll meet again in the morning." Andre looked intrigued. There was something to find out there, and they both knew it. He gave her a slight nod, dismissing them.

Outside of Andre's office, Darion grabbed Becca's hand and led her down into the private caves past the med unit.

"Where are we going?" Becca wasn't familiar with this section of rooms.

"Andre gave me my own room a couple nights ago."

"Really?"

"I was keeping odd hours translating for him, and he didn't want me to wake the others." He continued forward with a tight grip on her hand.

On the dim path, she realized maybe Darion had a right to be mad. She'd dragged him into this mess with Ryma, and now she had volunteered him for another crazy mission. He loved his magic, and he loved being here, able to use his powers for something positive he wasn't forced into. Now, she wanted to take it all away.

He entered a small room and lit a nearby lantern. A small cot was tucked into the corner, and there were a few other sparse belongings. He closed the door.

Before he could start, she said, "I'm sorry."

Confusion replaced anger on his face for a brief moment. "Why?"

Where to start, she thought. "I shouldn't have volunteered you to go with me. Here I have dragged you through the wilds with my possessed sister, and once we get settled, I'm ready to volunteer you on a half-brained idea, which may not even work. It's not fair of me to expect—"

He kissed her, briefly, but it was enough to send a warm jolt down her spine.

"You're wrong," he stated.

"That's what I was trying to explain."

"No. Yes, I wish you would have run the plan by me first, but I'm not worried about going south. I just don't want you to have to go." His frustration melted, softening his eyes. "I can't stand the idea of you throwing yourself into another dangerous situation, putting yourself at risk."

It was her turn to be surprised. "Really?"

A laugh escaped his lips, but it wasn't happy. "Have you not figured things out between us yet? You're pretty important to me. When we first met, I didn't tell you I was a magician because I wasn't about to drag anyone into my dangerous world. Then you got involved with the coven, and there wasn't anything I wasn't willing to do to pull you out." He reached for her hand, and she willingly gave it to him. "If you leave, and I know you probably will because I won't be able to talk you out of it, there isn't anything that would keep me from your side."

"Oh…" How could she have doubted him? "I'm—"

He closed the distance with another kiss, his arms weaving around her. "You better not say sorry again."

Lost in his kiss, her body lit with a fire all on its own. She leaned back slightly. "Thank—"

He raised his brows. "No thank-yous either. I'm a purely selfish beast at heart."

She knew that was untrue. He had helped her, her sister, Caleb, and so many people in this community. Embracing him, she whispered in his ear. "There is one thing you won't be able to stop me from saying… I love you."

Heat emanated from him, a warmth that enveloped both of them. "Of course not. As long as you know I love you more."

END OF BOOK TWO

Thank you for reading UNHOLY SUNDERING. DeAnna Browne will be back in Spring 2019 with DARK ALLIANCE, the exciting conclusion of Dark Rising Trilogy.

Don't miss out on the prequel novella, EVIL ETCHED IN GOLD, now available!

If you're looking for more from DeAnna, keep reading for a peek into her Young Adult Sci-Fiction Romance, HOOKED.

Do you want to share your exciting discovery of a new read? Help others add it to their To Read lists by rating and/or writing a review:
Goodreads
Amazon US

Amazon UK

Sign up for DeAnna's newsletter for the latest news, free releases, and new release information **HERE**

Or you're welcome to come for a visit Deanna's website at:
https://deannabrowne.com

HOOKED

HARD-WIRED TRILOGY BOOK 1

When virtual reality surpasses people's wildest dreams, many struggle to remain in the real world.

This isn't real.

Ari stood on a nearby hill above the familiar carnival with her brother, Marco. Rides spun endlessly in the distance, and neon lights flashed, illuminating the dark night. It stole her back to a time when the world was a different place, a place full of laughter. An uneasy sensation crawled along Ari's skin as she thought of her body tucked back in reality with wires streaming from the port in her neck.

"Remember how you puked on the Spinning Hammers?" A wide smile lit up Marco's face. Marco and Ari both took after their mother with their tanned skin, dark wavy hair, and chocolate eyes. Except for the smile— Marco wore their father's smile.

She couldn't figure out how her brother always appeared so put together, in and out of the virtual realm.

Ari wore a flannel shirt and beat up jeans, and not on purpose. The Virtual Reality, or VR, program let people change their clothes, but Ari never stuck around long enough to bother with fashion.

She turned back to the carnival, the rides antiquated and shedding their paint even in this computerized replica. The carnival had come around every spring when they were little. People lined up all day and night for rides, an event so popular someone made it into a VR.

"Please, Marco, I feel like I'm about to lose it." She dug her nails deep into her palms and welcomed the pain as it grounded her in reality.

"What? You don't like it?" Marco acted surprised. "I had to ask them to dig into their storage to find this virtual for you. Come on."

Marco grabbed Ari's hand and pulled her down the hill towards the rides. The cool night air brushed against her face as they raced down the grassy path, and she fought to keep her fear from bubbling over. She had never lasted more than two minutes in one of these programs, but today she needed to. Her future depended on it. Assignments for their continued education were coming soon, and if she couldn't pass the VR simulation, she might as well sign up for a life of kitchen duty.

Her breath came in rapid pants as they reached the entrance. A disfigured clown face with exaggerated eyes and teeth welcomed them, his mechanical voice scratchy. Her throat tightened as she tried to breathe. She panicked at the idea of being stuck here forever, trapped in this virtual world, spiraling into a VR coma like her father. The government limited the hours kids could be inside a VR, but people, young and old, still slipped, which left their family paying the bill in hopes they would return.

The clown image frizzed momentarily into a dark void

with specks of light replacing the creepy face. "Marco, what's going on?" She pointed at the distorted image. There had to be some sort of glitch.

Marco glanced at the clown. "What are you talking about, Ariana?" He tugged on her arm. "Snap out of it. I told Mom we would have fun." He yanked her toward the Tilt-a-Whirl.

An elderly man worked the empty ride, or so her brain told her. He wore a plain blue uniform and a smile that was a touch bigger than necessary. Holding the gate open, he welcomed them inside.

The virtual showed its age as the computerized character blinked constantly and tilted his head every three seconds like clockwork, but they couldn't afford anything more sophisticated. Ari wasn't sure if it was the uncomfortable memory of wires hooked into her unconscious body or this man's creepy behavior that made her want to run away.

She froze with fear at the gate. "I can't do this."

"Yes, you can." Marco's dark eyes locked onto her with a firmness that didn't suit him. "You don't have a choice. Get used to VRs or get used to cleaning toilets while Mom tries to marry you off. Is that what you want?"

Normally she would have smacked her older brother for talking like that, but the truth hit its mark. Biting her lip, she stepped toward the small compartment built for two. Marco climbed in and slid across the faded blue vinyl bench. She squeezed in beside him and fastened the thick black strap.

"I thought you loved being here. I always did."

Every spring, her father would empty the jar of coins on top of the fridge and treat Ari and Marco to a fun day at the carnival. They would fill up on fried bread and cheese curls, watching the night descend into a blur of neon lights. But, unlike her brother, this reminded Ari of what they didn't have anymore: a father and a jar full of savings. In a VR coma, their dad was more dead than alive, and the chipped jar now sat empty on top of a rundown fridge.

Chest tightening, she pushed back the memories. "I'm sorry. I can't, Marco. I gotta go." She clawed at the thick black safety belt as the ride surged forward.

"Are you really going to waste Mom's money? You know this is your last chance before your tests." If he saw the fear in her eyes, he ignored it. "Whatever. Go. I'm staying and getting my money's worth."

She bit her lip and faced forward, holding back her rising hysteria. The cart picked up speed and pushed her against Marco, who screamed in delight, arms raised high in the air. She wanted this so badly, wanted to let go of reality, to let go of the gnawing sensation in the back of her neck. As the cart continued to spin, Ari closed her eyes, hoping to endure. By the time her cart approached the aged man a second time, she was gone.

Her eyes opened to a water stained ceiling. The stench of old cigarettes and filthy bodies welcomed her back to reality. She strained to turn her head. Her neck pinched from the cords in her port. Disgust tasted sour as she clawed the base of her neck, pulling at the thick cable.

"Hey, girlie. You're going to tear your port, and I don't have the stuff to fix it." A man's thick hands turned the cable until a click sounded, and then he gently pulled the wires out. She wanted to scratch at the insertion site, to tear away the mechanical feeling that lingered inside of her. Instead she undid her ponytail and covered the port site with hair, smoothing it down.

Her brother lay next to her in a reclined chair, a smile pasted on his handsome face. His wavy, thick hair, often kept short, curled around his temple. He always appeared more innocent while unconscious.

Glad to see he's enjoying himself. She pushed back the bitterness boiling inside. He had been trying to help.

The large man, covered in old tattoos and smelling of yesterday's beer, winked at her. Revulsion rolled around in her gut. Before he could speak, she rushed out of the room. She detested this shop as much as the virtuals themselves. The VR center stood only a few blocks from her house, a permanent fixture in her rundown neighborhood.

Ari hurried through the metal doors, squinting as she welcomed the sun. The real sun.

Her sun.

"Missy, want to catch a trip with a real guy?" A withered man sat outside, his dirty clothes hanging off his body. "Trust me. I look a hell of a lot better on the inside."

She snapped her head back to the road in front of her, ignoring him.

"Don't be like that," the man said.

Someone reached for her, grabbing at her arm, but she swatted it away, quickening her step. *Please just leave me alone.*

The jeers of the strung-out VR addicts followed her for the rest of the block.

She tried not to imagine how her father had used to be there, hanging out with the bums to catch a free VR. She tried, but it didn't work.

Follow Ari and get HOOKED now!

ABOUT THE AUTHOR

DeAnna Browne graduated from Arizona State University with her BS in Psychology. She finds it helps to corral those voices in her mind and put them to paper. An avid reader and writer, she has a soft spot for fantasy with a touch of romance. Despite her love for food and traveling, she always finds her way back to Phoenix, Arizona with her husband, children, and pet dog.

Follow her at:
www.deannabrowne.com

facebook.com/deannabrownebooks

twitter.com/brownebooks

instagram.com/deannabrownebook

amazon.com/DeAnna-Browne/B074L9BH72

goodreads.com/DeAnnaBrowne